A Novel
ABOUT THE END OF THE MAYAN CALENDAR
Book One: *12* Series

By
JEFFREY MARCUS OSHINS

DEEP SIX PUBLISHERS
Santa Barbara, CA
www.deepsixpub.com

THIRD EDITION

Cover designed by Daniel Seman crowanimations.net

ISBN: 978-0615271453

Library of Congress Control Number: 2012945616

Also by Jeffrey Marcus Oshins

And We Shall Perish (Book Two - *12* Series)
Hippies in the Andes/Freedom Pure Freedom
Women in Politics

Acknowledgements

Thanks to Gia Esola, Bernard Baycroft

Every 25,800 the Sun makes a reverse cycle through the Zodiac and rests in the eye of Sagittarius (the archer). At this time the temporal and celestial planes touch creating a portal through which gods enter the temporal plane to battle for the elemental nature of the Earth.

The following is the story of the Water god, *Tatya-Masi*, who passes through the eye of Sagittarius to destroy the Age of Man and bring forth the Fifth and Final World of Water.

Preface

Clouds suddenly envelope the globe. Ceaseless rain or snow falls. Within days massive flooding washes away whole communities, sweeps millions to their deaths, and brings modern civilization to the brink of ruin.

As everyone knows, this was our planet's collective fate last year. Disappointment in the lack of scientific agreement on the causes for what has universally come to be known as the Great Flood has led to a spate of paranormal speculations. To this body of mythical pondering can be added the following firsthand account by seventeen-year-old Du Moss who claims to be *Tatya-Masi*, a deity sent to destroy the modern world and claim the Earth for Water.

So odd a tale is difficult to give much credence, but there is at least in Du Moss' account a cultural basis in the myths of the La'ku, a Mesoamerican culture that existed in the same geographical range and dates as the Maya civilization. The La'ku believed that every 25,800 years the celestial and temporal planes touch. At this time gods and spirits enter the physical world to battle for the elemental nature of Earth. The La'ku marked this date at a point where the Sun rests in the eye of Sagittarius, the constellation whose symbol is an archer, known to them as the mutable or change sign.

What we have left of the La'ku knowledge and prophecy of this event is contained in the following brief codex, written on a piece of bark, preserved in the Morales library.

The Sixth World, the Final World,

Sign of **12** *Ixchel* (Water)

It is the World of Water,

Because it flows.

According to what has been left to us,

Said by the old,

When the Sun rests in the eye of *K'iché* (Sagittarius)

Rain will fall without end,

And we shall perish.

Therefore, the following is offered with the caveat that there is only the slimmest scientific basis for its claims. But on the other hand we cannot fully dismiss Mr. Moss' explanation of the recent rains or warnings of what is to come when the Sun rests in the eye of Sagittarius at the winter solstice next year.

Editors

Foreword

A m I Tatya-Masi?

I am neither beast nor god, this narrative neither Sutra nor Bible. I ask those who think that I am *Tatya-Masi* not to take what I relate as gospel or apostasy. For what is divine and ordained for one is profane and insignificant to another.

In this universe of uncounted worlds, surely there are as many heavens as those who pray to them. The age we know *will* perish in its time, as have the civilizations of the Aztec, Maya, Inca, and La'ku.

As difficult as it is for the modern mind to accept, I must ask you to believe that a battle is taking place between the goddess of Water and Lord of Fire for dominance of the next Age of Earth. The Sixth and Final World will dawn when the Sun reaches the equiplane equinox, the exact center of our galaxy. Whether this World will be one of Water or Fire depends on the outcome of this elemental battle.

Ancient and yet frightfully modern, these gods seek to control the very nature of the planet. Will the Earth be as it has been—a place of Fire with mankind able to make steel, explode atoms and propel themselves and their machines around the galaxy with the force of Fire? Or will we return to an earlier age of Water when the oceans covered the globe and scarce land was buried beneath miles of ice?

Three spirits fight for an Age of Fire. They are: *Quetzal* the Plumed Serpent, *Kinchel* the Avenger, and *Mitnal* the Smoking Mirror.

Quetzal the Plumed Serpent can change shapes to appear as a fearsome fire-breathing dragon or as a beautiful bird. He wields a silver cross entwined with a snake as his totem to control the will of those he chooses to serve him.

Kinchel the Avenger is a nine-headed dragon who commands the Assassins of Fire. Recognized by their red eyes, the Assassins of Fire are humans and animals that relentlessly pursue *Kinchel's* prey in the physical realm.

Mitnal the Smoking Mirror, a spirit of war and human sacrifice, is the most devious. The servants of *Mitnal* possess great charisma, which provides them the ability to attract many followers. *Mitnal* feeds on the pain and suffering caused by his deceptions.

What is most difficult for me to explain and the reason I have written this book is this: the leader of the forces of Water is supposed to be me—a god able to live on land and in the water called *Tatya-Masi*.

Am I this god?

My difficulty in accepting this appellation is rooted in a full awareness of my own very human failings. But what is clear is that I have the appearance of this god, have certain amphibious qualities, and possess powers that cannot be easily explained. What is more troubling is that the goddess *Inika* Lordess of Water believes that I am *Tatya-Masi*, and seeks to use me to drown the Age of Man.

Other spiritual forces from the distant past have risen to claim me as their god. *Xucha* witches from the ancient city of Manoa have waited six hundred years for the coming of *Tatya-Masi*.

A necklace, called a *tunjo*, fashioned by Curratta, the Supreme Shaman of the *Xucha*, came into my possession. Whether or not the magic of the *tunjo* comes from the Jewels of Life embedded in the talisman, I cannot say. I can only attest to the Jewels' power.

Until recently, the La'ku prophecy that when the Sun rested in the eye of Sagittarius the god *Tatya-Masi* would vanquish the Spanish invaders and return their land to them was mostly the concern of cultists and anthropologists. Then the rains and floods came. Now growing panic and widespread despair compel me to share what I know.

In the end I am only...well, read for yourself and decide what I am.

Du Moss

Lake of the Frogs

CHAPTER ONE
QUETZAL THE PLUMED SERPENT

I begin my tale in the jungles of Central America, ten years before I was born, when ancient spirits possessed the bodies of three La'ku boys.

Red-bellied hummingbirds and hard-beaked toucans banked in the mist rising up in wet clouds. The air shook around jagged rock columns that thrust from swirling water thrown white from brown waves. The scent of the muddy river mixed with the ripe jungle smells of rotting leaves and flowers.

Small and furtive, Kare squinted his almond-shaped eyes and pushed back his straight black hair. He had begged his brother to take him on the adventure. Now, he had fallen behind and as always had to run to keep up with Norane.

His older brother was stronger, faster and smarter than other La'ku boys. When Norane was a baby, their mother had taken him to the top of Mount Susuprina to offer him to *Inika* Lordess of Water. Maybe it was there that the spirits who lived in the mountain had given Norane his speed and strength.

Ninety feet ahead, Kare saw his brother and Eduardo Morales descend on the first steps of the trail that ran down the face of the waterfall. Eduardo wore a small backpack with a fishing net and collapsible metal pole sticking out of the top. While Eduardo was dressed in clothes laundered by three women, Kare and Norane wore dirty, torn factory discards sold in the village market. Norane and Eduardo competed at everything from footraces to grades at the Cristóbal School. But it was Norane who had led them here, claiming that he knew where to find the greatest treasure.

This would not have been the first time that Norane had found something special from the ancient days. His knowledge of the jungle ruins had made him a favorite of Eduardo's father, Don Carlos Morales, the owner of all the land around them. Norane had a job as a groom in Don Carlos' stables and he often accompanied Don Carlos, Eduardo, and his sister Lilia on trips to explore jungle ruins. Maybe if Kare found an old La'ku pot or a black rock knife he would be able to go with *el Patrón* and his family on the exploring trips.

Kare stopped at the edge of the rain-swollen waterfall. The two twelve-year-olds had disappeared into the mist below. Kare filled his lungs and tentatively lowered a foot onto the steep, angled path. Once he started, the thought of going back up the wet wall was as terrifying as continuing. Down and down he went into a world of thundering water fists trying to knock him into the crushing whirlpools below.

His eyes watered with tears. This was no place for a ten-year-old boy to be. He pressed his trembling lips together to squeeze back the urge to cry out to his brother to take him back up the cliff. But Kare knew his words could not be heard over the unrelenting roar of the falling water—so loud he could feel but not hear his own moans. He reached a point where he was hanging from a narrow ledge, slick with condensation and slimy decaying plants, looking between his extended arms for another hold, searching for his brother in the vertical fog. He could not go down or up. He was stuck.

"Norane!" he screamed. "Norane! Help me!"

Like a miracle, his brother's hand reached up from the clouds and pressed against his back, guiding his foot to another step. And then they were standing together on soggy ground, both as wet as if they had been an hour in the rain, their clothes pasted against their skin.

Kare did not have time for gratitude or pleading. Norane gave him a flashlight and then with a quick excited gleam in his brown eyes renewed his race with Eduardo along a narrow path by the lake at the bottom of the falls. Kare considered whether to go after the older boys or expose himself as a coward. An old statue of *Tatya-Masi*—a kneeling half-man half-frog covered with jungle vines—faced the falls. Kare had heard that snakes filled the inside of the statue. The belching croak of ten thousand frogs mixed with the splash of water. Something moved in the jungle.

Kare skirted the riverbank, picking his way across the soaked ground that sucked his feet into the mud as if the Earth did not want him to go on, until he reached the base of the cliff. He watched his brother bend his head and pass through a wet curtain at the edge of the crushing fall. Kare closed his eyes, swallowed the bitter-tasting saliva choking him and followed Norane, ducking into the falling water that slapped him as if he'd been struck with an open hand.

On the other side of the waterfall a narrow passage ran between wet rock and falling water.

Eduardo—followed on his heels by Norane—entered a hole wide enough for them to pass abreast of each other without stooping. With a deep gulp to swallow his fear Kare followed them into the Cave of the *Xucha*.

The *Xucha* were witches from the ancient times when the statue of *Tatya-Masi* had been built. Some said the *Xucha* still lived inside the cave. If the damp dark place was not scary enough, the thought of witches caused Kare's eyes to twitch. If he met a *Xucha* he would explain that his mother and aunt Naj were witches. Maybe then the *Xucha* would let him go back to the surface.

Kare told himself to stay close to Norane. The sound of the waterfall thumped like a rumba in the dance hall. Light dimmed, from aquamarine, like being underwater, to darkness without stars or moon in the undeterminable depth of the hole in the earth. The cold air smelled as moldy as an old refrigerator. Kare trembled as he turned on the flashlight. The beam glistened on the wet rock. Norane and Eduardo had moved far ahead. The dark swallowed their flashlights. Kare ducked and crawled through a narrow crack in the rock. He *had* to keep the older boys in sight.

Norane needed little light to guide him. His brother ran through the dangerous cave like a ghost in this endless night.

Kare's flashlight suddenly illuminated a skeleton and a pile of pots buried in dirt. He gasped and crouched, looking for witches. "Hey," he whispered, and then shouted, "Look what I've found." Maybe this would be enough of a treasure for Don Carlos. They could find their way back to the surface and bring him some of these old things. There was no response to his echoing call. "Norane!" he screamed. "Eduardo!"

Where were they? He was alone. A terrifying solitude pressed in around him. His heart banged against his ribs so hard he thought it might explode. To show himself a coward seemed far better than coming to this place of death. He would rather have been anywhere but here trying to keep up with the two crazy boys who did not seem to know fear.

Ahead, Kare saw a faltering light. He squeezed through a small passage in the rock and stepped onto a narrow bridge. There were no walls to balance against. A pebble fell, echoing as it hit water a long way down.

"Norane! Don't go so fast." Kare's scream bounced off the rocks from ten different directions. On the other side of the stone bridge Eduardo's flashlight barely glimmered in the pitch black.

The sound of the other boys' footsteps disappeared. All Kare could hear were the desperate gasps of his own fear-clenched lungs.

He got on his knees and crawled forward, feeling in front of him with his hands until he reached the other side. "Norane!" he wept.

"What's the matter with you?" Norane stood near the dim silhouette of a jutting rock wall.

Kare reached for him. Norane pulled him around the corner and led him by the hand just as he had when their parents had been killed and they had gone to live with Naj. Gleaming, pointed, stone teeth hung from the ceiling. Others rose from the floor, some melding into towers. Kare wished that Norane were leading him out of this terrible place.

"There it is," Norane said. "It's still here."

"I can't see anything, I tell you," Eduardo said standing, beside an underground pond. Their flashlight beams reflected off a still, dark surface, lighting their faces from beneath their chins.

"It's there," Norane said and released Kare's hand.

From where Kare cowered behind his brother, he could see nothing but the black water that disappeared into a dark curving cave wall covered in white powder.

Eduardo handed Norane his flashlight, took the backpack off, and removed the fishing net. He extended the pole and lay on the ground, thrusting his head into the water until he looked as if he was cut in half.

Norane set the two flashlights on the ground, and then took off his shirt and shoes.

What was his older brother doing? Kare's pulse sped up. The beam of his light wavered in his nervous hold.

Eduardo rose and blew water from his lips with a sharp exhale.

Clothed only in his pants, Norane stood over the pool.

"Norane!" Kare cried out a warning and reached for his brother.

Before he could stop him, Norane dove through the flat surface. Kare leaned over the side of the pool watching his brother kick down through the thick water until all that was visible was the flash of the soles of his feet.

What could make Norane—anybody—jump into that hole? Kare held his breath, as if by not breathing he might help his brother. He'd watched Norane and Eduardo dive to the bottom of the lake behind the *estancia*, each surfacing with a handful of mud proving they had made the bottom. Was Norane trying to reach the bottom of the underworld, Kare wondered?

"Point your flashlight at the water!" Eduardo held a steady focus of his and Norane's flashlights on the surface that still rippled from the disturbance Norane had caused. The three beams of light only made it harder to see what was happening beneath the surface. Kare's teeth chattered. The beam of his flashlight jumped and moved. Kare pressed his elbows to his side partly to keep warm, partly to contain his fear.

The half-hour they'd been in the cave seemed like a week on the surface. Every second marked a point where Norane could not hold his breath a moment longer. What had happened to him? A minute, two, three minutes passed. Kare's mind filled with horrible images of his daredevil brother floating lifeless to the surface of the underground lake. He imagined a tree limb snagging Norane and holding him down. He thought of a monster, like the man-frog statue in the jungle, taking his brother.

Eduardo set his and Norane's flashlights down and took off his shirt and shoes. If Norane dove in the pool Eduardo had to follow. A La'ku could not be braver than he was. Eduardo drew a deep breath and dove in the center of the water.

Kare alone in the middle of the Earth, completely alone, inched closer to the rough edge of the pool but saw only the reflection of his flashlight on the rippling surface. The treasure Norane alone had seen—the attraction that had brought them to this nightmare—remained hidden. Kare shivered as he tried to hold his flashlight steady and keep his eyes locked on the underwater lake.

Eduardo finally appeared as a blurred movement before he burst through the surface—alone. Eduardo held onto the edge of the pool breathing in gasps. He pulled himself out with a rush of dripping water. "Stupid, stupid La'ku," he said as if angry with Norane for killing himself.

Kare wept out of fear and loss. How could he live without Norane? The idea was impossible to accept. Norane could not die. His older brother was too strong to drown in a cave. How frail and short must his own life be if Norane could die so easily?

Eduardo dressed, swung the backpack over his shoulders, picked up Norane and his flashlights, and left without another word.

"Wait!" Kare pleaded. "Leave his flashlight for him. He'll need his flashlight." Eduardo paid no attention. He'd made up his mind that Norane was dead and Kare was of no more value to the rich boy than a dropped *centavo*. "Wwwe can't leave him," Kare stammered. Eduardo walked around a blocking wall of stone. Kare looked at his brother's useless shirt and shoes before sobbing and hurrying after Eduardo.

"Please, please come back. Find him. Please find him," Kare wept, but Eduardo only seemed to be moving faster, causing Kare to hurry after him or be lost here forever. He couldn't be left here alone. Tears rolled down his checks, and flooded his throat, chocking back his useless pleas. Kare concentrated on Eduardo's feet, stepping where he had as they crossed the bridge over the deep underground canyon. Tears blurred his vision as he tried to keep sight of his one connection to the surface.

Kare was sure Eduardo was going a different way than they had come. He was climbing when they should be moving in the opposite direction. He squeezed through a crack in the cave wall Kare did not remember. Kare tripped over a rock. He extended his hand to break the fall. His flashlight fell, blinking out at once.

Infinite darkness closed in around him. He felt as if his eyes had been stolen. He reached for the flashlight, fumbled around in the blackness like the blind boy he had become, touching only dirt and rock.

"Eduardo!" he screamed, choking. "I can't see!"

Eduardo did not respond. What did Eduardo care if Kare found his way out or not–if he lived or died? Eduardo's father would look for his son. Even with torches and fifty men, Kare doubted anyone would find him. And if they did find Eduardo they would not bother to keep looking for a lost La'ku boy.

"Anhhhh! Anhaaa," sobbed Kare. Why had they ever come? If he could turn back time, he would beg Norane not to come to this evil place.

"Eeeeeeddddddduuuuaaaarrrrddddoooo!" His voice quavered.The echoes mimicked him like cruel ghosts. "Eduardo, Eduardo, Eduardo," he moaned and fell to the cold ground and released his racking sobs. He cried until through his tears he saw an ill-defined radiance. Sniffling, he rose to his feet. Careful not to lower his gaze and lose sight of the dim light, he shuffled forward. Once, he tripped and fell against a cold, damp rock wall, banging his knee so hard he was sure that he was bleeding. But he did not take his eyes off the saving light ahead. He groped his way around the barrier that had injured him and the light grew brighter.

At last he saw its source—a crack in the ceiling forty feet above him. The high thin opening looked no wider than a loaf of bread and as distant as the promise of heaven. Still he moved toward the illumination until the sound of rushing water made him stop.

For the first time since he'd seen the light, he felt confident enough to look down, and it was a good thing he did. The sun from the outside world revealed a cliff that fell into darkness. Too far down to see the bottom, he heard the watery pulse of an underground river. Had he taken another step he would have fallen into the rushing water. A canyon he could never jump blocked his way.

What was he supposed to do now? How could he ever hope to reach the other side? He looked into a grotto, a dark stone room. He could see no way forward. The idea of going back into the darkness was too much for him. What was left of his courage disappeared. A trembling weakness grew in his legs until he could not stand. Whimpering, he sank to his knees and fell to the side.

He shivered as if he had a fever. He felt cold and empty, already nearly dead. After lying on the dirt floor of the cave for a minute—or hours—who could tell—Kare moved his hand. He felt rock and dust and then something hard the size of a small melon. He grasped the round object and pulled it closer. Kare squinted into the hollow eyes of a skull. The sight so shocked him that he jumped to his feet and stepped back to run, but to where? He inched back in the dim light and saw a headless skeleton lying on the ground, its feet pointed toward the opening as if it had died looking at the light far above. Rib bones extended from a curved metal chest piece. A sword lay in the dirt beside a skeletal hand. A cross hung from the skeleton's neck.

This was a conquistador. Kare had seen pictures of these Spanish explorers and conquerors at the Cristóbal School. Eduardo's ancestors had been conquistadors. It was said that all the land called Omagua had been owned by Morales since the days of the Conquest.

Kare stepped closer to the remains of the dead conquistador. There was no reason to be afraid anymore. He was no longer alone. He was no longer blind. Soon he would become a skeleton like this one, and in a hundred lifetimes another lost boy would be drawn to the high opening to the sky and join them in their quiet grave.

Something stirred. His fear returned in a heart-squeezing rush. Where could he hide? There was nowhere else to go.

"Shhhhraaaaa!"

The cry of the ghosts combined the whistle of a boiling steam kettle with the warning growl of a wild animal. It seemed to come from the skeleton but at the same time from the rock walls and ceiling.

Terror turned to pain as if knives were stabbing Kare from the inside.

"Hello?" his whisper shook from him. Then louder in a wavering voice, "Is anyone there?"

"Shhhhraaaaa!"

The sounds of ghosts rustled from the ground, coming to claim him.

A faint glint like a dying ember broke the darkness.

"Shhhhraaaaa!"

The light brightened into the shape of the cross on the conquistador's chest.

Kare's eyes bulged and his mouth opened in a silent scream so wide that his lips pulled back around his teeth.

"Take the cross."

The voice was as quiet as wind moving through branches.

"Take the cross!"

Kare leaned over and held the pulsing metal necklace.

Energy spread through him like the pricking stings of a thousand fire ants marching into his brain. He tried to drop the necklace but could not open his hand.

"Shhhhraaaaa!"

A flaming serpent curled around his arm.

Kare jumped backwards and squealed.

"Shhhhraaaaa!"

A monster erupted from the cross, rising higher and higher. Its eyes burned like hot coals. Scales on its orange hide reflected a fiery luminance. Shimmering wings arched from its coiled back. In the bright light of the ghastly sight Kare saw other skeletons in old armor slumped against the walls.

Kare slowly backed away from the dragon to the edge of the cliff. At the last moment he stopped himself from falling over the edge by whirling his arms like a bird to hold his balance. A small landslide cascaded beneath his foot sending rocks and dirt splashing into the water after a long fall.

"Ahhh!" The hiss was a groan of relief as the rainbow wings of the creature unfolded and spread across the cave's stone roof. "That is better," the dragon spoke.

Kare bent his head back until he was arched over the deep drop behind him. The horrendous sight filled the grotto. The cross dangling from his hand was forgotten. His eyes would not close. His chest crawled with burning nerves.

The dragon's gaze narrowed and drilled into him. With ponderous depth, he spoke. "La'ku cub. Why are you here? To spend your last days gazing up at a crack that will never let you see the sun, with *Quetzal* the Plumed Serpent?"

Did the apparition expect him to answer?

As if understanding Kare's fear, *Quetzal* the Plumed Serpent shrank until it rested on a rock in front of Kare. The Plumed Serpent changed into the most beautiful bird Kare had ever seen, prettier than a peacock with a silver chest and golden beak. Tail feathers shined and danced with iridescent colors. How could anything be that terrifying and that beautiful? Was *Quetzal* the Plumed Serpent a dragon or this beautiful bird?

"Be not afraid Kare." A gentle familiar voice took Kare to a place he loved, a memory of his mother holding him in a hammock. "Mama is here, Kareisito," the bird said in her gentle voice. "I'll stay with you."

"No! No!" Kare wept and pressed his hands against his head, inching away from the edge of the cliff toward the darkness.

The bird spread its tail. "What is time?" the bird asked, its voice now like a rich man's from the capital. "For you, it is before and after you came into this cave. For me…" the bird lowered his luminescent head and sighed. "It is the same—before and after I was trapped here in this prison of no time and no movement. I need you boy. I need you to free me."

Kare shrank from the demon.

"Put on the necklace," the bird urged. "You want to die alone here in this cave? I'll leave you forever. You want that?" The feathers flapped. *Quetzal* was going back into his skeleton to wait for another lost boy.

Kare reached out.

The beautiful bird settled and tilted its head toward him. "The cross will be your guide out of this prison. You will never be alone again," *Quetzal* promised.

Kare studied the four-inch gold cross intertwined by a feathered serpent. Blood-red rubies inlaid into the eyes stared at him as if they possessed a life of their own.

What better chance did Kare have to get out of this cave but to trust the Plumed Serpent, whether a dragon or bird? An electric rush spread to Kare's brain. He hesitated, then lifted the chain and stared at the ruby-eyed pendent.

"Accept me," *Quetzal* hissed. "Give me your heart. Believe in me."

"I do," Kare mouthed.

Two streams of colored red and yellow smoke flowed from *Quetzal's* golden beak and surrounded Kare who rocked back as the fiery presence entered his body like peppers searing his throat.

Then the burning was gone. Kare winced and measured how little of him was left. *Quetzal* was inside of him. The world that Kare had known was pitiful and small, like looking at life through a pinhole. Kare now saw with the eyes of a spirit backward in time and forward to the battle for the next World of Earth.

"Now you must leave me," the bird spoke. "I shall stay here until you return with *Tatya-Masi.* Only the Water god can free me from the spell that has trapped me here."

Even with his new vision, Kare could not imagine how he could bring a god from another age to this cave. But he had no time to ask. With a twinkle of light, *Quetzal* the Plumed Serpent disappeared leaving a changed Kare alone with the dead conquistadors. Kare would be *Quetzal's* eyes and ears outside his stone prison. Wherever Kare carried the cross, the Plumed Serpent would be.

Kare placed the necklace over his head, turned from the boneyard, and moved without hesitation or doubt around the obstacles and false passages. He did not need a flashlight. Inner eyes pierced the black like a bat feeling his way with senses and an intelligence Kare had never known.

A weak light revealed a lost Eduardo, moving on a path that would never have lead him to safety.

Kare took off the necklace and put it in his pocket. He would share his treasure with no one. *Quetzal* was strong in him.

"Eduardo," he called to the older boy with a confidence he'd never before known.

Eduardo spun, his flashlight a pathetic tool against the all-encompassing black.

"You're going the wrong way," Kare said. "Follow me."

When the sound of the waterfall indicated the direction, Eduardo pushed Kare aside and stepped ahead of him.

A figure awaited them in the opaque light just outside the entrance to the cave.

Norane!

"Look," the voice of *Quetzal* the Plumed Serpent whispered in Kare's ear. "Your brother has been claimed by the Lordess of Water. See *Inika* in him."

Suddenly, Kare could see inside of Norane a jaguar with four heads swimming in a jungle pool. Four lilies were on the Lordess' heads. Norane had been changed in the cave as much as he had. *Inika* had saved Norane like the Plumed Serpent had saved him. Both of them were different now.

The Plumed Serpent's voice inside Kare's head spoke. "This is your first lesson. I am a spirit of Fire. Your brother serves the Lordess of Water. He is your enemy."

No. What was left of Kare's freewill rebelled. He could never hide anything from Norane. The part of him that was Kare wanted to cry with joy and hug his older brother, praise the gods for delivering him. Instead, he looked at the box Norane carried.

Eduardo too seemed overwhelmed by the miracle of their survival. He quickly regained his rich boy swagger and playfully punched Norane in the chest. "We did it!"

Norane took the light blow but said nothing.

Eduardo pressed him. "Where have you been? How did you get back here? How did you get out of that pool?"

Norane looked away in a manner that told Kare he would rather not answer the question. But Eduardo was angry as if he'd been tricked and it was best not to provoke him.

"I swam down and found the box," Norane said in a soft voice like describing a dream. "I couldn't get out. Trapped with no air, I was drowning. The box sparkled like a thousand fireflies and told me to not go up but down. I found my way to another passage that led me back to the air. You both were gone. I put on my clothes and tried to find you. I'm happy you both found your way back."

"What do you mean the box told you? Give me that." Eduardo took the book-size object from Norane in the manner of one who is used to having whatever he wants. The metal container was tarnished with age, and nearly black from being in the water. Eduardo held it up to the dim light. "What is it?" he demanded.

Norane turned away with what Kare thought was a moment of regret in his eyes, as if he'd already said too much. "It's old, very old."

Eduardo pulled on the top and bottom of the old box until the taut muscles in his arm quivered and his face contorted. Norane watched with a passive expression.

"Open it!" Eduardo ordered and handed the box back to Norane.

Norane held the container in both hands and looked down at it with a reverent expression. "It cannot be opened by us," he said.

"Well who can open it?" Eduardo demanded.

"*Tatya-Masi.*"

"The frog-god? You're *loco*. Give it back to me. I'll bring it to my father. He'll know how to open it. You'd better come. He'll ask questions." Eduardo put the container in his backpack, as if he was the one who had found it.

Kare followed behind Norane. He needed no help climbing the cliff beside the falls, knowing that he would not slip or fall. *Quetzal* would guide him. When they reached the trail to the hacienda, Norane slowed and walked beside him.

"What has happened to you?" Norane asked.

Scratched and muddy, Kare knew his brother was not asking him about how he looked. Could Norane see *Quetzal* the Plumed Serpent in him like he'd been able to see *Inika* Lordess of Water in him? The cross burned against his thigh. Kare felt a combination of fear and longing to tell Norane everything.

"How were you saved?" Kare asked.

Norane's eyes shined as he looked up at the volcano Susuprina rising from lush hills to the clouds that always covered its peak. "By a Water spirit. She gave me the box. It is for the god *Tatya-Masi.*" Norane stepped ahead to stay close to Eduardo and the box.

Now, Kare was beginning to understand how he would find the god. Norane would lead him to *Tatya-Masi* and Kare would lead him back to the cave to free *Quetzal*.

The Plumed Serpent whispered. "I have hidden myself from him. He cannot see me in you. He cares nothing for you now. He can think of nothing but *Inika.*"

The Plumed Serpent was right. Norane was changed as much as he was. They did not need each other anymore.

Kare hung his head. He hated the gods for taking his brother from him.

CHAPTER TWO
THE FRAILTY OF A MYTH

The three boys walked through the village of small neat houses with white plaster walls and red tiled roofs where the workers on Eduardo's family plantation lived. Everyone said that the workers of Omagua were treated the best of any estancia. Theirs were comfortable homes in a village with a school and a clinic.

They continued on a pathway through a central park, past where Kare and Norane lived with their aunt Naj. The brothers had been orphaned six years before when their parents had been killed by the paramilitary who thought they were leftists. The boys would have been happy in their aunt's home except for her son Hernando Rosas. His father was in the military and never around. Three years older than Kare, their cousin was the most handsome boy in the village; he was like a preening peacock as he grew into his teen body. Excessive charm allowed Rosas to escape blame for his many misdeeds. But Kare saw him as he was—as mean and cruel as their aunt was kind.

Rosas stepped from the white-walled house. "Come here, Kare," he ordered.

Kare ignored him.

"Hey, I'm talking to you." Rosas grabbed Kare's arm and spun him around.

All it took was one look with the eyes of the *Plumed Serpent* and the bully backed down. Rosas would never touch him again.

His cousin turned and walked quicker to catch Eduardo and Norane. And then it looked as if Rosas was hit by lightning. There was a bright flash and sparkles dropped from his head to cover his body. Kare thought his cousin was going to fall, but Rosas straightened up and looked around with a bewildered expression.

With *Quetzal's* eyes, Kare saw Rosas had been possessed by another spirit. It was something he wouldn't have believed before he took the cross. Rosas had been a stupid, vain boy, but now Kare saw something wholly different in him. Kare could see a beast with eight tentacles, each tipped with mouths that were lined with razor shark teeth.

Rosas was shimmering with his new power by the time Kare reached his side. The two boys didn't speak to each other. They were a silent audience to a conversation between the Fire spirits–*Quetzal* inside of Kare and a spirit called *Mitnal* the Smoking Mirror inside of Rosas. The spirits spoke to each other in a rapid series of chirps and squeaks barely audible to the human ear. The complete exchange was finished in the time it took to take a step. But Kare understood.

"Prince Quetzal, *I bring you greetings from your father* Xiulu *Lord of Fire and joy for your escape from the cave,"* Mitnal *said.*

"You mock me Mitnal. *I go only as far as this puny being can carry me."*

"You have a plan?" Mitnal *asked with deferential tone.*

"I do. I shall turn Tatya-Masi *to my bidding."*

"A Fire spirit will command a Water god. That is heroic." Mitnal said.

"Have you come to attend me? Be careful that your careless tongue does not reveal me to Inika."

"The Lordess of Water is weak in this world now. See how I've taken for my host a son of one of her witches."

That was true, Kare thought. His aunt Naj was a witch, just like their mother had been, who revered *Tatya-Masi* and served *Inika* Lordess of Water. *Inika* commanded the rains. When *Tatya-Masi* came to Earth, the Lordess of Water would send rains that would fall without end until all the fires of man were extinguished.

"The Lordess has eyes in the gulls and all creatures of water. I shall summon you when I need you," Quetzal said.

"My lord prince, your Father has sent me and Kinchel *the Avenger to secure the Sixth and Final World for Fire. If we can save you, we are to. If not...."*

Kare was surprised to understand what the Fire spirits were talking about. There had been five Worlds of Earth. If *Tatya-Masi* should come, there would be a war between the forces of the Lord Fire and Lordess of Water for the Sixth and final World. *Mitnal* had come to Earth not to save *Quetzal* but to fight *Inika* and to keep *Tatya-Masi* from being born or kill him if he did appear in a mortal body. But only a god of Water could free *Quetzal* from *Inika's* spell. For *Quetzal* to be freed, *Tatya-Masi* had to be born.

"When Tatya-Masi frees me, I shall bring the four Jewels of Life to my lord father," Quetzal said.

Whoever controlled the four Jewels of Life would be able to breach the barrier between the celestial and temporal realms and overwhelm the Earth with their spiritual forces. Two of the Jewels were inside the box that Norane carried. Two were in a scepter that *Quetzal* had stolen from *Inika*. The Lordess' spell on *Quetzal* could only be broken by *Tatya-Masi* when he held the four Jewels.

"Inika has sealed the box with a spell. Only Tatya-Masi *can open it. We are to kill the god before he opens the box. Without the Jewels* Tatya-Masi *will not have the power to bring* Inika's *rain and the Sixth and Final World will be secure for Fire."*

"Kill the god before he opens the box and you sentence me to eternity in this prison. If you serve my father, you serve me. You will attend me and not interfere until I call you."

"I know Xiulu *will grieve to sacrifice his bravest son to stop* Inika *from*

claiming the Sixth and Final World for Water."

"Do not challenge me, Mitnal. *I shall control the Water god. I shall be free of* Inika's *curse and secure the Sixth World for Fire."*

Rosas silently fell in with them as they walked up to the big house.

Kare thought he might as well have died and been reborn into a new life. Three hours before he'd been worried about keeping up with his older brother and now he had to comprehend the rivalries of gods and spirits, and the power of magic jewels and totems.

Eduardo led them through the kitchen and formal dining room. Norane and Rosas walked with the confidence of those who had no doubt of their right to be inside the mansion. Kare stayed a step behind, sidling past the reproving looks of the maids and butler, aware of the dirt and blood that covered him and his companions. Kare had never before been inside the house of *el Patrón.* Now with quick darts of his eyes, he took in the art, rugs, the rich polished wood—sights few La'ku boys had seen.

Lilia, Eduardo's younger sister, walked down a wide, curved wooden stairway. She and Kare were in the same class at the Cristóbal School. Even with his new confidence, Kare looked away.

"Hi, Kare," she said.

"Hello, Lilia," he meekly replied, his complexion red with embarrassment.

"Hi Lilia." Rosas puffed his chest out and stepped toward Lilia. Everyone knew he liked her. She turned her back on him and smiled at Norane.

"What have you found now?" she asked Norane.

"Something very special." Norane said in a matter-of-fact tone and followed Eduardo into the library.

"Papa, I've found a grand treasure," Eduardo announced and set the box on the polished surface of the great desk where his father sat.

Kare stood by Lilia behind the older boys.

Don Carlos was big in the chest, with graying hair and a mustache over a square chin. He picked up the container and turned it in his hands. "This is phenomenal. Where did you find it?"

"In the Cave of the *Xucha*," Eduardo said with pride.

"You went in there by yourselves? I've told you not to do that."

"It was in a pool of water. We had to swim for it."

"What do *you* think it is, Norane?" he asked without taking his eyes off the box.

Eduardo frowned as if worried Norane would know an answer he did not.

Norane didn't appear nervous to be questioned by *el Patrón.* He gazed past Don Carlos as if he could see through the walls into another dimension. "It is the *tunjo* the *Xucha* created to call back *Tatya-Masi.*"

"To drive away the Spanish?" Don Carlos asked with a hint of a smile at the corners of his lips.

Norane's returning stare was narrow and hard.

"So you think Curratta's *tunjo* is inside? That would be something." Don Carlos examined the box again. "We'll have to open it then."

Norane closed his eyes and cocked his head listening to a distant voice the rest could not hear. "Only *Tatya-Masi* will open the box," he said.

Rosas laughed with a high girlish trill as if he and Don Carlos would share the joke. But *el Patrón* did not laugh. He studied Norane for a moment with a serious expression.

Norane did not look down or appear doubtful.

"Let's take a closer look at it," Don Carlos said. He led them through a door at the back of the library to a laboratory. Kare quickly glanced at the shelves with boxes, skeletons, mummies, a large stone wheel carved with ancient La'ku symbols.

Don Carlos put the tarnished container on a worktable and shined a bright beam on the lid that reflected off the emerald eyes of the frog-god. *El Patrón* gently tapped the thin seal around the side with a metal chisel.

No matter what Don Carlos did, the lid would not move.

A servant came in and said that the *señora* wished to speak to him. *El Patrón* seemed annoyed to be called away. "Why don't you let me keep this for awhile?"

The four boys left the box in Don Carlos' laboratory and walked outside into the rose garden. Eduardo grabbed Norane's arm and spun him around, ready to hit him. "You show disrespect to my father?"

"He did!" Rosas egged Eduardo on.

A defiant gleam flashed in Norane's eyes before he lowered his gaze in appropriate submission. "I hope I did not offend him."

Eduardo frowned. "I suppose he would have said something if you had. How do you know so much about that box?"

Norane began to speak, then stopped as if he wanted to explain, but did not know how. He looked toward Susuprina. "I just know."

"How?" Eduardo demanded.

Norane gazed at him with passive assurance. "Some things I just know. I have always known."

Maybe his brother had always had the Lordess of Water in him. But if Norane had the power of the Lordess in him, he still had time to be a good brother. Now, they had become strangers to each other. Nothing would ever make Kare think that Norane was his enemy.

* * *

A week later when the servant from the house came to school Kare had no time to tell anyone where he was going. He was driven up to the mansion to the rear door of the laboratory and told to go into the library. There he saw Norane standing behind Eduardo. The rich boy was dressed like a little *hidalgo* in a suit and tie, seated beside his father at the long polished table. Across from Eduardo sat a *mestizo*, a hazel-colored man with round glasses and dark lips, who Don Carlos called Professor Matais. Kare stood behind Norane.

"These are the boys who were with my son when he found the box."

Professor Matais looked past Don Carlos at Kare and Norane and smiled in a quick polite manner.

Before *el Patrón* on black velvet cloth was the container, polished and as beautiful as if it were new. The frog-god on the surface was shiny gold, the base brilliant silver, and the jeweled eyes as bright as if the sun were shining through them.

The professor's eyes glistened with excitement, but he spoke like a priest at a grave. "As you can imagine, *Señor* Morales, we are ecstatic to be entrusted with this priceless national treasure. We believe it to be one of the greatest finds ever unearthed in this country."

Don Carlos nodded at Eduardo to give him the praise.

Professor Matais studied the box. "We were able to clean it with no trouble. But unfortunately we were not able to remove the cover. X-rays are of course insufficient. These are sonograms." He held out pictures showing the black and white, hazy outline of a small figure. "There appears to be a *tunjo* inside, a very fine one."

Don Carlos briefly lifted his eyes to Norane and then took the images.

The professor leaned forward with his hands held together before him on the table. "Because of the inestimable value of the piece, we propose a very cautious approach to opening it. First, we'll try solvents, and if that doesn't work, we may use heat to expand the lid. At last resort, we may have to make a small incision. In either case, the box might be slightly damaged. I wanted your permission before we proceeded."

Don Carlos studied the photos with a magnifying glass. "What do you think?" He turned to his son.

Eduardo sat more erect, and in a serious, slow manner, imitated what his father had said when they had first brought him the box. "I think we should see what is inside." He spoke with a city accent.

"And you, Norane?" Don Carlos looked over his shoulder at him.

Eduardo frowned at the equal consideration being given the La'ku boy.

"Only *Tatya-Masi* will open the box," Norane replied.

Don Carlos lifted the container, turned it over and studied the complex artwork and polished depiction of a man-frog.

"What would you do with the box?" he again asked Norane.

Norane did not reply, as if *el Patrón's* question was too difficult to answer.

"Go over there. Stand beside the professor where I can see you," Don Carlos ordered Norane. When Norane had moved to the other side of the table, Don Carlos asked, "What does the legend say?"

Norane looked at Don Carlos. He spoke as if reciting a poem to children, pronouncing each word so that they would understand. "The *Awkanakuy-Hauakuy* will find the box and give it to his true love, and from their union the Earthly presence of the god will appear. When *Tatya-Masi* opens the box, the World of Fire—the Age of the Spaniards—will end—and the World of Water—the new Age of the La'ku—will begin."

"Do you know of this myth?" Don Carlos asked Matais.

The professor glanced over his folded hands on the table. "It is the La'ku tale of the Warrior-Brother."

"Do you believe that the La'ku built the legendary city of Manoa where Dorado was their king?"

Matais smiled slightly. "I think that is highly unlikely."

"Then you don't believe in the Fountain of Youth?"

Matais raised his shoulders and searched Don Carlos' expression as if to see if he was joking. "I think that the legend of such a life-giving fountain was a powerful incentive for some early exploration but..."

Don Carlos interrupted him. "The source of the power of the Fountain of Youth was said to be four remnants of the comet that brought life to Earth. The La'ku called them the Jewels of Life."

Matais nodded with a hint of impatience.

"It is said that seven hundred years ago, a young La'ku girl named

Curratta discovered the Jewels on the snowy summit of Susuprina. Curratta grew to be a great shaman and ruled a sect of witches called the *Xucha* who worshipped and served *Inika* Lordess of Water. When *Inika* saw that the servants of Fire, the Castilian conquistadors were on the verge of conquering the La'ku, she hid Manoa beneath Lake *Itza Uo*." Don Carlos looked out the window to make it clear that he was speaking of the lake behind Omagua.

The professor's face impolitely revealed his scorn of Don Carlos' words. "Are you saying that there was a connection between the Castilians and the La'ku deity *Xiulu* Lord of Fire?"

"What drew the original conquerors, my ancestors, to this land was the rumor that they would find Manoa and the Fountain of Youth here." Don Carlos looked across the room to a glass case that held a collection of *tunjos*—castings in metal, carvings in stone, wood, and bone of the amphibian figure of *Tatya-Masi*. "According to the legend, *Inika* took the Jewels and placed two in a scepter, the *Cocatamia* Staff of Life, and two in the eyes of a *tunjo*. "

Matais vigorously nodded his head to indicate that he knew about the myth of the four Jewels. "You possess a marvelous collection of *tunjos*, unparalleled in…"

Don Carlos interrupted Matais. "*Quetzal* the Plumed Serpent, the son of *Xiulu* Lord of Fire came to Earth to steal the Jewels of Life from Manoa."

Kare leaned forward slightly.

"*Quetzal* placed his spirit in a four-inch gold cross intertwined by a silver feathered serpent with jeweled eyes."

The cross burned in Kare's pocket.

"Through this totem," Don Carlos continued, "*Quetzal* possessed the body of a conquistador named Gabriel Ayala. Guided by the Plumed Serpent, Ayala led a band of eleven conquistadors to Manoa. King Dorado and the Xucha repelled the invading conquistadors but in the fight Dorado was killed. In a rage at the death of her favorite mortal son, *Inika* Lordess of Water cast a spell that trapped the spirit of *Quetzal* and the eleven conquistadors in a cave within Susuprina."

Kare breathed deeply and kept his eyes down.

"Inika the Lordess of Water saw that the Spaniards were going to conquer and enslave the La'ku. She made this promise to the Children of Water. When the time came for the battle for the Sixth and Final World, she would send the Water god *Tatya-Masi* to Earth to lead the forces of Water. The god would be part-man and part-frog, able to live in many realms: water, air, and the celestial and temporal planes. The Lordess of Water told Curratta to place two of the Jewels of Life in a *tunjo,* a small likeness of *Tatya-Masi,* and to place the *tunjo* in a box that *Inika* would seal with a spell. Only *Tatya-Masi* would be able to open the box. The other two Jewels of Life were placed in a silver wand wrapped in golden fascia upon which rested a golden casting of the head of *Tatya-Masi.* The La'ku called this baton the *Cocatamia."*

They were now all staring at the box.

What they did not know, what Kare knew from *Quetzal,* was that the Plumed Serpent had stolen and hidden the *Cocatamia.* This was the treasure he would use to bargain for *Tatya-Masi* to release him.

In an ominous voice Don Carlos said, "The prophecy says that when *Tatya-Masi* possesses all four Jewels of Life, rain will fall without end and the World of Fire will drown."

Quetzal would not let this happen, Kare thought. This is why he served the Plumed Serpent, why his own brother was now his enemy.

Don Carlos said, "Professor, the legend says that when the Sun has completed a 360-degree circuit through the zodiac and rests in the eye of the archer Sagittarius, the celestial and physical planes—Heaven and Earth—will intersect. At this time, gods and spirits that have been forgotten a thousand years will walk the Earth. Professor, I've calculated that date. The equiplane equinox will occur in thirty-four years. I believe it perfectly feasible that inside this box are the seeds of the Earthly presence of the water deity *Tatya-Masi.*

Now, the professor did not look so sure. He peered uncertainly at Don

Carlos, suspicious that he might be toying with him.

Don Carlos continued, "The spirits of Fire or Water, depending on who holds the Jewels, will rush into the temporal plane and determine the elemental nature of the next World. The La'ku believe that *Inika* Lordess of Water will send a great flood that only they will survive."

Matais looked so distressed, Kare thought he might cry but he arrogantly tried to keep sounding smart and educated, "The deluge myth of a deity sending a great flood to destroy civilization is an archetypical theme. Noah, Manu, Gilgamesh are but a few of these diluvian figures."

Don Carlos said, "The La'ku were great astronomers. The stars gave them a date when the physical and celestial planes would touch."

If Don Carlos was expecting Matais to match his enthusiasm, he was wrong. The professor looked at Don Carlos with a glum expression.

Don Carlos' eyes shined as he shared his exciting news. "Seventeen years before the coming of *Tatya-Masi*, a mortal man, the *Awkanakuy-Hauakuy*, the Warrior-Brother, will bring to Manoa a mortal woman who will become the Earthly Mother of *Tatya-Masi.*"

Forsaking all manners, the professor looked at *el Patrón* as if he were a wayward student. "And?"

If Don Carlos noticed the professor's impertinent tone of voice, his excitement did not appear to be diminished. "I ask you to consider this, Matais. What if this box these boys have found does contain *Inika's tunjo* and what if two of the four Jewels of Life are inside?"

Matais maintained his joyful demeanor. "I certainly agree that this is a magnificent find, and I assure you that we will treat it with the care and honor such a magnificent artifact deserves."

Don Carlos was silent for a moment. Nobody spoke, waiting to hear what he would say. "Professor, what if this box these boys have found does contain Curratta's *tunjo?*"

Matais responded with a sincere, nearly reverent expression. "As I said,

Señor Morales, we think they have found a great treasure that we will treat with the care and honor such a magnificent artifact deserves."

Don Carlos held up his hand. "I'm suggesting we allow Norane to keep the box to see if he is the *Awkanakuy-Hauakuy*."

The professor shifted in his seat and his eyes squinted. "I apologize for my frankness, but I find that notion preposterous."

"I think we should not attempt to open the box; rather leave it with the one who found it, to see if the myth is true."

The professor cleared his throat in a nervous manner. "Do you mean to say, that this boy might be…?"

"Yes, exactly," Don Carlos said.

Kare glanced at Eduardo who grew red, embarrassed that his father knew who had really found the box. Eduardo would blame Norane for telling on him.

The professor looked as if he had swallowed a rotten egg. "I assure you, sir, we are most competent. We know what to do. We won't harm the box and will take very good care."

Don Carlos interrupted him. "I have no doubt that you would succeed in opening the box. But what about the myth?"

Matais sat back, blinked, took a breath, preparing to say a lot, but only repeated, "The myth?"

Kare thought he did not sound very smart for a professor. Couldn't they all see what was happening? The box was controlling them.

"Yes, the myth of *Tatya-Masi.*"

"I, no…I mean it's a *myth*, a mere legend. I suppose that there is some basis for it in history. That is why we want to open the box."

Don Carlos again cut his words off. "Professor, I ask you to ponder this hypothesis: that myths are like frail, gossamer creatures that are preserved in special atmospheres; like the fish that are sometimes found at great depths in the oceans–take them from their environment and they disintegrate. Or consider this analogy: what if we, by some chance, had come across a viable dinosaur egg that we had a chance to hatch. Would you suggest that we crack it open to see what was inside?"

"No, I suppose not."

"I'm going to entrust the box to Norane. Let us see if we can incubate this myth."

"You may, of course do what you wish, Don Carlos."

Norane showed no reaction to being talked about by the adults.

Kare knew Norane was the Warrior-Brother. That was why they could not open the box now.

Don Carlos placed both hands on the container. "I will keep the box here with the rest of my collection. Norane, you may come for it when you feel it is time."

Norane nodded.

The professor turned to look back at Norane. "How will you know what to do with it?"

Norane spoke in a low voice, showing proper respect to the professor. "The witches will tell me."

CHAPTER THREE
THE EARTHLY MOTHER

Kare left Omagua that day and did not return for fifteen years. Every day he had missed Norane, but his brother had not come looking for him. The spirits that ruled their lives commanded that they be apart.

Kare had grown used to *Quetzal* sleeping inside of him. At times, he'd wondered if the demon was still there, if he would ever call upon him to fulfill the bargain he'd made to escape from the cave. Then *Quetzal* was back, saying it was time to return to Omagua.

Kare arrived the day before Lilia Morales' wedding and within an hour had a job as a chauffeur. He was standing in the driveway with the other drivers dressed in black suit and caps when he saw Norane step from the garden doorway of Don Carlos' library.

The sight caused Kare to rock forward and stare in amazement.

He and his brother shared the same build and strong La'ku features—muscular in the arms and chest, with milk chocolate-flesh, and a long, flattened downward-tipped nose over a thin mouth and thick chin. Norane was dressed in a costume from another time—white pants, a jaguar-skin vest worn over his naked chest. His arms and head were decorated with feathered leather bands. He carried the jeweled box with the *tunjo* before him in his upraised hands. The sun sparkled off the silver and gold, flashing in sparks on the emeralds.

Kare followed Norane across the lawn of the *estancia*, forgetting propriety as he pushed through the elegant gathering to where beneath a white tent the bride and groom and their families were receiving the guests who passed before them to pay their respects and offer their own private words of endearment.

Lilia was a beautiful bride in a satin gown. Lace covered her bodice and arms. Her tanned complexion and pretty eyes shined with joy. Red lips and white teeth made a happy smile. Her expression changed to a curious half-frown when she saw Norane enter the receiving area and move to the front of the line.

Norane stepped past a rich doctor from the capital and his wife, and with a slight bow, placed the burnished container in Lilia's hands.

Kare saw her shiver as the spell was cast.

Norane lifted his gaze over Lilia's shoulder toward Mount Susuprina then stared into her brown eyes. "I can find nobody in my heart but you," he said in the La'ku dialect. He bent over and whispered something to her, then walked away from the party.

Don Carlos stepped from his place in the line. "Norane!" he called.

Norane did not stop.

The disturbance was so brief that most of the guests, including the groom, could not have guessed the significance of what had just happened. But Kare knew that Norane had just selected Lilia Morales to be the Earthly Mother of *Tatya-Masi*. Who would have ever expected Norane to choose a *castellana*, a descendant of the lobster-skinned men sent by the Lord of Fire to conquer the Children of Water?

"Lilia?" Don Carlos asked.

She ignored her father, and to everyone's surprise, clutched the silver box to the bodice of her pearl-studded bridal gown, and walked from the enclosure across the garden and out the gate.

"Everyone stay!" Don Carlos ordered. "I'll see what this is all about."

The groom, Theodore Moss, obeyed, but not Eduardo who, with hunched shoulders and lips twisted in fury, hurried to the house.

Lilia's mother, Beatrice, made unbelievable excuses about nerves to the murmuring and embarrassed guests who craned their necks to watch the bride follow Norane toward the jungle.

With the cunning of the Serpent, Kare followed Don Carlos and Lilia after Norane. Norane's action might make no sense to him or anybody else who knew the myth, but the Plumed Serpent saw and accepted–the *Awkanakuy-Hauakuy*, the Warrior-Brother, the Earthly father of *Tatya-Masi* had made his choice, and Kare must be there when *Tatya-Masi* opened the box.

Norane was moving quickly past the stables. Lilia, in her wedding gown, was a white figure moving at the same rapid pace past the security guards at the edge of the *estancia*. Don Carlos ran but could not catch his daughter.

Kare also hurried but not so fast as to pass Don Carlos. He instinctively knew Norane was going to the Cave of the *Xucha* below the waterfall fed by the lake.

The chase went past the community schoolhouse. People from the village who had gathered at the edge of the *estancia* to watch the ceremony followed behind Kare. Word of the strange occurrence spread and more hurried from their houses, stores, cafes, and bars to watch the spectacle.

Eduardo, dressed in a tuxedo, as was his father, came roaring by on his motorcycle, skidded to a stop by his sister, jumped off and stopped her. Kare slowed his pace and watched as Don Carlos also reached his daughter.

Lilia did not appear to resist. Her expression was peaceful but unresponsive as if she were having a happy dream. With an arm around her shoulder as if she might fall, Don Carlos led Lilia back to the mansion. She continued to press the jeweled box with two hands to her chest.

Eduardo climbed back on his motorcycle. He and Norane might have been best friends before they were men, but now Kare saw a cold fury in Eduardo's eyes for what Norane had done to his sister and family. His brother was about to die.

A buried loyalty and love made Kare want to save Norane, but the Plumed

Serpent overrode that concern. Kare had his own unalterable mission to perform. He followed Don Carlos from a distance of twenty-five yards and watched him lead Lilia through the door of his laboratory.

Kare walked past the guards as if he belonged there, waited a few minutes and opened the same door into the laboratory, and moved past the metal shelves on which lay tagged and bound pieces of La'ku history.

Not daring to go into the reception area, he hung back in the laboratory looking out into the library, waiting for the Plumed Serpent to tell him what to do.

After an uncomfortable hour hiding in the mansion, Kare saw Moss walk past the open library door with Lilia's younger sister, Matilde. Now, he knew what *Quetzal* wanted him to do.

Holding his cap in his hand, he moved past the empty display case that had recently contained Curratta's *tunjo* and into the foyer in time to hear Matilde say, "Wait here for a minute, and then come up to her room."

Moss was left standing alone.

When Matilde reached the top of the stairs, Kare approached the groom.

Theodore Moss acted shy but confident. He smiled in the open, egalitarian manner of people from the United States. Though not strong, he was handsome in a studious sort of way with sandy blond hair combed to the right over a broad forehead. Kare had heard gossip that Moss was a petroleum engineer who had met Lilia at a university up north. Lilia had agreed to marry him after a long courtship and many visits to Omagua. Kare was suspicious that Norane had always loved Lilia and could not bear that she had selected another man; that was why he had given her the box.

"Excuse me, Mister Moss," Kare spoke the English he had learned at the Cristóbal School.

Moss still looking around, trying to understand what had happened to his bride, nodded at him. "Yes?" he asked, expecting more terrible news.

Driven by *Quetzal*, Kare pressed the gift into Moss' hand. "Mister Moss,

Señor, I want to give you a present."

Kare followed Moss' gaze down to the ancient silver cross. A gleam flashed in the eyes of the snake and Kare felt the Plumed Serpent working his way into Moss' mind.

The *yanqui's* eyes narrowed from a soft focus to hard attentiveness, trying to resist and then succumbing to alien intrusion. Kare remembered the first burning sensations of sharing his mind and will with *Quetzal.* He wondered if Moss would be stronger than he had been.

"Thank you...?"

"Kare Kuwaru'wa, *Señor,* your driver. And may I say, *Señor,* that I am at your service." Pressing his case, he said, "I would be most honored to be your personal servant."

"Servant?" Moss looked at him in a manner that made Kare feel he had gone too far. Kare was uncertain how to say he wanted to stay near Moss and the cross. But he need not have worried; the Plumed Serpent took care of that.

* * *

Ten months after the wedding, Kare received a telephone call from Theodore Moss telling him to come to California. The next day, Kare was stacking cardboard boxes of supplies on the deck of an outboard motorboat moored to a dock on the Lake of the Frogs in the Sierra Nevada Mountains of California. The prow was covered with a peaked roof backed by a dashboard, steering wheel and throttle. The summer sun heated his skin to a dry crisp, more of a burning sensation than what passed through the denser humid air of Omagua.

Did *Quetzal* have a sense of humor? How else to explain traveling thousands of miles from the jungle to the mountains of California to a forest named after the ancient La'ku king Dorado, to a place called the Lake of the Frogs? There had to be something powerful about this mountain lake to hide the infant *Tatya-Masi* from *Inika* and the spirits of Fire. The sunlight seemed brighter and closer than what passed through the denser humid air of Omagua. The power of *Quetzal* spread between the mountain peaks forming an invisible screen over this lonely place, protecting them from the Fire spirits *Xiulu* Lord of Fire had sent to Earth to kill the Water god—*Mitnal* the Smoking Mirror who had possessed the body of his cousin Hernando Rosas, and *Kinchel* the Avenger with his nine human, snake, and wolf heads.

How long would the Plumed Serpent keep him in this land of pine trees and cold water, Kare wondered? Would *Tatya-Masi* remain here until the Sun reached the eye of the archer in eighteen years?

Kare worked alone. Moss stood on the dock beside Edgar Weinmann, an Austrian doctor, or nurse, or someone from the hospital where Lilia had given birth to *Tatya-Masi.*

Kare did not know how she had come to bear the god. Norane had never been seen again. The day of the wedding, Moss had taken the bride away, still holding the box with the *tunjo*. When they had reached the airport, it was Moss who carried the box. Moss had told Kare that if anyone asked about the box, he was to say that it had been lost. Maybe there was something in the container that had spawned the god. All the ways and powers of the spirits were not for him to know. But he had no doubt that Weinmann held *Tatya-Masi* wrapped in a thin white blanket in his arms.

The infant god was a horrible sight; a real freak, with a squished face, bulging eyes and distended lips that seemed to cut the head in a long gash from ear to ear. It had no legs, rather two bones inside a pointed tail. How could this thing destroy the world? Why didn't they just kill it now?

"Cruuahh, crrruuuaaa," the deity bawled, a helpless, plaintive, longing sound like a cross between the caw of a crow and the bleat of a goat.

Edgar rearranged the blanket around the deity's face.

Kare wondered about the Austrian. In his early thirties, frizzy blond hair on the sides of a head that looked too large for his body, his cheeks and the surface of his nose and the tips of his large ears already burned red in the thin air. He was a composer who had agreed to the job because he wanted solitude to write his music. Kare did not sense the Serpent in him. There was nothing of the Lordess of Water about him either, not like Norane. He just seemed like a kind man who cared for the helpless being in his arms.

The thought of Norane caused a reflexive pang of sorrow. Though nobody saw it or accused Eduardo to his face, everyone knew Eduardo had shot and killed Norane the day of the wedding.

"Ver are vee going?" Edgar spoke English with an accent that sounded like a Nazi in the movies.

That was a good question. Kare cocked his head to better hear what the Serpent had planned for them.

"I am taking you where that unfortunate deformity can live or die without notice or fanfare," Moss said. He was a different man now that *Quetzal* was inside of him. Others might think that it was the tragedy of having to commit his new wife to a mental institution that had hardened him, but Kare knew that what made him so dour was the Serpent working his will on the young *yanqui*.

Edgar pursed his lips, wanting to say something but resisted.

"As you can see," Moss looked at the thick woods surrounding the lake, "it is unlikely that anyone will bother you here."

When the boat was loaded, and Kare and Weinmann were aboard, Moss went back to the truck. Kare knew the real reason they were there—to be with *Tatya-Masi* when he opened the box so the Water god would have the power to free *Quetzal* the Plumed Serpent.

The silver and gold box glinted in the sun as Moss stepped onto the boat and set the cursed container on the dashboard.

There was not much room for standing. Kare stood in a small cleared space in the center of the deck. The engine started with a growl that disturbed the placid tranquility of the lake. The powerboat lurched forward, throwing Kare back so that he almost fell against Weinmann and the god.

They motored past steep mountains that fell to the shore, through thick forests, sheer cliffs and jumbles of boulders split at sharp angles. This looked like a good place to hide. He did not see a house, person, or boat, during the one-hour journey up the lake toward what looked like a wall of mountains. The Lordess of Water and the *Xucha* witches had to know their god had been born. Kare doubted the Serpent could shield *Tatya-Masi* from them. How long would *Quetzal* keep him in this land of pine trees and cold water? When would *Tatya-Masi* open the shell?

A lone gull banked above the boat, dipped and glided over them. Before he could react, Kare saw a single ray escape the box and reflect in the water bird's eye. Kare swallowed hard and wished he had a gun to shoot the gull down, but knew it would do no good if what he'd seen were a spirit of *Inika*. The bird squawked and flew upward into the blue sky, and began to spin in an unnatural circle. Dark clouds spiraled from its wings and expanded into a swirling storm that rolled down from the peaks through the Christmas tree forest. The dry mountain air changed to a hot clinging heaviness. Kare didn't care if they were in California. This was a jungle storm and he didn't need *Quetzal* to tell him that *Inika* had found them.

The Plumed Serpent spoke to Kare, "Protect the Jewels. Do not let the Lordess have *Tatya-Masi*."

Moss must have heard the same warning. He pushed the throttle to full power and steered the boat to shore, bouncing heavily over rising whitecaps.

"Cruuuu."

The sound was a wavering incantation from the spirit world, as if a chorus of voices were casting a spell. The witches were here. Within the spinning cloud Kare saw La'ku faces and bodies. The spout was made of thousands of dead souls.

"Cruuuuu!"

"Boom!"

Thunder exploded. Lightening bolts shot from the black funnel. "Aiieee!"

Kare screamed.

The boat was picked up and twirled through the air, lighter than a piece of straw, carried into the sky in a sickening spin that whipped Kare around and sucked the air from his lungs. He saw the jeweled box containing the *tunjo* lifted by the devil wind and carried away to the center of the lake.

From a height higher than the tops of the trees, Kare was dropped, smashed into the lake, plunged far into the cold, clear water. He kicked his feet dragged down by his shoes. Only the strength of the Serpent kept him from drowning. He pulled his way from the depths to the surface, gasping for air. Waves rolled over him. Through the whitecaps and rain, he couldn't see the boat or shore.

He heard a cry behind him, and paddled to find the Austrian calling that he'd lost hold of the "child." "Help me," Weinmann pleaded and dove, searching for the god.

The wind and rain lessened, and soon sunshine was moving from the mountains onto the lake. Kare knew he would have been dead long before he reached the shore if not for the warmth and strength *Quetzal* gave him. He abandoned Weinmann and swam to a rocky jetty that thrust into the lake. Moss was already on the beach watching the lake with a dumbfounded expression.

Kare staggered onto the smooth rocks, and fell to his knees, sharing Moss' agony, the twisting of their guts at *Quetzal*'s fury. They had lost the box. He looked far out into the lake where the prow stuck out of the water, surrounded by floating supplies.

What did this mean? This had to be the work of the Lordess of Water. But why would she destroy the god? How could the Plumed Serpent ever be freed now?

"Shrraaaaaaa."

Kinchel the Avenger was also here. He saw the nine-headed hydra and felt his fury cut him. How could Kare be there when *Tatya-Masi* opened the box? Kare shivered from a cold that was more painful than could be caused by ice or snow. He lay on the flat rocks wanting to die.

Then he heard the sound.

"Craaa."

He lifted his head from his arms and saw that the god had broken out of the membrane sheaf around its lower body. With bent legs and tiny arms held before it, in a position of prayer, the infant *Tatya-Masi* hopped from the lake with a happy smile on its amphibian-like face.

CHAPTER FOUR

TATYA-MASI

Sixteen Years Later – My Life.

My state of mind changes when I'm in the water. I feel more like an animal, living in the moment. My senses are heightened. My protruding eyes collect light so I can see in the translucent lake nearly as far as I can on land. Immersed, scents are fresh and pungent–like the smell of the forest just after a rain.

Feeling is my gift. My super-power is a great, boundless empathy. Edgar thinks that I have an excess of mirror neurons that enable me to feel what another feels to the point that I can read his mind and experience his memories. This allows me to create so strong a connection with someone that he or she and everyone else sees me as that person. Kare says that I'm *Mestaclocan*, Shapeshifter. Not that I get to use my empathy on that many people.

I can't reveal myself to anyone but Kare and Edgar because *Xiulu* Lord of Fire is searching everywhere to kill me, and his spirits might be lurking in any fire. Where we live is very isolated. Only a few campers come into the woods around our cabin. Once when I was eight years old, I'd peeked from behind the broad trunk of a sequoia at a family camping by the lake. They'd built a fire surrounded by beach stones. That summer day, I became intoxicated by all the many things I'd never had in the cabin: the scent of cooking hotdogs and hamburgers, cans of soft drinks, marshmallows, family and laughter. I'd crept closer until I could hear the crackling of the flames.

I took a chance and used my empathy to change my appearance to Edgar. I stepped from the woods, shape-shifting into my tutor so that campers saw a white-haired, small man, dressed in shorts. The family had welcomed me, and in full view of the fire, I'd approached them until I saw a burning log flare and a spark rise into the sky. I became frightened that a Fire spirit had seen me and hopped away into the woods as fast as I could. As I fled, I heard the father exclaim, "Will you look at that? He's hopping like a frog!"

I suppose I do look a bit like a frog, well, really, a lot like a frog, a very big frog. At six feet I weigh nearly two hundred pounds—cumbersome and heavy on land but swift and supple in the water. My bulbous eyes and nostrils protrude from a sloping skull circled by a tonsure, a monk's ring of short bristly hair. Olive skin runs taut over the veined bald dome of my head, falling to fleshy jowls, and secreting a slime that keeps my skin moist when I'm out of the water. This aids in the osmosis that allows me to breathe underwater. Still, I must immerse myself in water every few hours or my skin rapidly dries and peels.

Edgar was the one who named me Du—the familiar German pronoun for you—but it might as well be short for duality—land/water; boy/frog.

Usually being underwater calmed me, but the thought of Edgar so sick lying in the cabin on the shore haunted me. What would I do if Edgar died? He was my guide. I saw the world through his eyes. I had always assumed when I ventured from the lake he would go with me, introduce me, help me cope with what he had described as the undeniably profound impact I would have on those outside our household.

Underwater, the scent of fish is as clear to me as the aroma of pine on land after it rains. The fish can smell me as well as I can them. I rose to the surface, stuck out my nose to catch a breath, and with a kick of my webbed feet dove again, swimming to where Silver Creek flowed into the lake. My fist-sized eyes moved independently, up or down, left or right, searching for a trout.

The first rays of dawn penetrated the twelve feet of water above me illuminating bits of suspended dirt and algae. Seven yards away behind a boulder somewhat protected from the stream's flow a knot of trout fed on insects and other nutrients delivered by the creek. A plume of sand formed to my left where a brown trout stirred up the bottom, looking for frog eggs. There used to be lots of frogs in the lake before the browns had been stocked there for the fishermen. The California frogs had no defenses against this Scottish species and had been almost wiped out. It is perhaps another irony of my existence that just as the world's population of frogs is in severe decline—decimated by fungus and global warming—I should appear.

The oily scent of a brown caused me to sweep my nose through the water. Fifteen feet toward the dark of the deep water a shape as big as a log hovered just behind a boulder.

Brownie!

Here was one fish I had never been able to catch. The queen of the lake lived in the deep waters and only ventured into the shallows to spawn.

She had always sensed me before I could get close enough to successfully pursue her.

Today the huge brown trout was careless. I readied my spear but decided she was too far away for a shot.

We both moved at the same time. I sprang kicking as rapidly as I could; my head thrust forward, arms pressed to my side. I'm fast underwater, but I couldn't catch an old fish like Brownie by coming right at her.

Brownie flapped her massive tail—the size of a Red-tailed Hawk's wing—against the resistance of the water and shot toward the depths.

Extended, speeding, I couldn't see her, but I sensed her. If she turned, she would escape me. I had to intercept her before she reached the drop-off to the black water.

I narrowed the distance between us. The bottom sloped to an underwater canyon. The trout, a body-length from me, turned her tail to the surface and swam down the face of the cliff, a flying shadow melding into the darkness.

To follow her was to risk drowning. I can breathe underwater only for so long. The deeper I go, the harder it is for me to extract oxygen from the water. But what a feast for Edgar if I caught Brownie. I needed all the miracles I could muster. If my prayers had not healed Edgar, then maybe by eating the strongest fish in the lake, Edgar would be revived.

I beat my feet in an exhausting whir trying to stay close to her, downward into a dark world where I never dared venture. The pressure flattened my chest like a giant's hands. Panic and remorse tightened my throat as I told myself I'd stayed down too long, dove too deep. Go up!

The shade of a shadow of a leaf at night wavered against the ledge. I couldn't see her, but I felt her. I *knew* Brownie was there.

I stretched the sling and launched my spear. It stuck. As the wounded fish dove for the bottom, the shudder of steel passing into flesh rumbled up the line and tore the wooden handle to the tips of my fingers. Somehow, I managed to hold onto the sling.

I swam after my trout trying not to pull out the shaft. I was not going to lose her.

I'd lost fish before, but when the line went limp in my hands, I knew I'd never catch another. The spear drifted up toward me. I'd killed myself for a dream. I was drowning. The edge of my vision sparkled and faded to darkness. I was too far from the surface. My mouth opened in a reflexive gasp.

In my fading consciousness, a flash of green gleamed in the darkness like the first burst of moonlight over the mountain peaks.

"Cruuuu."

I heard a chorus of female voices echoing in the depths. The sound, a longing, keening, seemed to herald my death.

"Cruuuu."

I was out of air, dying. The singing altos vibrating through the water calmed me. My panic eased into acceptance.

With one last effort, I dove to the aquamarine penumbra and thrust my hand into the phosphorescent halo, touching something hard.

Energy coursed through my body; a rush of excitement, but more intense, every doubt or limitation had disappeared.

This was it! The box! I had found the box!

Kare had told me that there was a container in the lake that held a magic amulet that would turn me into a god. He'd said that some day I would find it when it was time for me to be *Tatya-Masi*.

The burning in my lungs and panic eased. I felt myself ascending, protected by a sphere of emerald light. In the uncertain time of a dream, I rose to the surface without the need for breath or sight.

I floated on my back, holding the container to my chest. I've sensed spirits in the rocks, trees and water. I've communicated with animals by their calls and a sharing of the universal exchange of energy. Now, the dimensional boundaries I've known, the borders between the spiritual and physical planes, waft in a supernatural breeze. The familiar landscape pulses with auras that breathe and shimmer with life flows I don't yet understand. My eyesight is sharpened so that I see the eye of a gull circling against the gray clouds spilling over the peaks of the mountains. I hear the sound of a fish splashing a hundred yards away. The empowerment, the altered interaction between my body and the atmosphere, made me wonder if I had died and been reborn in another life. Yet nothing was changed about the familiar landscape.

Heavy raindrops slapped my face. I rolled my left eye and saw the contours and rock formations of the shore I had always known.

A few strong kicks brought me onto the stream-rounded stones of the beach. The strange energy subsided and left me so exhausted I staggered ashore to collapse to my knees beside a driftwood tree.

"Cruuuu."

The reverberating chorus penetrated, filled my mind.

I fingered the tarnished surface with its relief of frogs and salamanders, and then turned the box over. In the center was a raised image of me.

"Cruuuuu."

The sound was a living presence surrounding the box. The space around the box shimmered like heat rising from hot sand. In the distorted air, ancient women reached for me, their mouths open, wailing.

"Cruuuu."

The plume of altered reality grew and coalesced into an ephemeral shape hovering four feet in front of me. I flinched back from a hag as old as a sequoia floating a foot off the ground. Tufts of white hair sprouted from her bald head. Her eyes protruded from thick round sockets on a frog face stretched tight with olive flesh. Lips curved from ear to ear. I guessed she looked like some ancient relative of mine. I knew she was Curratta.

Now everything Kare had told me had the immediacy of a warning. My feelings of joy were replaced by breath-stealing dread. This was no toy I was holding. The power in this box would decide the fate of the world.

"Cruuuuu."

The dimensional boundaries between time, celestial and temporal, collapsed around me. The borders between the spiritual and physical planes wafted like curtains in a supernatural breeze. Twelve witches, bent, ancient women, skeletons covered with parched and withered skin, emerged from the ether and formed a coterie behind Curratta.

"Cruuuu."

The witches chanted.

"Craaaack." Sharp peals of thunder barreled across the mountains. Lightning flashed as light-soaking clouds roiled in the sky.

"Cruuuuu."

A spirit glided through a waving tear in the physical fabric of land, atmosphere, and water.

I recognized her with certainty. Mother.

Of all my dreams my favorite fantasy was to see my mother and to feel her touch. I had pestered Kare and Edgar for descriptions of her, constructed a thousand images from the collage of their memories. She was not frog-like. Beautiful raven hair fell over pale complexion, brown eyes. Red lips smiled at me. Edgar had told me that she was unconscious and had not spoken since she was brought to the hospital where I was born. Was she really here?

"Cruuuuu."

The witches parted around the vision coming toward me. Peace spread through my body. Unwavering trust enveloped me like a welcoming hug.

"Open the box."

Mother's voice inside a celestial wind sang in my ear, harmonizing with the "cruuuuu" rustling in the breeze. The spirit intoned: "Your power is inside the box.

She extended her hand to my cheek. I could not feel her touch. She turned her palms up in supplication, raised her shoulders and faded into the gray horizon. The vision of Curratta and the witches dispersed, blown away by the metaphysical wind.

Thunder ricocheted off the sides of the mountains and rolled down the valleys. The warm rain incited the aroma of pine and sage. But there was another, more sinister, scent in the unusual humid air. The forest was burning; but I saw no flames or smoke among the evergreen pinnacles. Lightning flashed and crackled. Static charges raised the villous down on the back of my neck.

To the north erupting clouds blending from gray to purple to impenetrable all-absorbing black overpowered the last sliver of sunlight.

I watched the waves rushing toward me on the shore of the Lake of the Frogs; dark-backed with a shining face reflecting the sky, the shades of the forest and rocks on the mountainsides.

If I opened the box then I was *Tatya-Masi*. I could heal Edgar.

My hope of curing Edgar was tempered by a deep sense of danger. The unnatural rain—warmer than a summer thunderstorm, dense from another climate—extinguished my euphoria within a damp squeeze.

"Craaaack!"

A bolt of lightning struck the remains of the cedar beside me. Shockwaves threw me onto my back upon the stone beach. The bleached wood burst into flames.

"Shhhhraaaaa!"

If the "cruuu" sound came from the air, this disturbance arose from the earth—a hissing that vented from beneath the mountains, a threatening guttural growl that caused adrenalin to race through my veins, a beast ready to maul me.

In the searing orange heat, the slanted eyes of a terrifying apparition burned. A dragon with nine heads, some human, one of a wolf, weaved and darted, leathery wings tipped with flames, focused its many ember eyes on me. The terrible specter caused my mouth to drop, my eyes to press outward from my sockets, my urge to flee overwhelming any sense that flight was possible.

Fiery forked tongues flitted and scorched my hand. Searing pain shot up my arm. I dropped the box and cringed in agony and terror, overcome with weakness, burning yet unable to move from the fire.

With a slap, as if a giant upturned hand had struck the surface of the lake, a ball of water shot over the shore and landed on the burning tree, leaving a smoldering wisp where the apparition had appeared.

I cautiously rose to a crouch ready to leap in any direction. My eyes moved in full-range arcs scanning the air, lake, and woods. The fuming remains of the embers blew past me and finally I was released. I jumped back, twisted in the air and landed in a full gallop back to the cabin. Abandoning the box and my spear, I bounded home, head extended so far forward only my momentum kept me from falling over.

I wanted to share Edgar's amused discrediting of Kare and his primitive beliefs, but what I had just seen was not the myths of a distant Latin American Indian tribe. This was real, here, now. Every concept I had of myself, heaven and Earth felt blasted apart in shards, shattered like the breaking of a mirror, leaving distorted refractions of rationality, of science and religion, their physical and spiritual planes.

As I raced back to the cabin, the story of a coming war between the Lord of Fire and Lordess of Water had the immediacy of a warning I'd failed to heed. The war for the next World was not supposed to start for another two years.

I hadn't opened the box, I repeated to myself. I'm *not Tatya-Masi*! I am *not* a god! I rotated an eye to search the gloomy sky for a supernatural presence to which I could plead my case, but saw only rolls of plum-colored thunderheads. What if I had already made the choice through ignorance and inexperience? Who was going to tell me how to be a god? All I had to go on were Kare's stories of magic and miracles, of battles between the Lordess of Water and Lord of Fire for domination of the Earth, of a Fire spirit named *Quetzal* the Plumed Serpent who was protecting me from the other Fire spirits because he needed a Water god to free him.

I raced out of the woods across the meadow to our lakeside cabin, leapt over our winter supply of stacked wood, hopped past a scratched table flaked with dry fish scales, jumped headfirst through the rear door of the cabin, and landed naked beside the kitchen table.

Kare was cooking at the wood-fired stove. His long hair was pulled into a ponytail; he wore a traditional blue La'ku shirt, colorfully embroidered with quetzal birds. His hooded eyes expanded from the dark shadows of his heavy brows when he saw the box in my hand.

"*¡La encontré! ¡La caja!*" I cried.

Kare refused to communicate in English. Edgar, like so many other things, had taught me English. As soon as I could talk, I had become their multilingual translator.

Kare backed against the counter, his hands held before him, to stop an attack. "Did you open it?" he gasped.

"No, but something came; something horrible, a dragon with nine heads. There were heads of humans and a wolf. It was the scariest thing I've ever seen."

"*Kinchel* the Avenger." Kare's voice quivered.

Kinchel was one of the three Fire spirits who had come to battle *Inika* Lordess of Water for rule of the next World. He commanded the Assassins of Fire–humans and animals, to do his bidding on the Earth.

"I saw my mother. She wanted me to open the box."

"Lilia? Are you sure?"

"She was with Curratta and the other witches."

A deep disturbance of thunder rolled across the lake. Kare looked at the rain through the window over the sink. "Lilia," he whispered. "Was there a man, a La'ku, with her?"

I held onto the thin tabletop to keep from sinking to the floor. "I don't think so."

He grabbed a worn and hand-shaped cowboy hat from a peg on the wall beside the rear door. "Take me to the box."

I shrank from him toward the doorway to the main room. "No. I can't. The dragon is there."

"You must bring the box to *Quetzal*. Remember what I have told you. Inside is a *tunjo*. When you hold this *tunjo* rain will fall without end and the Age of Man will drown. *Quetzal* will tell you when and how to open the box."

The ways and motives of the La'ku gods and spirits now meant everything to me. I wished I had asked more questions, taken Kare more seriously when he had described their complicated shifting alliances. Now, I had to hope Kare was right and there was some way to appease or escape these terrible demons.

"Go now." Kare pushed me by the upper arm.

I leaned against his impetus. I felt weak, feverish. I did not want to go anywhere near the box, certain *Kinchel* the Avenger was waiting there for me to return.

"Why can't you go get it?" I whined.

"Hurry!" Kare shoved me so hard I fell against the door and stumbled outside.

"You bring the box to *Quetzal?* It's on the beach, by the creek."

"Only you can control the power of the *tunjo.*"

"But what if I'm not *Tatya-Masi?*"

Kare ignored my doubt that I was the god, staying behind me, herding me with staunch purpose.

"Let me get dressed at least." I stalled finding and putting on my wet pants by the dock where our sixteen-foot powerboat bobbed. Rain was falling harder. What if just by finding the box I had started rain falling all over the world? I had no more idea of how to stop the rain than how I or anybody or anything could start it. I thought of asking Kare if he thought I should take the box back and drop it into the bottom of the lake where it had been hidden all these years, but that would mean my having to carry it. I still hoped to convince him that he should be the one to retrieve the container.

I searched the horizon for any sign of a break in the clouds. The dark masses seemed to be trapping every ray of sunlight. Boulders I could easily have hopped over blocked the shortest route back to the box. I was in no hurry. Moisture pasted Kare's black bangs to his forehead. Beads of water rolled from his hooked nose and square chin. I had more sympathy for him now. He had lived with these terrible spirits since he had first held the Serpent's cross. No wonder Kare had always seemed distant, studying me with a hunter's focus. If he was to be believed, *Quetzal* had protected me from *Kinchel* because the Plumed Serpent hoped that someday I would free him. But if I could free *Quetzal* that would mean I was a Water deity. I was *Tatya-Masi*. If this were true then *Kinchel* the Avenger would never spare me. I was in no hurry as I crept through the last stand of Jeffrey pines, and pointed. "There it is."

"Get it."

"No! It's…it makes me feel…"

Kare shot his sharp brown-eyed gaze from the magical container to me and back, leaning away, ready to run. "*Quetzal* will protect you, as he has always done."

The idea that a benevolent spirit was watching over me gave me little comfort. Fear caused my thoughts to rush too fast to sort or make decisions.

"I can't."

"You must," he harshly whispered, trying not to be overheard by unseen spirits. "Bring the box to *Quetzal*. He alone can teach you how to use its power. Go now." He shoved me from the back, managing to knock me a few inches away from the tree I was hiding behind.

The air seemed to be growing warmer, more humid. What if the prophecy was true about rains without end drowning the fires of men and women? The rain slapping my face, making small craters in the mud, and bending the grass took on a more terrible aspect. I looked quickly at Kare. He was staring at the box. He would not help me. I had to do this myself.

Taking one final deep breath, and trembling so much I wobbled when I landed, I hopped to the intricately fashioned container, watching it as if it were a coiled rattlesnake. My vision spun and I swayed with the overload of senses. A sudden longing to feel the power I had when I held the box became a craving more demanding than the dread of my apprehension.

"Pick it up," Kare ordered from the edge of the forest.

I bent over and tentatively reached for the container. At the touch of the cool, wet metal my thoughts cleared. My strength increased. The shapes of pinecones on distant trees were visible again. The scurry of small forest animals came to me on the rush of the wind.

"Cruuuuuu."

Curratta and her host of witches swirled around me.

I looked at Kare. I was certain he couldn't see the *Xucha*. Otherwise I doubt he would have been able to maintain his focused concentration on the box.

The image of Curratta, the high shaman of the *Xucha*, wavered before me. Her voice cackled a hoarse, high singsong.

"*Tatya-Masi*."

The chorus of female voices vibrated the air.

"Cruuuuu."

Longing nearly overwhelmed me. I ran my tongue across the cartilaginous edges of my lips and stared into the emerald eyes of the relief of *Tatya-Masi* on the cover. To hold and possess the *tunjo* would answer every question, and give me the knowledge I needed to safely find my way through the conflict into which I had been cast. The rush of new awareness gave me confidence. I would learn to use this power. Inspiration would guide me. I was at the beginning of a great adventure. My life would be filled with excitement, my former dull existence a lamentable memory. I could open it right now. My eyes shifted to Kare. His warning that only *Quetzal* could tell me how to open the box without causing a worldwide flood made me hesitate. Where was the Plumed Serpent now? Curratta and the witches hovered before me. They wanted me to open the box. They promised that I would have the power to heal Edgar. What was I waiting for? Clearly, I was the god.

"Hold me."

The witches' spell entwined my will.

I had to become what I was meant to be. Just as the box brought into focus the blurred ephemera of the spiritual world, I could see into the future and knew what would happen if I opened the box. I saw the result of rain without end. Men, women and children drowned in swirling brown floods; walls of water-destroyed homes, collapsed churches; schools, art galleries and museums washed away. The new World of Water would come with widespread destruction and ruin.

"Come, Du. Hurry!" Kare implored.

I moved in slow careful jumps, carrying the box with both hands before my chest. Curratta and her covey of ghosts followed me, casting spells, trying to reach from the celestial realm to influence me.

"Tell me about *Kinchel*," I said to Kare.

"He is a Lord of Fire. *Kinchel* the Avenger protects the World of Fire. He commands the Assassins of Fire."

I dropped lower and looked around. "What are they?"

"They can be humans or animals. You will know if you ever see one."

What would the *Xucha* do if I brought the box to the Plumed Serpent? "What about Curratta?" I asked.

His wet face spun toward me. He slipped in the mud and pushed himself onto one knee, grabbing the stripped limb of a fallen sugar pine, and propelled himself down the trail. "Do not listen to her. Hurry. *Quetzal* will protect you."

From whom? *Inika*? *Kinchel* the Avenger and the Assassins of Fire? Or from myself? I knew I could not resist the lure of the box for long.

CHAPTER FIVE
THE IDOL

Kare led me straight to his room. Candlelight flickered in its dark corner and shined on the altar to *Quetzal*. Against the wall beside his bed was a platform set on four black volcanic rocks. Parrot feathers, dried palm leaves, and seashells framed a three-foot high carving of *Quetzal* the Plumed Serpent: a dark red mahogany snakehead with the body of a landing bird, flame-tipped wings spread.

A golden cross wrapped with a winged serpent with red jeweled eyes hung from a silver chain from the statue's eagle-like neck. Here was the cross that Kare had taken from the conquistador's skeleton in the Cave of the *Xucha*.

Even inside the cabin, the air had grown unnaturally hot and muggy. Rain drummed against the boards on the roof and splashed against the windowpanes. If I opened the box, how long before the log cabin was beaten down by the rain and covered by the rising lake?

"Present the box to *Quetzal*." Kare pointed at the foot of the auburn bust.

I hesitated. The idea of giving up the box was as grievous as being asked to cut off my hands.

"Lord *Quetzal*," Kare intoned. "I have brought you the *tunjo*. The Water god is here. He is ready to serve you. Show us your will."

A bolt of lightening struck a tree not fifty yards outside the window.

"Shhhhraaaaa!"

The corpse of a dead pine burst into flames. I shrank to the ground, breathless, shivering with fear. If I tried to open the box, *Kinchel* the Avenger would never let me live long enough to be a god.

"Hurry Du, there is not much time. Tell *Quetzal* you will serve him."

I rotated an eye and kept it on Kare as an anchor to keep me from being swept away by the magic around me. Holding the vessel of the destruction of the Age of Man, I knelt before the idol of the Plumed Serpent.

The witches' response to my betrayal was to increase their chanting.

"Cruuuuu."

"Cruuuuu."

"Save us, please save us," I babbled and dropped the box. As soon as my physical connection with it was broken, I fell backwards to the floor. I groaned, my forehead and underarms wet with clammy sweat.

Nothing happened. The sound of rain beat on the roof like the fall of approaching steps. I rose to a crouch and looked at Kare, expecting to see disappointment. I had done something wrong, had not known the correct way to contact his Fire spirit.

But Kare's constant focus remained on the statue. I followed his gaze and gasped. On Kare's alter, the ruby eyes of the Serpent flared. A stream of red and yellow gas streamed from the carved snakehead's pearl nostrils.

I shrank toward the door. Numbing, trembling fear caused my eyes to bulge.

The wooden body transformed into a living, vibrant presence. *Quetzal's* golden reptilian head turned; his magenta eyes followed me. The silver breast expanded. Long feathers spread behind him in a tail of dancing colors.

If this was what was going to protect me, the ally seemed no less terrible than the enemy. Kare blocked my escape or I would have fled in blind terror to the bottom of the lake. The serpentine form horrified me. I saw myself in the reflection of his lambent eyes—my round lower jaw hanging limply in a stupid and confused expression.

Quetzal's hollow voice echoed inside my brain with a distinct courtly,

Spanish accent. I felt appreciated and protected by him.

"You understand. We can help each other. Our common good is the good of the many."

"Cruuuuu."

The witches screamed for my attention, for my devotion. But I could not take my eyes off *Quetzal*.

"Together we will save the Age of Man. Take the box. Inside are two of the Jewels of Life. Carry them to Manoa. There you will find *Cocatamia* the Staff of Life. Imbedded in the Staff are the two remaining Jewels of Life. Only when you possess all four Jewels will you be able to stop the rain. Only then will you be able to free me."

Either by *Quetzal's* magic or through the strength of my newly empowered empathy, I saw a vision of *Cocatamia* the Staff of Life—a one foot wand on which the eyes of *Tatya-Masi* held the other two Jewels of Life—two small translucent jewels that reflected light in bright flashes and at the same time emitted their own internal emerald radiance.

"How...?" The thought barely formed and the Serpent responded, his voice quietly urgent. "Find your mother. Her body lives, even as her spirit is in Manoa. Give her the *tunjo*. She will guide you to Manoa. Beware. *Kinchel* seeks the destruction of the tunjo and your defeat. Do not wear the *tunjo*. The Assassins of Fire are near."

Even under the intoxication of *Quetzal's* envelopment of my will I could not imagine finding my way to Manoa. How was I supposed to reach a mythical city in Latin America when I was not certain if I could find my way to the nearest town? I had no idea of how to find my mother. If I had known how to find her, I would have tried long ago.

Curratta hovered between *Quetzal* and me. "Do not heed the lies of Fire," she entreated in a high-pitched voice that cackled with rage.

Quetzal grew until he filled the room.

The bald shaman ignored the Plumed Serpent, watching me with eyes set above her cheeks so similar to mine.

"Be strong, *Tatya-Masi*. Open the box. Unite with those who revere you."

"Cruuuuu."

The chorus of female voices vibrated the air.

Quetzal the Plumed Serpent became a dragon whose head reached as high as the ceiling. Red flames flared from the tips of his wings.

The spiritual armies formed battle ranks around the box. Then, choosing a better time and place to fight, the Plumed Serpent spread his wings, and disappeared into a gaseous stream that flowed back into the nostrils of the statue.

The vision of Curratta faded.

Alone with Kare, in the familiar four-room log cabin, the container on the dais seemed the most dangerous object on the planet.

Kare reverently removed the conquistador's cross from around the statue and lowered the necklace over his head. He sighed deeply, reuniting with an elemental source of wellbeing. The translucent eyes in the snake that was wrapped around the cross glinted and then grew placid.

I inhaled deeply with the first breath that seemed my own and not squeezed from me by the pressing spirits.

"Take it," Kare said. "You must carry the box."

He had been the one who had brought the box to California—who had worshiped *Quetzal* all these years. Even as I tried to convince myself I was not to blame, everything I knew about Kare told me he was too small and weak to have been anyone but the servant of the Plumed Serpent. The hellish spirit had lain waiting all these years for the moment that I would find the container. But what then?

"I can't," I whined. "There must be some other way. You carry it."

"No human can be trusted with its powers."

No human. Then what was I? One thing I knew certainly, human or not, I could not bear the burden of the fate of mankind.

"Craaack!"

"Shhhhraaaaa!"

Kinchel was near, waiting for me to hesitate.

Kare pushed me toward the riser where the box lay. But I resisted.

I pulled away from his powerful grip of my shoulders, trying to reach the door. "No," I cried.

When I was small, Kare had taught me how to wrestle. I knew what was coming before I had time to counter his move. "Obey *Quetzal!*" Kare grunted, wrapping his leg behind mine, and using my own weight, spun me around and threw me onto his temple.

With a heavy crash, the shrine collapsed beneath me.

"Hold me," the spirits of the container pleaded.

"Craaak!" *Kinchel's* thunder shook the house.

My hand fell on the box. All feelings of weakness disappeared. I could do anything!

I rose up so strong I could throw Kare from here into the lake if I wanted.

"Good. Good," he said, sensing my transformation. "*Quetzal* will protect us if you do as he says. We must hurry. The Assassins of Fire are near."

Who or what were the Assassins of Fire? Despite my new strength, I did not want to find out.

Kare handed me a wallet. "If we're separated, there is enough money there for you to reach Omagua. Find your way to the cave I have described to you."

"What would I do without you?"

Kare looked me in the eye with great love. "These years I've spent with you have not been wasted. What I'm trying to say is come what may, you are a good, strong boy–a   man, who will do fine anywhere. Just be yourself. A man lost to himself is lost to the world. You have the power to do great good at a time that sorely needs goodness."

He pulled me to him and gave me a quick hug. I suppressed a sob. This was not a time for weakness.

"Come. Come." Kare lead me through the living room.

We were going now. To find my mother, to Manoa.

"Wait." My own voice awoke me from the dream. "What about Edgar? We can't just leave him."

"He has served his purpose. There's no time." Kare cocked his head and looked toward the lake, sensing someone or something approaching.

"I must see to Edgar."

Kare did not dare try to stop me, but followed close behind as I moved past the piano where Edgar had taught me to play into the bedroom we shared. I stopped in the doorway, the box, the fate of the world forgotten.

Edgar lay still on the bed, an arm fallen limply over the side.

Kare watched over my shoulder.

No. Please, no. No, no, I prayed and knelt beside the bed. Lifting Edgar's lifeless arm, I knew the one who loved me best in this world was dead.

"Come," Kare put his hand on my shoulder. "We must hurry. Come. Come."

"Edgar?" I called hesitantly. He might just be asleep. I ignored Kare and looked at my friend and mentor. A suffocating lump rose in my throat. Tears hung on the edge of my lids.

"Hold me," the witches whispered in my ears.

Yes, there was a way. The Jewels of Life give the holder immortality. Inside the box was a power that could resurrect Edgar. If I opened the box...

I held the embossed container over my friend's corpse and as *Inika's* rain fell, I betrayed the Age of Man and whispered, "I am *Tatya-Masi* Bringer of the Sixth World of Water."

"Cruuuu. Cruuuu."

Beams of energy shined through the emerald eyes of the raised image on the lid, focusing straight into mine. With a sound like wind gusting through a crack, the cover lifted and a stream of pulsing light formed into a watery image of *Inika*. The four-headed jaguar surged skyward, leading a swarm of frog-faced *chacs*—their fangs exposed as they joyfully dispersed in every direction.

"Cruuuuuu."

A powerful storm broke hard over the mountain. Lightning struck around the cabin.

I was amazed, but not fearful; thrilled, but not surprised when the swirling cloud cleared enough for me to see, on a cushion of colorful woven fabric, a small gold statuette half as big as the palm of my hand. The head, feet, and legs—every detail—were perfect portrayals of me.

The eyes of the *tunjo* radiated with an awakening power, a power that would end the Age of Fire.

No warning, or memory of doubt or concern for the destruction of modern civilization could stop me from reaching for the *tunjo*.

My strength swelled as I took hold of the heavy gold necklace. Energy arced from the Jewels of Life into my brain, increasing the magnification of my senses a thousand times. I was aware of dimensions I'd only suspected existed...time, memory, transmutation of matter. Life was a web through which I felt the tremble of every strand.

I could see through Edgar's chest the arteries and muscles, to his still heart. I saw the sickness as a multiplying mass that had spread through his liver and taken his life. Heal, I willed.

Charged particles flowed from the *tunjo* and surrounded Edgar's body like a sputtering fire.

His eyes shot open, transformed; split—the witches' jade on the top, Edgar's blue on the bottom.

"Cruuuuuu."

Edgar's bifurcated eyes bulged over his sunken cheeks.

"What have you done?" Kare wailed. "He is possessed by Water. You've unleashed the forces of Water."

"Cruuuuuu."

A wind rushed from behind me.

Edgar's body flew out of the bed. *"Cani wa satay Tatya-Masi yaswa Awkanakuy-Hauakuy!"* he screamed in the voice of the box.

"¡Brujas! Aiiee, the *tunjo!"* Kare turned and fled.

Edgar chased him, eyes shining like nightmare lanterns, a vengeful specter calling out incantations in the dead language that inconceivably I understood.

"With the power of *Tatya-Masi* and the Warrior-Brother I banish the spirits of Fire."

The sight was so shocking I dropped the *tunjo* and box on the bed, and hopped into the living room, knocking a stack of Edgar's musical scores from the piano onto the floor.

A crackling beam of energy flashed from Edgar's finger into Kare's room. The statue of *Quetzal* exploded.

Edgar flew after Kare through the kitchen and into the backyard. I chased him and saw Edgar fall to the ground beside the entrance to his garden.

I hopped out and knelt beside him.

Kare scurried down the dock, pursued by unseen demons. He gunned the motor, not waiting to untie the line and pulled until the cleat ripped from the boards.

Even if I had jumped, I couldn't have swum fast enough to catch the speeding craft disappearing into the gray haze ahead of a widening wake and a rope dragging the skipping cleat.

Death was not strange to me. I had lived in the wild all my life; I had seen the drop of an eagle, the final shudder of a chipmunk in a king snake's coil, the decomposing remains of the animals of the forest and lake. But this was death beyond death. I had wasted the chance to bring Edgar back to life and misused a power I could not control. I had condemned the world to drowning and broken my pact with *Quetzal.* Guilt and anguish pulled at me. Who or what would protect me now from the vengeance of *Kinchel* the Avenger?

I gently put my arms under Edgar's body and cradled him to my chest. He had never been a large man. But now he weighed no more than an armful of books. Rain pasted his pajamas to his emaciated body.

He stirred in my arms. I gasped and my lungs felt pricked with sharp ice. Was he coming back to life?

I dared not evoke the power of the necklace again.

The spirit that had infested him would not allow him even a final word to me. The reptile eyes flashed open.

Curratta's voice spoke through Edgar's unmoving, breathless mouth. "This is the World of Fire, born of the World of Earth. You are the Caller of the Earth of Water. Command the legions of Water, *Tatya-Masi*. The *tunjo* is your weapon. You must wear the *tunjo.*"

With that final effort, the host could no longer accommodate the parasite. The bulging, unnatural eyes closed.

Shamefully, I dropped his body and leaned away.

I fearfully studied Edgar and then bent forward to regather him in my arms. What did I care about new worlds? Let this world drown in a thousand deluges. Only end this pain. A trembling, pitiless loneliness swallowed me. I rolled back my head and wailed at the stormy sky.

CHAPTER SIX
THE ASSASSINS OF FIRE

"You've unleashed the forces of Water." Kare's words floated through my mind. I blindly wandered to the end of the dock where I sat in a daze, my feet dangling over the water. A seagull atop a wooden piling studied me with a cocked head. A chipmunk rose up on its haunches on a rock along the shore. Everything had changed.

Edgar's corpse remained where it had fallen. Muddy puddles were deepening among the reeds and fescue. I should have buried him or taken him inside, but did not move. All I had wanted to do was heal him. What did I know of being a god, and what a terrible god I would be if terrible destiny were my fate.

The weight of the decisions I had to make and the sudden, radical changes in my life, burdened me with such inertia that I stared helplessly at the sheets of rain falling in striated lines from the dark clouds. I was sixteen years old. Edgar had provided me with a good education. There never had been a shortage of books in the cabin. But I'd also never been to school and had never had contact with anyone but Kare and Edgar.

"Craaack!" A lightening bolt danced on the water just offshore.

I had not done this. This rain was only a passing storm. A cold, crisp breeze would soon blow the unusual damp warmth in the air away. The necklace and box in the room were certainly strange and had powers that could not be easily explained, but this was not my fault. There was nothing

I could do about it.

Never mind trying to find my way to Manoa. What was I supposed to do to survive? Never mind saving humanity—as if I could. Edgar was dead. Kare gone. What was I supposed to do now? Live as a hermit? Go find a father who had never once visited me or sent a letter? All I knew of my mother was that she was at a hospital somewhere in Oregon.

"Hold me."

"Wear me."

The voice drifted on the whipping wind from the house. What had I done? What force had I unleashed on the world?

"No! No! It can't be. Edgar, Edgar," I wept. "What should I do?" My unheard voice fell weak and useless in the vast dome of the lake and mountains, a now empty void. Maybe it was the deep feeling of loss that came from Edgar's death, but this world already seemed destroyed. What of the Eldorado Forest, my world? The animals of this place that had nurtured me, that I loved, would drown along with the cities and people I had never seen, never known.

Edgar would not have believed this. I could easily imagine his voice calling it superstitious nonsense. Just this morning I could have asked him, talked to him about it. Now he was gone, and I was alone.

I did not want to live in a World of Water. I wanted a family and friends. I didn't want to live like an amphibian—a freak of nature— alone in the wild. But what could I do? I had never been beyond the woods. How was I supposed to save a world of which I knew so little?

The rising pitch of an outboard motor coming from the narrows overpowered the hold of my grief.

"Shhhhraaaaa!"

The terrible sound of *Kinchel* the Avenger shook the air and dispelled my momentary hope that Kare was returning.

With a yelp, I hopped past Edgar's body into our bedroom. I did not know where I was going, but I could not stay here.

The container and the *tunjo* lay on Edgar's bed. I glanced at it and steeled myself. No spirit or inanimate object could possess me. I had free will.

"Hold me. Wear me."

"Cruuuuuu."

Curratta's ghost floated before me, arms extended, beseeching, beguiling.

The sound of the boat was growing louder.

I dressed, put the wallet Kare had given and some clothes into Edgar's red day pack, put on my wide boots, and left the *tunjo* on the bed.

As I hopped out the door, a squall of rain lashed me and I stopped. To abandon your child, your most precious possession could barely begin to equal the guilt and sorrow I felt.

Curratta's words haunted me.

"The *tunjo* is your weapon. You must wear the tunjo."

I craved the talisman, though I knew the pendant was a window to the celestial plane through which the Lord of Fire could see me. I wanted to conceal myself, but could not leave the necklace.

I hopped back into the room and grabbed the *tunjo*. With an exhilarating rush, I was uplifted in mind and body, swept into the euphoria of union with the power of the Jewels of Life.

"Shraaaaaa."

Kinchel the Avenger dared me to confront him. I had but one path to follow, the one planned for me by *Quetzal* the Plumed Serpent. My only hope was that the son would protect me from his vengeful father. I must find my mother and together we must find our way to Manoa.

My arm trembled as I placed the *tunjo* back in the box. My powers dissipated. A deep remorse and unrequited desire added to my sense of weakness and abandonment. While the lid fit snugly, the break between top and bottom was evidence of the curse I had unleashed. I put the container in the pack, slung it over my shoulder and abandoned the only home I had ever known.

"Cruuuuuu."

The witches lamented. Just as the *Xucha* were my conduit into the celestial world, I was theirs into the material.

The sound of the outboard motor revved down to an idle. With a foolish hope the approaching craft only carried fishermen, I peered around the doorway into the kitchen and looked through the window.

The red pupils of four Assassins shined through the rain. The wolf *Xolo* howled and hurdled from the prow, splashing ashore; he searched for my scent as he ran toward the cabin. Sheriff Titus Creation and Hunter Assassin, both tall, heavy men carrying rifles, climbed out of the boat. Caterpillar-sized red eyebrows highlighted Hunter Assassin's gaunt face. Blond Assassin, a teen who might have been no older than I, with a mane of reddish-blond hair, tied the boat to the dock. Carrying multiple guns, he ran after the other Assassins, led by the bounding *Xolo.*

"Shraaaaa."

I hopped out the door fast enough so if they saw me they would only catch a glimpse. But the wolf barked and launched himself from the boat, scrambling onto the dock to get at me.

I bounded up the steep trail through the woods, past lichen-carpeted granite boulders, winding up to a pass between the mountains, not stopping until I was out of sight of the cabin, sucking the full scent of the pine air into my straining lungs.

The mountainside was shrouded in low-hanging clouds. The wind and shadows were a shifting presence moving across the landscape. My senses reached out to catch every nuance of the land and air that had nurtured me.

"Shhhhraaaaa!"

The sound of *Kinchel* shook the woods and prickled the skin on the back of my neck. I rotated my eyes in different directions, looking for danger.

The Assassins of Fire came out of the mist—the wolf loping up the trail, followed by the lean man with a pump-action shotgun.

"Shhhhraaaaa!"

The wolf's ruby eyes blazing. Barking wildly, she closed on me with swift, fluid, relentless strides.

I planted my feet and jumped, slipping sideways before regaining my balance. With my head thrust forward, an eye turned toward my pursuer, I vaulted onto a fallen tree, then into the forest where I moved in low hops to keep from hitting overhanging branches.

Every time I thought I was ahead, the wolf seemed to gain speed, leaping or running under obstacles, her ruby-colored eyes piercing the mist, her tongue flapping beside her mouth like a wet flag, her powerful muscles rippling beneath her wet pelt.

The few times I had encountered people in the woods, I never had trouble avoiding being seen. But I'd never tried to outrun a wolf like this. She was closing with a methodical, constant effort.

"Shhhhraaaaa!"

The eerie sounds mixed with her hunting growl causing me to tremble and waste energy and momentum in clumsy, flailing motions and panic.

Though I no longer had direct contact with the box, my increased empathy remained. I reached into the wolf's mind, and saw *Kinchel's* nine dragon heads, fangs exposed, his flaming wings spread like a hawk landing on its prey.

Was the world filled with Assassins of Fire trying to kill me? What was the use of running?

I had only opened the box to save Edgar; I cast my thoughts back as desperate pleas to be spared.

The wolf was close enough that I could hear her panting. A hundred yards behind her, the hunter raised his gun.

"No!" I cried.

"Pow!" The reverberation of the shotgun coincided with heavy impacts of projectiles into a tree trunk beside my head.

Xolo howled in victory. Carrying my daypack in my right hand, head thrust forward, an eye turned toward my pursuers, I vaulted over a fallen tree, then into the forest where I moved in low hops to keep from hitting overhanging branches. I thought I'd gained some separation from the wolf only to turn my right eye back to see I was losing ground. *Xolo* ran under a partially fallen tree, tongue hanging from her mouth, and without breaking stride, leapt a six-foot outcrop of granite. With swift, fluid, relentless strides she closed the fifty yards separating us.

My movements became panicked. I slipped on the wet ground, pushed myself up and jumped, nearly falling again.

Shots echoed across the mountainside. A tree trunk exploded as Hunter Assassin's bullet plowed into it. I jumped off the trail onto a ledge and goat-hopped down the foggy slope. *Xolo* pursued me, skidding, falling, until I reached a precipice, turned and with expanded chest and arms outstretched, bellowed in a defiant, animalistic cry that I would be chased no farther.

"Croar!"

My challenge incited my foes. *Xolo* jumped to a ledge ten feet above me, flexed to make a final lunge, her gums pulled back over sharp white teeth. Above her, Sheriff Titus Creation fired his weapon. Rock splintered beside my head and I vaulted backwards, twisting froglike in the air. Falling headfirst thirty-five feet, I leaned back to put my legs out, but landed off-balance and crashed to the ground. Stunned for a minute, I lay hidden by fog, rocks, and trees, while *Xolo's* bark drew closer.

"Pow! Pow!" The reports shook the air.

I was going to be killed. I needed the power of the *tunjo.* I reached for the bag.

"No!"

Mother's spirit appeared beside me, kneeling over me, a hand that I couldn't feel rose over my shoulder.

"Do not wear the tunjo. You are part Fire. *Kinchel* will use the necklace to destroy you. Cunning and stealth are your strengths."

I had no time to ponder this new, confusing information, or to determine if I had seen Mother's spirit or a trick of *Inika* or *Kinchel*.

"Shhhhraaaaa!"

The hunter and wolf were approaching.

Driven by terror, I slung the bag back over my shoulder and headed back to the lake, on the other side of the mountain. I had no time to take out the container even if I had wanted to ignore Mother's warning. Water was my only hope. Like most of my abilities, my cunning and stealth would increase in the water.

I heard the wolf panting, her paws scratching the earth in a rhythmic pursuit, her devil eyes burning through the fog. The hunter called to the wolf to wait for him.

I concentrated on short goals—reaching a patch of trees, then the crest of a hill, passing over a summit, and down the other side. The day melded into darkness as the black clouds blotted the last of the light, giving me increasing cover from the hunter but not the wolf. Night would not hinder her.

The slope lessened. Rain fell in concentrated streams from the branches of pines. A sharp stub dug into my calf, causing me to shift my weight and tilt to the right. My ankle turned. I cried out and crumpled to the ground; almost rolling, I pushed myself into a sitting position and listened. The sound of water falling from trees, rocks, and new waterfalls everywhere mixed with the rain and my deep gasps. The touch of my hands on my wounded thigh was a contact with the physical world, a handhold to keep me from being sucked into the abyss of devil wolves and fiery reptiles.

My overalls were heavy with water and mud. I studied the shadowy outline of trees, my irises dilated to see into the darkness. I was near seasonal homes and a boat launch where our boat bobbed unattended. Where was Kare?

The shortest way to the lake was through a small area of habitation. The homes were empty during the cold months. If nobody was there, I could reach the lake unseen. Any other route would have added distance, and I did not feel I could survive an extra ten feet.

I rested against a tree and listened for my pursuers. The sound of the running wolf was gone. Where were they? Had I escaped?

"Shhhhraaaaa!"

The evil calling crushed my frail hope. How could I possibly escape the Assassins of Fire? Only underwater would I be safe.

When I'm not being chased, when I'm not staggering from exhaustion, I pass through the woods as quiet as a cougar. But my injuries and fear caused me to scrape against trees, and push pebbles against each other as I slid my feet forward, hoping I had enough stamina left for a final burst of flight. My eyes spun. With weak leaps, I skipped to the edge of a two-lane road.

The scent of wood burning, a sweet tint on the moist breeze, blew through the forest as the wind swirled in a momentary shift, mixed with the unnatural smell of oil.

A car rattled toward me. The chirps, squeaks, and quick darts and hesitations of the forest altered in nervous anticipation as the machine came closer. Lights coming from the car shined on the falling rain and trees around me in a sweeping arc.

From behind a narrow cottonwood trunk, I watched a van turn into a break between the trees. I continued forward, until I came to a clearing.

Bright lights illuminated a sign, *ROADHOUSE BAR - Halloween Freakers Ball. Best Costume Prizes. Let Your Freak Out*. Halloween was one of the many holidays I'd missed, known only through descriptions I'd seen in magazines and books.

I had never before attempted to cast an illusion to many people at once. I'd never been around so many people. Because he was so much in my thoughts, I chose to project the image of Edgar. This was a chance to participate, and perhaps to be obscured among the partying crowd. I looked over my shoulder into the darkness of the wet forest before moving into the parking lot, passing between rows of cars and trucks, to the entrance to the Roadhouse Bar. Rain streamed off an overhang where costumed young men and women, some not much older than I, were standing. The scent of burning sage came from what they smoked.

"Shraaaa." The sound of *Kinchel* echoed in the woods.

"Did you hear that?" asks a girl dressed in a black pointed hat.

"Sounds like a werewolf," said a man wearing a cape, his mouth distorted by bloody teeth.

These costumed images didn't compare to the real horror I brought.

A hologram flared around the bag in my hand. Even if I could disguise myself from the Assassins, the *tunjo* would still pull them to me.

Just as I feared, over my shoulder I saw *Xolo* lead Hunter and Blond Assassin out of the woods. Their red eyes gleaming, the Assassins moved through the parking lot toward the bar. I pushed into the crowd, looking for a place to hide. The Assassins would recognize me as Edgar. I needed a new disguise. But to assume another's identity, I had to be able to achieve a strong empathetic connection with them.

"Excuse me," said a man in a big straw hat as I brushed past him.

I looked him in the eyes, trying to see into his thoughts so I could possibly assume his identity, but I heard only a rush of static. I lowered my head and moved deeper into the crowd.

Colored lights hung from rafters pointed at the stage. A turning ball of mirrors reflected patterns of rainbow lights.

A man dressed like a duck addressed me. "What costume is that?" He grinned as I stared into his eyes, trying to find a strong enough connection to adopt his image.

A wall of people blocked my progress, and I could go no farther. The music was so loud I was forced to close the flaps in my ears as when I'm diving.

In the center of a stage, risen three feet off the floor, stood a young woman in a short dress and rose-colored glasses, her blonde hair held back by a scarf. She played a bass guitar and sang in an alto voice that was loudly carried with the sound of the music. Behind her, a frenzied drummer hit an array of percussion instruments. On the front of the kick drum the name APOKAFUL was written above an image of an erupting volcano.

On the left side of the stage, a man costumed as a doctor in a white jacket played three different keyboards. On the right, another man played a guitar, and a woman a saxophone. The band ended a song to great applause and whistling.

"Shraaaa!" I turned an eye to see Hunter and Blond Assassin pushing through the crowd toward the stage and me. I needed to change my appearance.

The tall, curly-haired keyboard player turned from the audience and looked at a cell phone in his hand. I've read about these devices and talked about them with Edgar, but I was seeing one and so much else for the first time.

"People! People!" His urgent voice was thrown loud over the room in a manner so insistent that some around me stopped talking to listen to him. The others in the band looked at him with curious expressions.

His amplified voice was the loudest I'd ever heard. "For those of you who don't know it, I have to tell you something," he yelled into the microphone. "It's raining or snowing all over the world. On every continent, in every country, it's either raining or snowing. The planet is covered with clouds, man! Nobody has ever seen anything like this. In the deserts, the mountains, everywhere …it's raining or snowing. This is it folks…."

I lowered my head in shame and remorse. I'd opened the box to save Edgar and released *Inika* and the *chacs*. Before the musician stood the one responsible for bridging the physical and celestial worlds. Through my shame, my connection to him was strong; I had no trouble entering Jerry Forrest's mind, sharing his thoughts.

"This is it, the end of days." Jerry spread his hands, reaching out with a sad expression. "This is the Flood. God told Noah he'd send a flood in seven days, and seven days in the Bible is seven thousand years. The world is to be washed clean of all our sins. Let us rejoice! Let us repent!" He looked out at the laughing crowd and held out his hands. "Accept Jesus Christ as your Lord and Savior."

"Oh yes, praise Jesus," a woman next to me shouted. Others hooted and laughed. A man hollered, "Just play some music!"

The female singer leaned toward the keyboard player. My hearing was sensitive enough to hear her say, "Jerry, time to play some tunes, OK?"

"This is it, MG. We don't have much time. We've got to get to higher ground."

MG, the singer, turned a palm up. "Jerry, we're in the mountains. We need this gig."

The other musicians were looking at him. Jerry spoke to them. "I'm telling you all. This is big. Bigger than anything you've ever known."

The drummer leaned over and said. "Man, this ain't no revival meeting."

"Just play the damn song, Jerry," MG said. "*Someone I Know*." She counted a beat.

Except for Jerry, the band began to play. Jerry shrugged and walked down the stairs at the edge of the stage. He moved toward me as Hunter Assassin closed from the other direction. I shoved my way forward and looked into Jerry's eyes, achieving a complete empathetic connection. As I passed him I became him. A girl beside me did a double take as the two Jerry's parted and moved in opposite directions, me toward the stage, Jerry to the door.

MG saw me as Jerry, and moved her head as she sang, indicating for me to get back on stage and play.

Hunter Assassin had made his way through the crowd. I sensed him searching my mind using his own powers of empathy to see through my new disguise. There could be nothing of me in my thoughts. I had to become Jerry. And I became Jerry. The Assassin's red eyes passed over me, searching elsewhere. As long as *Xolo* didn't come inside and catch my scent, I thought I could project a strong enough image of Jerry to stay hidden. I had no choice but to climb the steps to the stage and pretend that I was the musician.

While I was worried about Hunter Assassin, Blond Assassin had moved to the foot of the stairs and was studying me.

I positioned myself behind the keyboard where Jerry had stood with the band, set the daypack between my feet and hoped the *tunjo* didn't reveal me to my pursuers. I pantomimed as if I knew the music. I'd played piano all my life. The musical scores Edgar brought back for me when he made his occasional trips to town had been a passage to the outside world. But I'd never imagined sounds like I was hearing now. I touched one of the keys. A loud note boomed from the speakers behind me. I touched another key and produced the same sonic result.

The band continued to play. I tried to accompany them, but had trouble with the rhythm.

MG frowned and glanced at me as she sang, "Someone I know can't let it show."

In desperation, I resorted to employing the same mental abilities I'd used on Edgar's music. By the age of three, I could perform anything he'd written. He would only have to think of something and I would play it as he sat at his desk, furiously marking up his scores as they were manifested through my reading of his thoughts.

The *tunjo* magnified my ability to hear what the band Apokaful was performing. The music drew the costumed revelers closer to the stage. The harmonies they had in their souls were pulled into a cauldron of sound.

MG was pleased with my performance. She smiled at me as she sang,

"Like him a lot."

The minds of the audience opened to me. I took in their thoughts and became them. Like the light-refracting ball on the ceiling, I dispersed my image into a hundred different realities.

The Assassin turned, changed direction, and followed the confusing mental reflections.

A nurse, dressed in white, her red hair pulled up under a small cap, moved past the stage carrying a box. I recognized Nurse Assassin, another of *Kinchel's* heads that had been detached to hunt me. The words on the box read PYROTECHNICS STAGE EFFECTS.

Suddenly, a brilliant beryl-colored light pulsed through the fabric of the bag at my feet. It reflected off the swirling globe on the ceiling, and cast a stream of flashing colors that become the ghostly forms of the *Xucha*, who flew over the crowd. Nurse Assassin jerked and twisted as she was struck by the witches' spells. The spirits of the other Assassins rose from their bodies to fight the *Xucha*.

MG's fingers rapidly plucked the strings as she watched the ghostly shapes of the Fire demons and witches chase each other in a fantastic display over the heads of the audience. The guitarist played a slashing stream of notes and as the song gathered in intensity, so did the battle inside the bar.

"Shhhhraaaaa!"

Xolo's howl reverberated through the room. "Raaarroooo."

Revelers in the audience gaped in amazement as they looked up into the fifteen-foot ceiling to watch the watery images of *Xucha* flit and dart amongst the shapes of the Assassins surrounded by flames. The dancers wildly swung one other around by the arms, entranced by the music and the spectacle.

I used my empathy to bond more deeply with the band, playing the keyboard like a shovel tossing music onto a levee in an attempt to stop the flood of energies trying to wash me to hell. But no matter how thick the bulwark of sound Apokaful created, the Assassins knew I was here and they would murder me even if they had to destroy everyone in the club.

The box Nurse Assassin had been carrying exploded at the foot of the stage. There was an acrid scent of chemicals and flames. The curtain hanging behind the stage and a banner printed with a pyramid and stars and the word Apokaful were on fire. The happiness of the crowd turned to panic. The weak or unfortunate were pushed to the ground by those trying to reach the small passage to the exit. The Roadhouse was burning. The band was the closest to the source of the calamity and farthest from the door.

Still appearing as Jerry, I grabbed my daypack and slung it over my shoulder. I looked up to see a burning beam falling toward MG.

"Croar!"

I reached for her and leapt away from the killing inferno. Lifting her across my arms, another jump carried us over the heads of the people pushing through the door.

Outside, I jumped again and landed in a clear space among the parked cars and trucks. I set MG down and concentrated on appearing as Jerry, while keeping an eye out for the Assassins.

She gaped at me in amazement. "How did you do that?"

The fiery form of the nine-headed *Kinchel* the Avenger rose in the conflagration above the Roadhouse. I turned from MG and fled into the woods, carrying away the bag with the *tunjo*.

"Jerry!" she called after me.

I ran into the dark forest where MG couldn't see me, then stopped to look back at the burning building, expecting to see the Assassins following.

"Jerry!" she called again. "Where you going?"

I watched as the real Jerry came up behind her. "Here I am." He tapped her on the shoulder.

"How? What?" MG stepped back from him in confusion.

Jerry cried, "Oh this is terrible. Terrible. How could this have happened? Wait here. I'm going to go back and see if I can help."

MG was dripping with rainwater. She looked at Jerry, the burning Roadhouse, and then she followed me into the woods. I watched her pick her way through the pines. "Hey! Jerry or whoever you are, where you going?"

I was completely exhausted, near defeat. Lacking the mental strength to project a disguise, I leaned against a tree, reverting to my real appearance. I could go no farther.

"Hey you!" MG called, but I didn't respond and she moved past me in the woods.

I knew I should let her go, but when she turned to leave the forest, I weakly called, "MG."

She came to my voice and, by the flames of the burning bar, she saw me as I am and screamed.

CHAPTER SEVEN

MG

"**P**lease don't be scared. I would never hurt you."

She inched closer to me. "What are you?"

"Raaarroooo," *Xolo* howled at the edge of the flaming building searching for my scent.

I turned and fell to my knee.

"Shraaaa."

"What's that?" MG cowered with her hand over her mouth.

My accent was different from hers. To sound like her, I rounded my vowels and sharpened my consonants. "That's the thing that burned down the Roadhouse."

"Somebody did that on purpose?"

"Shraaaaa!" The woods echoed with the haunting cry.

"What *is* that? What are you? Are you an alien? How many of you are there?"

I pulled myself to my feet and leaned against the wet bark of an oak. Many times I'd wondered how I would be perceived if I ever left the woods. I knew I was different, but somehow the proof that I am so odd as to incite this kind of reaction made me feel embarrassed, shy nearly to the point of speechlessness.

"It's hard to explain," I mumbled, my voice a pale whisper, "but please believe me when I say I'm alone and I'm just a boy."

"A boy what?"

"A human. I'm human." My voice quavered. "I just look different."

"Shraaaa!"

"I have to escape."

"From what?"

"That!"

MG squared her shoulders and said, "Let me get my truck. I'll get you out of here. Just wait. OK?" She held up her hand in a motion for me to stop, as if I had the strength to go anywhere.

From the shelter of the woods, I watched her run through the rain toward the Roadhouse. Sheriff Titus Creation and *Xolo* were standing at the edge of the inferno, thirty yards from MG on the far side of the parking lot. They watched her, their pupils red. The wolf howled.

MG kept her head down as she climbed into a black truck with a raised chassis. She drove slowly through the chaos and pulled off the road to let fire engines and police cars pass. The big wheels of her truck cut a swath through the mud until she was beside me.

"Get in. It's me," she softly called through an open window.

If I moved, *Xolo* would sense me.

MG stepped from the truck as more fire engines rolled past with lights flashing, sirens bawling.

Knowing this was my best chance, I focused on casting the image of Jerry and jumped from the woods. MG held a door open for me. "Get in," she said.

I climbed up and sat on the bench seat of the only truck I'd ever been in, looked out and saw police and firemen in yellow jackets moving among those who'd escaped or had been injured by the fire.

"Shraaaa!" *Kinchel's* hunting wail rose above the sounds of the rescue vehicles.

MG flinched as she got behind the steering wheel. *Xolo* ran at us while Titus Creation shouted at a police officer directing traffic. "Stop them."

"Shraaaa!"

I looked through the rain-obscured rear window to see the red eyes of the chasing *Xolo*. We were going too fast for the wolf to run us down. A rush of exhilaration that I'd escaped momentarily revived me.

MG leaned toward me as she sped through water pooling on a sharp bend in the road. Yellow lines flashed by–faster and faster. But I knew the Assassins would not be far behind. They would have cars and trucks too, but each mile increased my chances of surviving.

I released the image of Jerry and appeared as myself with a single eye turned to look at MG. She stared at me, and then back at the road. Her rain-soaked hair was pasted against her skull. Her clothes were soaked. She reached for a towel beside her on the seat and patted her face before using it to wipe the fog off the inside glass.

I'd read about and imagined riding in a car or truck, but I was too exhausted and scared to feel excitement. Dashboard fans pushed dry heat at me. Wipers swept the rain off the outside of the windshield.

"Cruuuuu." The witches chanted. Radiance spread from the daypack in a dancing eerie light.

"What's that?" MG made a sharp correction to stay on the road as a verdant penumbra flared and burst around me.

"Cruuuu."

I had to say something. I should at least warn her of the risk she'd taken to aid me. Beams of green light shined into my chest. The *tunjo* gave me the confidence to ask, "Do you believe in gods?"

"God or gods?"

"Ancient gods that were known to people who knew this World would end and a new World would begin."

"Oh man, you mean that stuff Jerry was talking about?"

"Jerry is correct. This rain will not stop. Being in the mountains won't help you for long."

"What do you have to do with this rain?" There was mockery in her tone and deservingly so. "Are *you* one of these gods?"

The notion of my being superior in any way seemed so preposterous that I lowered my head and confessed, "I am *Tatya-Masi* Bringer of the Sixth World of Water."

"Sounds like a god to me. But OK, uh, Tatya, is that why those people are chasing you?"

"Yes, and please, my name is Du."

"They're trying to stop you from drowning the world, Du?"

She believed me now. I sounded childish as my voice whined, "I didn't mean to. I mean I don't want to."

Her right eyebrow rose in another incredulous look. "So, I'm helping you destroy the world?"

"No, just drown it." I sounded like an idiot.

I turned away to watch emergency vehicles speeding past the truck toward the Roadhouse.

A ringing sound came from the dashboard. MG pushed a button on the steering wheel, and Jerry's voice came through speakers. "MG, where are you? The cops here at the Roadhouse are looking for you. They want to talk to you."

"Oh man, why?"

Jerry's voice caught. "It's bad. Anybody still in there is dead. Kirsten and Dennis are missing."

"Oh…." Her whole body slumped. Tears glistened on her cheeks.

I looked at her and then focused on the road. This was my fault. She had every right to hate me.

Jerry's voice also carried a sob. "People are saying it wasn't an accident. They say we had stage effects. You know we never had anything like that."

"No, it wasn't us."

"Well, all of them in there are just going a few days early. This rain is for real. This rain's gonna take us all, wipe the Earth clean. We've sinned against each other and too many of God's creations."

MG wiped her face with the back of her hand and sat straighter behind the wheel. "I've got to go, Jerry."

"What should I tell the cops?"

"Tell them I'm coming back."

"I won't be here. I've got to get home and be with Laurie and the kids."

"OK, I'll see you back there after I deal with the cops." She pushed the button again ending the call and then looked at me. "What do you know about this?" MG asked. There was nothing mocking in her tone of voice now. "You say you know who started that fire?"

"*Kinchel* the Avenger started the fire."

"One of these gods?"

"No, *Kinchel* is a spirit who serves *Xiulu* Lord of Fire.*"

Something I'd said, or everything I'd said, was wrong. She reacted angrily. "I don't know what you are or who you think you are, but a lot of my friends are dead or burnt to hell. If you know anything about who did it, you should be talking to the police."

"One of them *is* a policeman."

She braked sharply and pulled over to the side of the road. "Get out of here. I have to go back."

I found the latch and opened the door while she watched me climb out into the rain. "I'm sorry. Please tell your friends, I'm so sorry." I swayed and was ready to faint but managed to shut the truck door and staggered into the dark, wet woods.

The sound of her truck steadily diminished and was replaced by the familiar night sounds of the forest. I watched as her pickup crested a hill and the red brake lights came on. She turned around and headed back toward me, but overshot by fifty yards where I was hiding in the woods.

She stopped the truck, stepped out, wearing a black leather jacket and cap, and walked up the road away from me in the rain. "Hey! You there? Hey. You still there?" A police car with lights flashing sped past in the other direction. She called louder. "You out there?"

Would MG tell the police I was to blame? I knew I should let her go. But I was too weak to escape on my own. When she walked back toward the truck, I staggered from the woods and weakly called her name.

She waited for me until I was beside her. "Can you stop this rain?" she asked.

"I don't know."

"You started it, didn't you?"

She was right. I hung my great, heavy head. If I could unite the four Jewels of Life, I could free *Quetzal* and he would tell me how to stop the rain. But first I had to find my way to the Cave of the *Xucha*. Without Kare to help, I only had Mother to guide me to the other two Jewels in the *Cocatamia*.

Quetzal had said that Mother she would lead me to Manoa. But what was his end game? Surely it was not to see me unite the four Jewels of Life and drown the Age of Man as Mother and the *Xucha* wanted.

"Well?" MG's hands were on her hips.

I couldn't anger her. She was my best hope. I tried to make my voice sound confident. "Yes. I started the rain. And I know how to stop it."

"Good. Get back in the truck."

Inside the cab, the air was warm and humid and I felt safer. The engine was running but we remained stationary on the side of the road, as if MG was still trying to decide what to do with me.

"Cruuuu." The witches' chant was a demanding, invisible presence in the truck cab. The daypack was surrounded by a dancing corona of light. I hugged the glowing pack to my chest but could not smother the flaring manifestation of the witches.

MG puts a hand to her mouth. "What is that? What do you have in there?"

"Cruuuu." The witches demanded my allegiance to the destruction of the Age of Fire. Light rose in spiraling patterns from the bag. The *Xucha's* ghostly energy fluctuated in the air between MG and me.

"This is what started the rain." I reached inside the pack and remove the box.

MG touched the gold image of *Tatya-Masi* on the lid. Magical light flared around her hand.

"Whoa! You can really feel its power. It's beautiful. Is that supposed to be you? Who made it?"

"It was made by people a long time ago who knew what was coming."

"What's inside?"

"I don't think you want to see that."

"Well what is it?"

Reluctantly, I opened the box. *Chacs* swirled up and, undeterred by the closed windows, flew into the night. Immediately, the rain increased in intensity, drumming against the truck's metal roof. The windshield was covered with flowing water. I removed the necklace with a light-fingered grip.

At my touch, the spectral forms of the witches coalesced into focus. Their ghostly forms hovered over the box. The witches resembled Curratta in the way their tufts of white hair sprouted on moss-tinged skulls. Old skin hung in folds. Knobby joints and crooked fingers spread from bony wrists. Their distorted chorus called, "*Tatya-Masi. Tatya-Masi.*"

Energy rushed into me. I was empowered. Hunger, fear, and self-doubt were forgotten. The golden likeness of me spun on its chain of woven silver and human hair. The Jewels of Life pulsed with an internal power.

"Cruuuuuu."

"It is called the *tunjo*," I said.

"Man! Look at those eyes. What kind of jewels *are* those? They look like emeralds and opals rolled into one. I can see the world inside of them, the ocean. It's like looking down from outer space." MG reached for the necklace.

I couldn't stop myself from pulling it away from her in an angry possessive manner.

"Ok, ok, you don't want me to touch it. That's cool. What is it, the ring of power or something?"

"You can hold the necklace," I said, releasing the *tunjo* into her hand and collapsing into the seat with the weight of my temporal woes.

I could see how the Jewels filled MG with their power. She sat straighter. Her eyes sparkled with excitement. "Whoa, this is a trip. Man. I'm hearing things. Seeing things. What a rush!"

"Put it back in the box. It calls the Assassins of Fire and brings more rain, more destruction." I held the container open beneath the dangling necklace.

Her eyes were locked on the Jewels.

"Do it now. Let it go," I said in desperation.

"What?"

"Let it go."

"Oh. OK."

She shuddered, blinked rapidly and released the chain, allowing the *tunjo* to fall into the box. I slammed the lid shut. The vision of the witches faded and disappeared into the darkness of the truck cab.

MG was looking at me with new understanding and respect. "Don't ask me how, but I get it now. You have to find a way to control the power in the necklace."

"Yes, yes. You understand."

"Is it from outer space? What is it?"

My mouth was dry. My head spun from exhaustion and hunger. "Please help me," I gasped.

She observed me for a moment, started the truck, and we rode away from the Assassins of Fire.

CHAPTER EIGHT
FROGGY HOLLOW

I was dreaming about my father. I used to dream about Moss a lot. I called him Moss because that's how Kare always referred to him. When I was four, Moss had left the lake and hadn't returned. One of my haziest memories was Moss telling me that he loved my mother very much and some day we would be together as a family. Maybe I only dreamed that he'd told me that. I used to ask Kare where he was. Kare had said he was alive and served Quetzal.

I awoke with a start. My eyes rolled around in separate arcs searching for danger. MG looked over at me, her pale face marked with the shadows of raindrops cast in the light of approaching cars. I exhaled with relief.

"You all right?" she asked.

I was confused by the question. Was she asking how I was at this moment, or how was my overall situation, which I think she knew was desperate. But then her future, and the future of all mankind, was at risk if I couldn't stop the rain.

"Yes, I feel better." I straightened in the seat. We were driving on a busy highway now. I didn't know how long I'd been asleep. Were the Assassins close? Had the box and my lack of disguise revealed my location to them?

MG pulled into a gas station and parked the truck.

I reached into the bag and took out the wallet that Kare had given me this morning. The aura flared around my hand as I brushed against the box.

"Cruuuu," the witches moaned.

I handed MG a hundred dollar bill. "Will that be sufficient?"

MG smiled. "Sure. I'll use it for gas." She took the money and stepped from the truck.

I projected the image of Jerry.

MG frowned. "That's creepy. Just be you," she said in an unknowing paraphrase of Kare's words from this morning. "There's nobody out here this time of night."

"It's to hide from those who are following us."

"Who's following us?" She looked about fearfully. There were only a few cars and trucks driving down the highway.

"It is better if I don't look like myself."

"All right, go ahead, look like Jerry. Man oh man," she muttered. "What have you gotten yourself into now, girl?"

My skin was dry and itching. I left the truck to stand in the light rain, and projecting the false image, turned my head to the night sky, and with the pack in my right hand extended my arms to catch the moisture on my blotched skin.

MG zipped up her motorcycle jacket and worked the pump to put gas into her truck. "I need some coffee. Want anything?"

I wanted to stand beneath the water pouring off a corner of the roof to give my skin a good soak. But I hadn't eaten for over twenty-four hours. "I'm very hungry."

MG led me inside the station store. An elderly woman behind a counter surrounded by knickknacks ignored us. I was amazed by the rows of packages of food, all the things I'd dreamed about eating—candies, chips, cakes.

I followed MG into a room marked with a figure wearing a dress. "You need to go into that one there." She pointed to the adjacent door.

A flush of embarrassment spread across my face and chest. I mumbled an apology and stepped through the door with a man on it. Alone inside the men's bathroom, I didn't see the disguise that everyone else did. My froglike face, tapered body, and amphibious hands caused me to wonder if I was a man. No, the rebellion and pride rose in me. I am a god, *Tatya-Masi*. Someday I wouldn't have to fear the Assassins and whoever was left to share this world with me would see me as I am.

After I was done and had changed into the fresh pair of overalls from my pack, I carried an armload of food to the counter.

Two teenagers came into the store with watch caps pulled over their faces and holes cut out for their eyes. They pointed a pistol at the lady behind the counter.

I stared into the eyes of a thin boy wearing baggy pants, a t-shirt, and a wool jacket. He turned the pistol at me and then aimed at the woman behind the counter.

"Sorry, lady," he said, "but we need the cash. *Coge la feria,*" he said to his friend who started to move behind the counter.

I reached out with my thoughts, and in a burst of empathy I made contact with the boy holding the gun and achieved a strong empathetic connection with Victor Magallanes.

"What're you looking at?" Victor pointed the pistol at me.

As soon as he turned the gun away from the lady, in one swift motion, she lifted a pistol and shot Victor. An ugly wound exploded in the middle of his face. The woman behind the counter was screaming hysterically and firing wild shots at the other boy who somehow made it out the door.

MG was pushing me while I was staring in shock at the dead boy on the floor.

"Get in the truck. Hurry," she said.

Inside the store the woman could be seen with a cell phone up beside her face.

"She shot him," I said. "He was looking right at me when she shot him."

"Get in." MG's tone of voice was urgent.

I'd been in his mind when the bullet tore through his brain. He might be still alive if he hadn't been looking at me.

MG sped out of the gas station. "Man oh man, this is one crazy night," she said.

"Why did she shoot him?" I asked.

"I don't know, man. What am I going to do with you?" She shook her head and her face was pale in the lights of oncoming cars.

"I'm sorry. I didn't mean to do anything."

"Oh man, it's not your fault. What a crazy night," she repeated.

I thought it better to remain silent until we'd driven for ten minutes. "I'm still hungry," I said.

She nodded and drove to a restaurant where she lowered her window before a sign showing pictures of food and prices.

"What do you want?" she asked.

Dizzy with hunger, I stared at the images of the food, my mouth watering. "I shall have number one, a number three, and a number four."

"That all?"

"I am very hungry. Do you require more money?"

"No, I've got enough."

We got the food–hamburgers, French fries, chicken, fried fish, salads, and tacos–and headed back to the highway. My large mouth was so stuffed that my cheeks were bulging. Edgar had taught me manners, and I tried to slow my consumption. But beside me on the seat, more boxes of food waited to be eaten. MG sipped a cup of coffee and watched me from the corner of her eye as she drove.

I finished much too quickly. What tasted so delicious in my mouth had turned to something hard and indigestible in my stomach. I couldn't help but emit a small groan.

"What's the food like where you come from?" MG asked.

"We had a garden and there was fish from the lake. We gathered mushrooms and berries when we could find them."

"They have woods where you come from?"

"I grew up on the other side of the forest where I met you."

"You did?" Her brows drew together in an incredulous expression.

"I'm a boy. I just look different." My voice rose in pitch.

"How do you make yourself look like Jerry?"

"It's a trick, an illusion. I don't know how it works. I can look like anyone whose thoughts I can see."

"And you could see Jerry's thoughts? What was that like?"

"Scary."

"Yeah, scary," she said.

"I mean, I could read what he was seeing and thinking about the rain."

MG sipped the coffee and steered with one hand. "How did you know what music to play?"

"I play piano at home."

"You're good."

I looked down and blushed at the unexpected praise.

"Can you read *my* thoughts?"

I nodded, feeling as if I'd been caught doing something sneaky.

"Mind me asking you, what's it like inside, I mean like inside my mind?"

"It's...it's very musical."

Not understanding why, my comment seemed to have pleased her. Her laughter was light and modest. "I got a lot of music in me."

"There's more. You're kind, soft, but strong. I've never known anyone like you." I didn't tell her that she's the *only* woman I'd ever known.

She appeared to blush with pleasure at my innocent compliment, and softly sang a beautiful *a cappella* spiritual. "What a mighty God. Hallelujah, what a God you are...Come on, sing along," she said to me.

I heard the song in her thoughts and joined in a bass harmony. "You are a mighty God. Let's bow before him, Heaven and Earth adore him."

"That's it!" She took her hands off the wheel and clapped a beat. "Heaven and Earth, Heaven and Earth."

We drove another two hours before crossing a bridge over a swollen river. Flares in the road marked a dented car with a shattered windshield. A large machine worked to clear rocks and mud from a slide covering part of the paved surface.

I am the bringer of the Sixth World. I am bringer of death. Everywhere I go, people are dying.

Stop the rain, I silently commanded, as if I really was a god. The sound of rain falling on the roof of the truck told me that my prayer were no more effective than the one I used to say when I was a child asking for my mother and father to come get me. To stop the rain I had to learn to control the Jewels of Life. But to succeed I would have to battle the forces, including my mother, who owed their allegiance to *Inika* Lordess of Water. Kare had said I should find my way to Omagua, but how could I get there?

With her own empathy, MG said, "You don't have anywhere to go, do you?"

"No," I said in barely a whisper.

"You can come with me. I live with Jerry and my sister, half-sister, Laurie. So, you can't be Jerry." MG's expression brightened. "But you can be yourself. Laurie is nuts about frogs. She's in the frog business."

I should have warned her that wherever I went danger followed, but I remained silent. She should have already known that death and destruction followed me.

She drove down a quiet street that was surprisingly familiar. A stone sign on top of a hill read Calaveras High School. With shock I realized my entire running and MG's driving had been to circle the Eldorado Forest back to the town closest to the cabin. Rotating my eyes independently, I swept the tree-lined streets, at the stores, restaurants, and gas stations I would haunt during my long night journeys when I would swim down the lake and go exploring. In the center of a lawn facing the courthouse was a statue of a man with an ax.

Thunder was again rolling across the sky. Rain lashed against the windows. What *Quetzal* has warned me would occur if I opened the box was happening. All the fires of man would be extinguished and my weakness was to blame. And what had I gained by opening the box? I'd come not twenty miles from where I was raised.

The main street was only a mile long. At the edge of the town, we pulled into a driveway marked by two large frog eyes carved in arches over a sign: *Froggy Hollow, Lake of the Frogs*. The two-story house was set in a clearing in the forest. A corral with three horses in a nearly flooded pasture stood behind the house.

"I have to see about my babies," MG said.

The horses neighed and trotted over to the fence when MG stepped out of her car. After she put hay and oats in their feeding troughs, she led me to the back of the house where she removed her jacket and hat in a mudroom.

"Wait here, for a minute OK?" She left me in the kitchen and went into the next room.

"Oh, honey," I heard a woman say. "I'm so glad you're home."

I recognized Jerry's voice. "I just got back," he said. "I couldn't deal with it. I guess the cops will be looking for both of us now. But it doesn't make any difference. It's over. All over. We should all be together now. I'm glad you're here."

"Listen, I've brought someone home," MG said. "You know how you've been saying someone is coming that's going to change the world? I think he's here. I mean here in the kitchen. I'm going to bring him in, but don't freak out too much, OK?" MG raised her voice. "Du, come on in."

Carrying my pack in my hand, appearing as myself, I hopped into the other room.

Jerry and a woman stared at me with stunned expressions.

"You know Jerry," MG said, "And this is Laurie, his wife."

Laurie, smaller than MG, had an oval-shaped, pale face with straight brown hair parted in the middle. She and Jerry looked at each other, clasped their hands and fell to their knees, with lowered heads.

"Get up," MG says. "I told you not to freak out."

"It's the rapture, isn't it?" Jerry said. "The end of days."

I looked to MG, not knowing how to reply.

"Get up, get up," MG insisted. But they stayed on their knees with their heads lowered. "Oh for goodness sake," she threw up her hands and said to me, "Don't mind them. I know you're tired. I know I am. Let's just get some sleep and we'll figure out what to do in the morning."

Scenes of flooding on the television screen riveted my attention. A reporter talked over images of hurricane clouds photographed from outer space. His voice was agitated. "I repeat, a mandatory evacuation is in effect for the entire eastern seaboard of the United States. These storms are extremely dangerous. The National Oceanic and Atmospheric Administration is advising…"

MG turned off the television, leaving me standing before the kneeling Jerry and Laurie.

"I'm sorry to disturb you," I said to them. "My name is Du Moss." I extended my arm.

Laurie reached out and lightly held my hand before releasing it.

"Oh for goodness sake, would you two please get up," MG said.

They climbed to their feet and Jerry gave my hand a more forceful shake. Laurie stood beside him, her words tumbling out of her mouth. "We just… just, well you know, we weren't expecting you to come back in this form. I'm sorry. It's beautiful, really. You look so natural. I understand. Like all the frogs are disappearing because of the ozone layer and then you come back as a frog. It's perfect, of course. I've always loved frogs." She waved her arm at shelves crowded with frog knickknacks.

"Show time's over," MG said. "Go up to your room. Leave him alone."

She herded Jerry and Laurie up the stairs to a second floor balcony-hallway over the living room.

"How do ever you expect us to sleep?" Laurie complained, looking over her shoulder at me.

"He needs to be alone. Go in your room. You can talk to him in the morning," MG said.

They went to a room at the end of a hallway and MG closed a door behind them. But the couple immediately opened it again and peered around the doorframe, first their eyes, then full faces.

"Leave him alone," MG said as she removed sheets, blanket, pillow, and a towel from a central closet and carried them down to me.

"Clear off the toys and sleep on the couch," she said, handing me the linens. "It's pretty comfortable. The kids will be up before you know it. I have to get some sleep."

She was so matter-of-fact, and so sensitive to my needs, that all I could do was stare at her. "Thank you, MG," I said to her back as she returned up the stairs.

"See you in the morning, Du," she called, and closed the door at the opposite end of the hallway from Jerry and Laurie.

Before I could sleep, I *had* to be in the water. I returned to the mudroom and took off my overalls so I would have at least one dry pair of pants. For modesty sake, I kept my underwear on, and hopped across the meadow behind their house to the Lake of the Frogs.

When I'm underwater, my metabolism slows. The intensity of my injuries, throbbing from every cut and bruise, subsided in the cold water. Fifteen minutes underwater was more refreshing to me than an hour of sleep, and usually, my mind cleared. But my separation from the necklace kept me from relaxing. I rose to the surface with only the top of my head and eyes protruding to see Jerry and Laurie standing huddled together under an umbrella watching the lake.

"I need to put on my clothes," I called.

"Back up! Back up! Give him room." Laurie pulled Jerry by the arm to the steps of the house.

I slipped out of the water, and hopped past them into the mudroom for my clothes.

They followed, staring so intently that I held my pants in front of me to cover myself.

"You are so beautiful," Laurie said.

Jerry said, "We have this band—or we used to have this band— called Apokaful. Apokaful means having thoughts of the end of the world. I made the word up, apokaful. People have been saying I'm crazy for a long time, but I knew, I just knew. That's why we live in the mountains. We can survive here a long time. We have children, you know—a boy and a girl. I don't want them to suffer."

"Is it the rapture?" Laurie asked, her hands clasped in prayer. "The tribulation?"

"I shall try to stop the rain," I promised as I stepped into my overalls and picked up the bag. The closer I was to the *tunjo,* the stronger I felt. I was beyond exhaustion and wanted to lie on the couch in the bedding MG had provided for me. I understood there was nothing I could say or do to Jerry and Laurie that would make them leave me. They silently followed me into the living room.

Laurie spread the sheets and blanket across the couch for me. I said goodnight and lay down. She turned off the lights and they sat in the dark silently watching me. Strangely, I found their presence comforting and quickly fell asleep.

When I awoke to the first sounds of dawn, Jerry and Laurie were still kneeling on the floor along with a little girl and boy.

"This is Margo and Bert." Laurie held each of them by a hand.

The wide-eyed boy smiled and said, "Hi. I'm Bert."

His blonde sister mimicked him in a whispered voice, "I'm Margo."

I rose up, holding the blanket across my stomach and shook their tiny hands. "I need to go into the lake," I said. "If you have a spear, I can catch some fish for you."

Laurie and Jerry looked at each other. "No, we don't have a spear," Jerry said.

"I have a fishing pole," Bert said.

Laurie wouldn't let the children go outside until she dressed them in raincoats, hats and umbrellas. Bert offered me a small fishing pole that I explained to him wouldn't work underwater.

"I knew that," he said as we crossed the swampy lawn behind their house. I heard him cheer when I jumped and landed twenty-five yards off shore. I went for a fifteen-minute swim and saw a lot of fish but returned empty-handed to find them waiting for me.

After I dressed again in the mudroom, Bert and Margo led me into the kitchen where Laurie prepared a breakfast.

"Don't stand so close, Bert," she said.

He disobeyed his mother, not leaving my side. The mother-son interaction fascinated me. Had I really seen my own mother in the vision by the lake when I found the box?

The box had been strangely quiet since last night. I'd not heard the witches or seen the telltale incandescence. As with so much about the power of the *tunjo*, I did not understand the meaning of this lull.

"You like flapjacks?" Laurie asked.

The thought of food drove all mystical thoughts from my mind. "Oh, yes!" I licked my lips.

Laurie carried a plate piled high with pancakes to the table. I stood beside her, my stomach twisting with hunger.

"Please sit," Jerry said.

They bowed their heads, held hands, and prayed.

I was seated between Bert and Margo and enjoyed the feeling of their hands in mine.

"Dear God," Jerry said in a voice that was soft and loving. "I know we've sinned against You. We've mistaken ourselves for You, and now You have sent your son again to remind us that this is heaven, right here and now. And Heaven will endure, even if we do not."

When he was done, they all looked at me as if to see if I thought he'd made a good prayer. But the truth was I could not take my eyes or thoughts off the food piled on the table. I mumbled something about forgiveness and waited for Laurie to serve me. We never had orange juice at the cabin, only coffee and tea. I savored the crisp bacon, the sweet syrup and butter on the golden flapjacks.

"It's good," I said.

"You look like a frog," Bert said.

"I know." I lowered the piece of bacon I was about to eat.

"Do you get teased a lot?" Bert asks.

"No. Not really. I mean, I don't know anyone to tease me."

"Let Du eat," Laurie said.

Bert blinked. "Nobody is going to believe me when I tell them about you." He looked at his mother, pleading with enlarged eyes. "Can I take him to school with me, Mom?"

"No!" Laurie said.

Bert was filled with so much emotion, his words caught in his throat, "But I *love* him."

I looked at my plate.

"You gotta let me keep him, Mom!" Bert begged.

"He's not a pet," Laurie said gently.

"I know," the boy whined, "but I could tame him." He persisted, looking across the table at his father. "Can I keep him, Daddy?"

"No," Jerry said. "Du belongs to us all."

"Then, I can take him to school with me. The kids will never believe me unless I show them, cause he…he belongs to them too."

There was a ringing sound and Laurie picked up a cell phone on the counter. I'd read about them in the magazines Edgar brought back to the cabin and was curious to see one used. "Yes, she's here. But she's still asleep. OK, I'll tell her."

Laurie closed the phone and said to Jerry, "That was that sheriff who called last night. Titus Creation. He's on his way over."

CHAPTER NINE

THE SERVANTS OF THE CROSS

I'd been thoughtless to bring the threat of the Assassins of Fire to their home. I made them promise not to tell anyone they'd seen me, especially Sheriff Titus Creation.

"Be careful of fire," I warned over my shoulder as I fled with my pack out the back door into the rain.

"Du!" Bert called and ran after me, but was caught by his mother on the back steps.

My first instinct was to head for the lake. The *tunjo* would not suffer for being returned to the water, but I didn't want to abandon the rest of my stuff either. I was bounding back up the driveway when I heard the warning.

"Shhhhraaaaa!"

A police car turned into the long driveway. Its side was marked CALAVERAS COUNTY SHERIFF'S DEPARTMENT K-9 UNIT with an emblazoned emblem of a snake-wrapped cross. *Xolo* barked from the back seat, her snout pressed against the metal grates covering the rear window. If the glass blocked my scent from the wolf, I might escape.

"I am the wind. I am invisible," I repeated to myself. As an undisturbed pond reflects the sky and woods, I tried to be still, calm, to blend into the dripping branches, a trick I had learned from the animals. But I was too scared, too out of place. This was not the forest, and I was not a pond.

To disguise myself as Jerry might cause more harm to him and his family than I'd already inflicted. Instead, I adopted the disguise of the boy

I'd encountered last night in the gas station; the one's whose mind I'd been in when his life had ended. I didn't know if it was because of that tragic encounter or if I was getting better at assuming others' personality, but I felt as if I knew everything about Victor Magallanes—his short life, not much longer than mine, his sweetness, the confusion and pain that has led to his ill-fated attempted robbery of the gas station.

I am Victor Magallanes, I repeated to myself as I hopped a thousand yards through the forest and emerged on the road into Calaveras just as Blond Assassin sped past in a red pickup. A surge of hope that my disguise would hold disappeared when the truck turned around at the next corner and headed back toward me.

Where was Kare? I would go with him to find my mother, but I could hardly do it alone. I was afraid the Assassins of Fire had scared him off—or worse. Maybe it was the *Xucha* who were keeping him away. I did not understand exactly why Kare and the Plumed Serpent had run from the possessed Edgar. Perhaps the forces that had taken over Edgar's body were more powerful than the Plumed Serpent. I could not put together the relationship between *Quetzal* and the Assassins of Fire. I felt like a wounded mouse batted about by playful cats.

I pressed the pack to my chest, and emitted the low moan of a trapped animal. How could I find Mother, when I could not move down a street without being chased?

Head lowered, looking like Victor, I leapt around the brick corner of a building, crossed a hard black surface painted with lines, and jumped a chain fence into a schoolyard.

"Shhhhraaaaa!"

The Assassins were near. Knowing that hopping away would call attention to myself, I repeated, "I am Victor, Victor, Victor Magallanes."

Glowering beneath the ski cap, I rocked and sauntered, the backs of my hands and tops of my arms pointed forward, looking as menacing as I could.

Paths leading to the high school were crowded with students. I fell in with a group heading toward a set of doors. The students glanced at me, then away. I was not sure if their fear was of Victor or the faulty illusion I was casting of the boy.

Blond Assassin stopped his truck, scanning the students.

I moved into the school, surrounding myself with other students. If Blond Assassin had not been able to penetrate my new disguise, my best hope seemed to be to secret myself amongst the students.

Imitating the nonchalant air of two boys ahead of me, I sauntered along until I saw a painting on the wall of a huge snarling, muscular frog wearing a sweater with the letter "C." I stopped, my jaw hanging open, almost losing concentration on the image of Victor.

Three boys pushed by me. I followed them past glass cases in which trophies, pictures of teams, and inspirational sayings were displayed. A banner read CIF Western Division Swimming Champions.

I came to a room filled with gray metal closets and wooden benches.

"You new?" asked a boy with a wispy physique.

I reached into his mind and saw idle curiosity. Reflecting a diffident attitude, I nodded. "Yeah," I said with a Hispanic slur.

"What's your stroke?" He took a bathing suit out of a bag.

What did he mean?

"Crawl? Backstroke? Breaststroke?"

I didn't know how to answer.

The boy squinted at me with suspicion, shut the closet, and joined other boys in bathing suits walking into a room of showers. The sound of the water made me long to bathe my drying skin, but I could not take the risk. As soon as I had the chance, I'd escape and find my way back to the Lake of the Frogs.

The suspicious one I had been talking to pointed at me and whispered something to a man carrying a clipboard and watch.

He came over to me. "I'm Coach Thompson. You want to come out for the team?"

I looked around, then back at him and nodded. "Then get suited up."

Coach Thompson moved to an office with glass windows looking out on a hallway leading from the room. To escape I would have to walk right by him. He was watching me.

Could I project a presentation of Victor dressed in swimming trunks? I took off my shoes and overalls, placing them in an empty locker. What was I supposed to do with my pack and the *tunjo?* If I were separated from the container, my ability to project an illusion would be limited, if not extinguished.

So far, my empathetic mass manipulation seemed to be working. But what were its limits? At any moment I expected the man to come rushing out of his office to confront me, or to see Titus and *Xolo* burst through the door.

To give myself courage, I invented a koan: *When I go to school, my friends will greet me because we have never met.*

Disorder and illogic had their place in the world, why not me? How I saw myself would be how I was perceived. All I had to do was keep a clear idea I was a boy from San Ysidro transferring to a new school, wearing the same elastic trunks as the other boys wore, carrying goggles in my hand as they did.

I carried the pack, but projected an illusion of Victor dressed in swimming trunks, quickly passed through the showers, and moved up a sloping ramp to a beautiful pool.

Seats were folded against a wall and diving boards of different heights stood over the water. A banner read CALAVERAS SWIM AND DIVE TEAM in which the snarling frog was featured; another was lined with silver five-sided flags proclaiming that year after year the school was swimming champion of the CIF Western Division.

Coach Thompson followed me out. Students lined up at the edge of the pool and jumped in when he told them. They seemed to awaken from their lethargy, bow into a tense ready position, and leap into the water with a flat dive, performing their strokes, trying to make the school swim team. If I could have escaped I would have, but at the same time I craved the moisture of the aquamarine water on my skin.

Acid bile of nervousness burned in my stomach as my turn came. I was trapped. To leave would only draw more attention to myself.

"Name?" the crew cut man asked me.

"Victor," I whispered, with my head down, clutching what I hoped was the invisible bag, keeping my focus on casting the image of Victor.

"Victor what?"

I misunderstood the question, thinking he was asking me the same question he had the other students. "Breaststroke."

Boys and girls laughed around me.

"Victor Breaststroke?" The string of a stopwatch wrapped around his hand, he shared his amusement with the other swimmers, smiling at them over the clipboard.

"I am a boy named Victor. I am from San Ysidro. I have come to live with my aunt." I reflected the image to him and all the other students watching me.

"Well, Mr. Breaststroke, let's see what you can do."

I couldn't take my pack into the pool with me. They were studying me, waiting. In my panic I felt the disguise starting to waver.

The coach looked surprised when I set the pack at the edge of the pool. "Where did you get that?" he asked.

The fastest way to end this was do what I have to do and get back to my backpack. I only hoped the distance between me and the *tunjo* would not weaken my powers enough to reveal myself.

The water was choppy from the swimming. What would happen to the illusion if I were wet?

"Go!" The coach shouted in my ear, startling me so much I leapt half the length of the fifty-meter pool. The quicker I was in, the quicker I would be out. I slipped beneath the surface, contracted my legs, and arms, hit the wall, pulled twice more and returned to where the coach was standing, reached up and touched the bag.

The look on his face told me I had made a mistake. I figured from his expression, he was seeing a large frog-like creature in his pool. But using my empathy, I saw his vision of standing behind Victor while thousands of people cheered and three-ring flags hung over the pool.

He looked at his stopwatch, then at me. "Do that again."

I hopped up to the edge of the pool.

"Go!" he said, with less energy than the first time, almost like a prayer.

I jumped and swam in a manner I thought was more in keeping with my disguise, using mini-strokes, and wafting my hands through the water to slow my progress, before returning to the coach.

He clicked the watch, and studied me in the water. Students standing in the other lanes were watching. I concentrated on the idea I had black wet hair, was sixteen. I had come from the border because it was too dangerous in my neighborhood.

"What's your p-b?" the coach asked.

I did not know what he was asking me.

"Your personal best?" a boy beside me in the pool whispered.

"I'm sorry, I don't know."

"Who have you swum for?"

"Nobody really."

He smiled and knelt at the edge of the pool so his face was closer to mine. "Well Victor, unless we're all seeing things, you just broke the Olympic record for the 100 meter breast by four seconds." He stood up and shouted at the other students, "OK, that's it. Practices start at three this afternoon." He stayed close to me, standing beside my bag, his manner solicitous. "Victor, I want you to be on my team. If anyone should be named Breaststroke, it's you." He extended a hand. I impolitely pushed myself out of the water without reaching for him.

He slapped his hands and smiled. "How ever you want to do it, Victor."

I grabbed the bag and clutched it to my chest, hurrying before him as he escorted me into the showers where boys washed themselves beneath the steaming streams of water.

"You know where my office is," he nodded across the room. "See you there in a few," he said and thankfully left me alone.

I returned to my locker and put on my shoes and overalls.

The boy I had first talked to said, "That was something. You sure can swim."

Others looked at me with envy and admiration. I could not help but enjoy the feeling of acceptance. Maybe as Victor I could have had some friends.

I saw myself dressing in Victor's baggy pants, cap, and blue ski jacket.

"Where did you learn to swim like that?"

"In a lake," I said. "I'm sorry, I must be going." I hurried past him toward the doors to the locker room before he could ask me any more questions.

"Hey, Victor!" Coach Thompson boomed across the locker room.

I rocked to a stop, looking for a way to escape.

"In here!" the coach ordered.

Trapped, I forced the projection of Victor through my doubts and sidled across the changing room to his office.

Coach Thompson was smiling, his teeth white and big between thin lips, his cheeks high and red as he closed the door behind me and pushed me into a seat. He said, "Boy, you're the swimmer I've been looking for." He pointed at the wall where rows of pictures were displayed showing teams he had coached with captions that identified the year and level achievements: State finals - 1998; State Semifinals Girls...

Only the loud insistent ringing of a bell seemed to distract him from his intense focus on me. He excused himself, saying he had to go teach a driver's ed class, but hoped I would make his office my second home. Escorting me out of the gym, he finally left me with an assurance he was in my corner a hundred percent. "We got practice after school today. I want to see you there."

I nodded and hurried away. The risk of staying in school and making more mistakes was outweighed by the threat of Titus and *Xolo* outside. But what was I going to do in the school? I could not take any more chances of blindly walking into a class.

The hallways emptied, changing quickly from bustling noise to muffled voices coming from behind closed doors. The polished plastic floor reflected bright lights running down the center of the ceiling. I crouched, looking up and down the line of metal lockers.

A man turned the corner and focused on me. I turned to move away from him, but he called, "Hey you."

I had to stop. He was broad-shouldered and his chest protruded strongly over a flat belly. I stared at my feet, not knowing how to answer, concentrating on appearing angry like Victor.

"What class are you supposed to be in?"

"That one." I pointed at the door beside me.

"Everyone treating you all right?"

I nodded.

"You let me know if any of those Servants of the Cross boys tries anything. I know who they are and we aren't going to tolerate racism. You understand?"

Not knowing anything about the Servants of the Cross, I continued to project Victor's diffident appearance and stepped into a classroom where students sat on stools arranged around raised tables with sinks and outlets marked *water* and *gas*.

Keeping my head down, I sat on an empty stool with the students.

Anne Lau, an Asian girl, sat in the seat next to me. Beside her was Randy Plough, a large boy who looked both pudgy and strong at the same time. His head was shaved and he wore black boots with silver chains on them.

Our teacher Mr. Rascos, a fat man with curly black hair, stood behind an array of plastic containers on a crowded tabletop.

I kept my head down, looking like Victor.

Mr. Rascos spoke in a deep basso, stopping all conversations in the classroom.

"I'm sure some of you have been looking forward to this day, while I am equally certain that some of you have not. Nevertheless, the fabled moment of the high school experience has arrived. Today, we shall dissect a frog."

Some of the girls groaned. Boys were smiling and slapping each other's raised hands. I looked around to see if anybody was looking at me.

"Come get your trays," the teacher said.

Anne Lau brought back a preserved frog in a pan filled with what looked like black wax, goggles, a sharp cutting tool, scissors, and pins.

Anne put on the goggles. I and the rest of the table crowded around to watch her pin down the frog's splayed legs and arms, and then slice through the pale belly with a scalpel. I could not help but look down at the formaldehyde-cured creature and wonder, do my insides look like that?

Anne used scissors to snip the translucent flesh up to the frog's neck. A girl screamed. I looked over to the next table. A giggling boy had his fingers in the open corpse of a frog and was scooping out the small intestine.

Blond Assassin, his reddish-blond hair falling over his eyebrows, sauntered into the classroom. Up close he looked heavier and stronger than the other students.

"Brian Miller–nice of you to join us," the teacher said.

Brian's glare seemed to intimidate Mr. Rascos.

Brian sat in the empty seat beside me, and I could not help but shy away from him, a motion he encouraged with a menacing contraction of his lips and hateful glare. An open denim shirtsleeve rode up on his arm. Tattooed on the top of his forearm was a black cross with a flaming snake wrapped around it.

Brian's eyes gleamed red.

"Shhhhraaaaa!"

I grabbed my backpack to flee.

Brian lifted a scalpel off the table and took a vicious swipe at me.

I fell back against Randy who grabbed me with strong hands.

Brian stabbed, and a sharp pain tore through me as if burned with a hot stick. I lost control over the illusion, jumped straight up out of Randy's grasp, hit the ceiling, emitted a loud "Croar!" and fell back among the startled class.

The *tunjo* radiated through my red pack.

Brian came at me with the scalpel raised to cut me again.

Disbelief emoted through thirty-five pairs of eyes. Screaming teenagers ran for the door. Terror spread from the room and out into the hall. No use in trying to recover my lost appearance of Victor. I rose in a crouch between two tables.

Brian jabbed at me with the knife.

Holding my backpack with my unwounded arm, I leapt over him and the heads of the other students, landed in the hall, looked right and then left, and with two head-thrusting leaps, reached the stairs, jumping down them as I had the switchbacks on the mountain. On the first floor, I leapt past the display case of student art and trophies and out the door.

The disguise of Victor was useless. I had to find another way to hide. In the rain, I regained enough composure to recall the illusion of Jerry.

Shuffling away from the school as fast as I could without hopping, I looked about, wondering from where the next attack would come. Sticky, warm blood ran down my fingers as I reached the stairs leading to the street.

A car with flashing lights was parked on the street. A policeman climbed toward me. "Hey, Jerry, been looking for you," he said.

I had no choice but to stop and do my best to hide my cut arm from him, concentrating on being Jerry Forrest.

The officer wore a long yellow raincoat with Police Department stenciled on the back. Water dripped from a wide-brimmed hat covered with plastic. "The sheriff's office in Dorado wants to talk to you about what happened last night at the Roadhouse. You better come with me."

Frantic bells rang throughout the school. Speakers beneath the roof broadcast a message that echoed across the campus. "All teachers go to their assigned emergency evacuation posts. All students go to your emergency evacuation locations."

More police cars—the lights atop their roofs flashing and reflecting off the rain-slick road—sped up and stopped in front of the school. Sirens were approaching. How long before Titus and *Xolo* would arrive?

From a small black box attached to the collar of the policeman questioning me, a voice said, "10-18 at the high school, possible hostage situation. All units respond."

His manner changed to a more authoritative tone. He unbuckled his raincoat to reveal a gun strapped to his waist. "Jerry, I'm afraid I'm going to have to ask you to turn around and spread your legs apart. Put your hands up against that tree."

I moved behind the thick trunk of a redwood, spread my legs, and raised my arms. I couldn't imagine what I would feel like. Blood ran down my arm and dropped to the ground.

"What's going on Jerry? You're hurt."

The voice from beneath Esola's coat said, "Suspect at high school is a young Hispanic male."

"Esola going into the high school," he said in a rapid clip into his microphone. "Gotta go. Get in touch with Dorado Sheriffs Department, ASAP, Jerry."

He glanced at my bloody hand and hurried away from me, his gun drawn.

Three more police cars converged on the one already parked in front of the school.

I was going to continue my escape when a gang of students, including Brian and Randy, rushed from the building. I pressed myself behind the tree.

The barrel-chested man who had questioned me in the hall stopped the boys. I leaned out slightly to watch them.

"Mr. Feldman, there's an alien in the school!" Brian shouted.

"I warned you about bringing that Servants of the Cross stuff to school." Feldman glared at them.

"Mr. Feldman," Randy whined, "It's a real alien, like the movie, *Predator.* It can appear as a human, change shapes. It would have killed us if we hadn't had a scalpel."

Students, some in costumes ruined by the rain, and teachers were rushing out of the school around them, their heads and shoulders stooped against the unnatural tropical downfall. "The alien killed that Mexican and is using his body," Randy said.

Feldman snorted in disbelief. "If that boy is dead, it's not going to be any aliens that are going to be the first suspects. It's you knuckleheads!"

Brian clenched and unclenched his fist.

"You boys find your stations."

"I'm telling you, Mr. Feldman, you'd better be careful. He can look like anyone. He could be you."

They menaced him for an instant before he made them back down with a curt, "You boys get back to where you're supposed to be or you're all expelled for the year."

In unison, the boys looked across the fifty yards of wet grass to where I hid. Red eyes bored into me. I pulled back and tried to make myself invisible. Blood dropped to a puddle by my feet.

"I am wind. Nobody can see me," I silently repeated to myself.

Crouched ready to hop away, I watched the Servants of the Cross boys walking across the lawn away from me. No doubt the cross they served was the conquistador's. "Calaveras" meant skull in Spanish. I had the feeling that the skeletons from the cave where Kare had found the cross haunted the whole town.

"Get the guns," Randy said, and hurried toward the parking lot.

Two officers hurried by me. One hesitated and I moved past him, ignoring his suspicion. Anxious parents were arriving at the school. I was ashamed to think I was the root of their terror. Anywhere I went, those around me would be in danger. Mortal lives meant only slaves to be collected, devotion to be gained by *Inika* and *Kinchel*.

I silently prayed, "Jesus Christ and all spirits and angels who want the good of man, protect them and me."

I reached the center of the town, moving through decomposing red and yellow oak leaves toward the statue of a lumberjack, not looking into passing faces, afraid I would see the red eyes of the Assassins of Fire. My vision spun, and I did not think I could make it to the mountains.

A man in dirty, old clothes, pushing a metal cart filled with blankets and stuffed plastic bags stared at me. He was drenched, but did not lower his head against the rain. "Injured, private?" he asked in a clipped manner.

I stopped and looked at him, sensing no evil.

"Better let me have a look at that. Sit down on that bench."

I did as he told me.

He reached into his cart and pulled out a canvas bag with a red cross on it, took out a pair of scissors and cut away the sleeve of my shirt. He treated my wound as well as Edgar would have.

As he bent over me, I empathetically reached out to him. He called himself Corporal Bob. The images of his life were shattered and projected into his consciousness in ill-fitted shards, some so sharp that they cut any sense of peace and well-being. I saw images of Corporal Bob, a young man in a uniform, handing a flag to a weeping woman in the company of sad-faced people at a gravesite. The casket was closed. An insidious question had come into Corporal Bob's mind...where are the bodies? He never saw the bodies, only the coffins draped in the stars and stripes. He would fold the flag into a tight triangle, present it to another wife or father in agony, and wonder, where is the body?

I wondered how someone like Corporal Bob could live in this world, and then admitted that he was doing a better job than I. The longer I stayed in his mind, the more confused I felt, the more like Bob I became. While I was in Bob's thoughts, he was in mine. As he taped a bandage over my wound, he said, "I hope you find your mother."

He put his bandages and antiseptic into his canvas bag, and pushed his cart away from me.

"Wait! Thank you," I said when I had moved in front of him.

He pressed his rain-streaked face close to mine, trying to look behind the illusion of my disguise. "Where are the bodies?" he asked.

"I don't know," I said with a heaviness that gave my words a husky tone.

"Then be on your way, private." He flipped his hand and pushed by me.

As I watched Corporal Bob blend into the buildings and trees and disappear into the town, I wondered if only insane people would stop to care for a wounded stranger. His empathy was the strongest I had encountered. He had seen that I must return to the task of finding Mother and reaching Manoa. But where was my mother?

* * *

According to Edgar, my birth had been earlier than expected. I had been born at the Balfore Institute, a private hospital near Grants Pass, Oregon.

Edgar had been working there as an orderly. A female nurse, the only other staff person awake at that time, had been tending to Mother. The nurse had come out with a basin covered with a cloth. "It's a still birth," the nurse had said. "I need to tend to her. Send in the paramedics as soon as they get here."

"Have you called her family?" Edgar had asked.

The nurse, an elderly woman, already retired from a career in a medical hospital, had looked flustered. "I can't do everything. Look at her chart. Call them."

Edgar had dialed the only number he could find and had reached Theodore Moss in San Francisco, several hundred miles away.

"Is it alive?" Moss asked.

"No. I don't think so."

"And my wife?"

"I don't know. The ambulance is on the way."

Moss then made an extraordinary request. "I want you to take the birth matter and keep it for me. Nobody must see it. You understand? I am willing to pay you very well for this service."

By the time the ambulance personnel and police had arrived, Edgar had hidden the basin in a storage cabinet. When asked where the fetus was, he had said that he had thrown it into the Rogue River behind the Institute. Since my mother had been eight months pregnant, the fetus was considered a missing body. Edgar had nearly been arrested for murder, but the nurse vouched that the baby had already been dead. Moss arrived near dawn and after being told what had happened asked to speak to Edgar in private.

"Do you have it?" he asked.

Edgar had described Theodore Moss as twenty-eight, appearing younger in body and older in face, a tall, slender man with straight brown hair worn in a part on the left side of his head. Handsome in a studious sort of way, but obviously deeply disturbed, Moss and Edgar had managed to sneak my supposed remains out of the Institute. In the passenger seat of Moss' car, Edgar had lifted the white cloth to show my father. Through Edgar's description, I had seen myself as they had, in the first daylight shining through the pines—still in the amniotic sac, my legs undifferentiated from a vestigial tail, looking like a large slug, but moving. "I think it's alive," Edgar had gasped.

Moss had showed no reaction, neither surprise nor joy. "I want you to help me care for it," he had said.

"Care for it? But...but."

"I will pay you a hundred thousand dollars a year plus all your expenses. By the time it is ten, you will be a millionaire."

"What is...it?" Edgar could not take his eyes off me.

"That remains to be seen," Moss had said. "Do we have a deal?"

Edgar had chosen his path. He went to work for Theodore Moss. I think at first Edgar did it for the money, then to write music, and finally because he loved living at the Lake of the Frogs, and I believe because he also loved me.

Two days later, Moss, Kare, and Edgar had taken Curratta's box and me by boat to the cabin by the Lake of the Frogs. When I was twelve, Edgar and I had climbed a peak that looked out over the side of the mountain that led to Calaveras, the same trail which four years later I would be chased down by *Xolo* and Titus Creation.

"If Mother is alive, then why has she not come to see me?" I had questioned, knowing I was asking more for reassurance than information.

Wearing a pair of gray lederhosen and seated with his bare knees pulled up to his chest, he'd remained silent so long, I had doubted he was going to answer me. Then he had said, "I think your mother, any mother, would come to her child if she could."

Was she still at the Balfore Institute? How could I get to Oregon? The future lay before me like a path straight into the clouds, hazy and uncertain. I looked across the park and extended my senses to the school. Titus and *Xolo* were searching for me there. Turning the other way, I waddled out of town, staying close to the road, ready to leap into the woods at the first sign of the Assassins. Rain continued to fall. I wanted to be in water, to have the oblivion of my animal side stop my questioning. The philosophy I had studied with Edgar at the lake had misinformed me. Noble thoughts were not for the hunted. I'd been relying on the wrong source. Better that I use the lessons of the forest and live as if another stronger beast was always close, ready to take my life.

As I walked toward the lake, I heard my name. "Du!" MG stopped her truck at the edge of the town square. I slumped into the passenger seat as she drove away.

Bent over the steering wheel, her mouth twisted in rage. "I knew it was you. The real Jerry is back at the house. They just burned down Froggy Hollow."

CHAPTER TEN
THE JEWELS OF LIFE

"What happened to your arm?" she asked.

"I...I had an accident."

She leaned closer to inspect the wound and the soggy dressing. "You'd better let me see about that."

"I heal quickly, really."

"Your shirt's ruined."

"It's OK. Do you know how I can get to Oregon?"

"Where in Oregon?"

"Grants Pass by the Rogue River. I think I might have some family there–my mother."

"Your mother?" Her blue eyes narrowed, wondering if I was joking.

"I think she's there," I said, embarrassed because I was not certain where my own mother was.

"This have anything to so with stopping the rain and those bastards who burned down my house?

"I hope so."

"Then I'll drive you, no charge." She grit her teeth and sped out of Calaveras on the same road we'd driven in the night before.

MG seemed very adept at maneuvering her truck through sheets of rain. She spoke to Jerry through the magical phone so both their voices came through the radio speakers in the dashboard of the truck.

"You can't tell anyone about him. Got that?" she said.

Jerry and his family had narrowly escaped the fire that had destroyed Froggy Hollow, the latest to suffer from me.

"People got to know that there's some hope," Jerry argued.

What hope did I have of stopping the rain? I stared at my daypack sitting before me on the floor of the truck. The urge to put on the necklace was constant. I was torn by duality. The Jewels would give me the power to stop the rain. The necklace would also lead the Assassins to me.

The atmosphere in the truck was momentarily still once MG said goodbye to Jerry. But then the radio crackled and the volume suddenly rose with the urgent tone of the announcer. "Widespread civil unrest is spreading as coastal areas of the world evacuate…"

MG reached out and turned off the radio. "We don't need to hear any more of that," she said. "So how long we got?"

"I don't know. I thought it was two years."

"You thought?"

I explained to her about the 25,800-year intervals it takes for the Sun to complete a 360-degree circuit through the zodiac before coming to rest in the eye of Sagittarius. And I told her about Kare and my grandfather. How Kare had said that the sun would pass through the eye of Sagitarrious on the winter solstice in two years.

"So, what's with all this rain now?"

I sighed and hung my head. "I don't know. The real battle for the next age of Earth is not supposed to be for two years."

"Yeah, well I'd say the battle has started and rain is winning right now. Keep talking. Let's see if we can figure this out."

During the long drive to the Balfore Institute, I told MG what I knew.

"Sixty-five million years ago this was a World of Water. The Lord of Fire sent a Fire rock that destroyed almost all of the creatures on the planet."

"I know about that," MG said.

I leaned back in surprise.

"A large meteorite hit the Earth near Chicxulub, Mexico. It left a crater about half-a-mile deep and 100 miles wide, sent tidal waves so high that it washed away everything within a hundred miles of the coasts. Firestorms raged around the globe. It was so hot even underwater plants burned. Killed the dinosaurs and almost everything else. Made way for the mammals, humans."

"The servants of Fire," I muttered. MG's confirmation caused my sense of guilt to deepen. If the Rock of Fire was not a myth, then the rest could be true; a god of Water, *Tatya-Masi*, would come to bring an Age of Water.

"OK let me get this straight," she said. "You're a Water god but you want to save modern civilization, the World of Fire, right?"

"Yes."

"Well, that sounds crazy, but okay…hmmm. So—there are four Jewels. You have two, and this *Quetzal* the Plumed Serpent—who's a Fire spirit—has the other two. And whoever controls the four Jewels will be able to say whether the next World, the final World, will be a Fire World or a Water World. Right?"

"That is correct. *Quetzal* had a spell put on him by *Inika* and only a Water god can free him. That's why he's going to show me where he's hidden the other two Jewels he stole from *Inika* so I can free him. Then, he will show me how to stop the rain."

MG turned her gaze from the road and looked at me with her aquamarine eyes. "Here's *one* of the things I don't get. Say you make it to the cave and bring *Quetzal* the *tunjo* and he gives you the what…?"

"It's called *Cocatamia* Staff of Life.*"

"And *Cocatamia* is what gives the Fountain of Youth its power?"

"Yes. It's a scepter and the other two Jewels are embedded in it."

"Got it. OK, say you get the four Jewels and free the Plumed Serpent. And then you can stop the rain?"

"Kare has told me that *Quetzal* will show me how to stop the rain."

MG slowly shook her head. "Look, I know Kare raised you. I know you're missing him, but I've got to ask you—do you trust him? You say he was possessed by *Quetzal*. Maybe *Quetzal* was only using him to trick you into bringing him the other two Jewels. Did you ever think of that?"

I hesitated before saying firmly, "I trust Kare." Then in a lowered tone of voice I said. "I have to. There's nobody else I can trust. Except you, I mean."

"Yeah, but what if Kare is being duped? If you want to stop the rain, and *Xiulu* wants to stop the rain, why is *Xiulu* trying to kill you? He should be helping you."

She had a good point. Now I wondered if it *was* a ruse. *Xiulu* Lord of Fire would have known *Quetzal* was protecting me. I would not have been that hard to kill. My voice was soft as I answered, "The Lord of Fire wants the Jewels in the *tunjo*. He will get them any way he can."

"You say you trust me. Great. But, honey, I can't tell you jack-all about what's going on here. What about your mother? You say she's a witch. What does she want?"

"The *Xucha* want me to reunite the four Jewels too."

"And use them to drown the world. Great. We don't want that. If you know your mom is going to use the Jewels to drown the world, why are you bringing her the *tunjo?*"

"Because she asked me to. And *Quetzal* said she would take me to him."

MG smiled. "You're a good son then—just doing what your mama asks?"

Her mocking tone made me feel foolish and immature. "Maybe she just wants me to be the god and imbue my spirit into the World of Water."

MG turned to look at me. "That still leaves everything underwater. I thought we were trying to stop that?"

"There are things I can't control…yet."

Her tone softened; it sounded genuine. "Well, you know, it's not like it's all you. I mean you can do some freaky things—that's for sure, but you're not the only one who's bringing this show to a close. Humans have been doing a pretty good job of it themselves. And it's not like we haven't been expecting it. Look at Jerry. You think he's alone? And there are plenty of other people that think we're due for a big house cleaning. This *Xiulu* Lord of Fire sounds like the spirit of white male domination, the bastards who screwed this all up to begin with."

She spat out her words and turned toward the rain-smeared window. "Bunch of greedy pigs who always want more." She smirked. "Yeah, the god of *Fire*. That makes sense. Fire made the steel, the oil wells, the bombs; it burnt the rain forest. That's what this Plumed Serpent wants you to help him save. The *hell* with him!"

I was shocked by MG's righteous anger. She sounded as if she blamed *Xiulu* more than me.

We rode in silence for an hour. She was quiet for so long I thought she didn't want to talk about it any more. Traffic was slow on the highway. We were stopped in a long line of cars caused by road closures and accidents. Rain had filled the pastures and fields, turning them into swamps where crops drooped in forlorn surrender to the steady unrelenting downpour. The farms and small towns we'd passed seemed to be trying to withstand a broken cycle until the sun came out. If I obeyed Mother and gave her the *tunjo,* would that only increase the rain, release more *chacs?*

MG cleared her throat and said she thought we might not reach the Balfore Institute until the next morning. Then she began to speak again in a tone of reflection and sadness.

"A lot of us for a long time have been thinking this all has to come to an end. People have been worried about global warming, terrorism, economic collapse, when actually it was something bigger coming. The signs were all there, but we just couldn't see them." She raised her hand toward the window and the rain. "It makes sense when you think about it. Fire messed up this world, now water is coming to wash it clean, start all over again.

Maybe it's for the best," she said with a wistful tailing off of her voice.

I studied her face as she stared straight ahead at the road. I wanted to tell her that I'd do anything to save her, but she started talking again, and so I stayed quiet.

"I'm going to miss some things, the band, playing music, making love, having children. I always wanted to have a kid, but you know that only makes things worse; one more American to eat twenty pounds of meat and generate sixty pounds of garbage a month. Yeah, start over again. We just got too destructive, messed with Mother Nature too much–she's saying... *that's it for you humans.*"

"No!" I implored. "This is a beautiful, wonderful world. What about Bert and Margo? What about you? I'll die to protect you."

She looked sad as she said, "Die for our sins? That's already been done, sweetie. He just didn't tell us not to mess up the planet."

I stared at the bag. The urge to put on the necklace was constant. Ever since I'd opened the box and held the *tunjo*, I craved the powers the necklace gave me. But I also recognized the *tunjo* as a portal into the netherworld. I could be strong in this plane. I didn't have to battle ghosts to prove who I was.

Maybe others were feeling my dread that a dam protecting the temporal plane from the nether realm had been breached. I could not discard the Serpent's accusation that this was my fault.

Edgar had told me the Fountain of Youth was a myth. He had said eternal life was one of those dreams that incited the imagination of most mortals. He had thought Kare's belief in the ancient city and witches was a combination of native superstition and psychosis. I had liked it when Edgar had refused to believe the story that was the foundation of my being a god. It made me feel more normal.

"Do you think Manoa really exists?" I asked MG.

"Maybe–the lost city of El Dorado, the Fountain of Youth. Plenty of people were looking for it when the Europeans first came to the New World. Ponce de Leon was searching for the Fountain of Youth when he discovered Florida."

I frowned. "Have you ever heard of the *Xucha* witches?"

"No. But I *know* they exist. I've been hearing them, seeing them ever since I held the *tunjo*."

"Cruuuu."

The *Xucha* stirred. I hugged the pack to smother their intrusive presence.

The boundary between reality and supernatural wavered. The seen and imagined blurred, hiding the border between physical and paranormal. I cringed at the touch of the unseen, at the call to become *Tatya-Masi*.

MG looked at me. I didn't want to distrust her. Was she now a servant of the *Xucha*?

"Cruuuu."

The *Xucha* commanded recognition. Their presence in the car was palpable. I kept my head lowered over the bag, resisting acknowledgment. "Do you believe there are spirits, forces that can try to make us do things?" I asked.

"They can try," she said. "But nobody can make you do something you don't want to."

With the bag shimmering, the witches crying, the spiritual world had breached whatever barrier hid it from most of the living. The wipers swept like a metronome pushing aside the rain. Was she reading my mind? Maybe our thoughts were intertwining through the power of the necklace. MG's observation raised a question I had been pondering since I'd opened the container—how much power could the celestial entities hovering in the miasma at the edge of reality exert over us? I had evidence of the difficulty the spirits had in reaching into the material plane. They needed me to exert their will.

"Cruuuuu."

Sparkles hung in the radiance filling the atmosphere around us. To recognize their materialization was to bring them farther into the realm of the living.

MG adjusted a fan blowing air on the windshield. Her blue eyes focused on me with a questioning expression, then back on the road. "It's just energy. You can use it. *We* can use it to stop the rain. Be strong." She reached over and touched me gently on the arm.

Her touch thrilled me.

"It's going to be all right," she said. "You can do it. You can stop the rain."

Breath-stealing warmth flushed my skin. "I love you." I exhaled.

"That's what it's all about," she said. "That's what it's all about."

CHAPTER ELEVEN

LILIA

MG steered the pickup off the Interstate onto a twisting, two-lane road bordered by woods and farms. We came to a twelve-foot fence of metal spikes alongside a broad flooded lawn. A guardhouse blocked a driveway beside stone pillars. A sign read Balfore Institute.

"I'm going to change," I warned.

"Change?" she looked at me.

"The way I look."

Even with the warning, MG flinched at the sight of me in the guise of Victor Magallanes, wearing baggy coat and oversized pants. By her response, at least I knew it was working.

We were stopped at the guardhouse by a wooden gate painted with white and red stripes. An elderly man in uniform leaned from the small enclosure. Loose red-tinged skin wrinkled his face. White curly hair pushed from beneath a cap.

A small gray car stopped behind us.

The guard stepped out from the small building, looked at us and nodded at the occupant of the other car. "Just a minute, Doc," he said with a wave of his clipboard. "What can I do for you, folks?" he asked.

MG looked at me, then said to the guard. "We've come to see his mother."

"What's her name?"

MG waited for me to speak.

"Lilia Moss, or maybe Morales. I think Moss," I said.

He opened an umbrella and stepped closer to the car to look at me. "What are your names?"

There were two short beeps from the car behind us. The guard looked back and frowned.

Again, MG looked at me.

"Du Moss. I think I'm her son," I said.

"You think?" Suspicion tightened his mouth. He wiped a raindrop off a bushy sprout of eyebrow with the back of his hand.

"I haven't seen her for...a long time."

"She's not expecting you?"

The horn behind us honked with more insistence.

"Ah fer Christ's sake," the guard muttered. "Listen, you folks got to call ahead and make an appointment. This is a private care facility. The docs got to OK you visiting."

The horn blared this time.

"All right! All right!" the guard shouted. "You folks going to have to turn around," he said, motioning forward with a sweep of his hand.

The driver of the other car pulled a white raincoat tighter around himself, and bareheaded, ducked against the rain, approached on MG's side of the car. "What's going on?" he asked, stepping beneath the meager shelter of the guard's umbrella.

"Hey, Doctor Brimley." The guard said with forced politeness, reluctantly leaning the umbrella closer to the doctor. "Just some folks wanting to see a patient."

Brimley studied MG for a moment. "Well, let them in," he snapped at the guard.

"They ain't got an appointment. This one says he's ah...Lilia Moss' son, that is, he *thinks* he's Lilia Moss' son."

Mother was here! They knew her name. I had to find a way to see her.

Brimley's dark hair, black beard and glasses were beaded with rain. He bent closer to the window.

With as much certainty as I could muster, I said, "Edgar Weinmann said I might find my mother, Lilia Moss, here."

Brimley studied the projection of Victor with such intensity, I wondered if he might not be seeing some of me beneath the disguise. He cleared his throat and said in a soft, even tone, "Lilia is a patient of mine. We've been expecting you."

I was dumbfounded that he knew I was coming. I reached into his mind for evidence that he might be a servant of Fire, but only sensed professional interest.

"Raise the gate, Harry."

The guard hesitated, seemed to be ready to argue, then stepped in front of the pickup to block our entry. He wrote down the number of the plate in front of the truck, closed the umbrella, stepped back into the guardhouse, and opened the gate.

We drove up a driveway that snaked in two long bends past a shallow lake that had formed on the lawn. MG parked in a space beside Brimley's car before a large brick building surrounded with mature trees and bushes.

I stepped out, a young Hispanic boy. The roar of the Rogue River into which Edgar had supposedly dumped my body was so loud beyond the rear of the estate, I wondered how long it would be before it crested its bank and flooded the Balfore Institute.

Brimley held a square, tan briefcase over his head against the driving rain. "This way," he said and hurried into a foyer where buckets were catching water from a leaking ceiling. A black woman sat at a desk. She was dressed in the same type of dark pants and shirt as the guard at the gatehouse.

Brimley extended his hand to shake mine. I shied away, afraid I would not be able to disguise the physical sensation of my webbing and nails.

If Brimley was insulted by the unrequited greeting, he did not reveal it. He focused on me. "We've been expecting you, Charles," he said to me. "Or would you rather be called Du?"

Nobody has called me by my given name since my father left.

"Du," I mumbled.

"What do you know of your mother's condition?" the doctor asked.

He took my silence as an admission of ignorance, and continued. "Lilia had not spoken for seventeen years until three days ago when she said that her son was coming. She's also called her family. I've just been told that your uncle Eduardo is expected later today. And I've notified your father, Theodore Moss."

I flinched. "When? When is he coming?"

"He will be here by evening. But with this weather, perhaps he will be delayed."

I hadn't seen my father since I was four. Was he going to bring Kare? Did Moss share Kare's fear of the *tunjo?* And Eduardo. Kare had told me about my uncle. He had been there twenty-six years ago when the box was brought into the modern age from the Cave of the *Xucha.* When Norane, Kare's brother, had given Mother the container at her wedding to Theodore Moss, Eduardo had shot Norane. I feared him without ever meeting him.

Brimley continued as if we were making a plan together. "I want to stimulate your mother's conscious activity. On the other hand we must not overwhelm her after such a long time. Do you understand?"

"Yes, I understand," I said.

"Very well, but please don't expect too much. We're very encouraged by Lilia's recent improvement, but sometimes these things take time."

"Cruuuu."

Brimley cocked his head and looked quizzically at the aura of pulsating light that surrounded my pack.

"What's that you've got there?" he asked.

"I have a present for my…for Lilia."

"It will definitely stimulate her," MG said.

"And you are...?" He looked at MG.

"I'm with him," she said.

Brimley looked at her with undisguised suspicion before shifting his gaze back to me. "How is Edgar?"

"He died two days ago." The words caught in my throat. My disguise dimmed.

Brimley blinked rapidly.

"I *am* Victor Magallanes," I repeated to myself, strengthening the thought of how I wanted to appear.

Brimley looked at the guard then back at me. "I'm sorry," he said. "Edgar was an old friend of mine. We started here around the same time. He was a good man."

Brimley led us past the guard through two white doors with small planes of glass reinforced with wire mesh.

"Cruuuuu."

The witches rustled in my pack like stalking animals in the brush. If they caused another disturbance I might never see my mother. I was so close. I just wanted to see her.

I mentally reached out, scanning the minds in the room beyond the closed metal doors. She was there! I sensed her waiting for me, as impatient as I to be reunited.

Brimley unlocked the doors. We entered a large room filled with groups of people of varying ages; some were in white coats and others in pajamas.

I focused on a pale, thin figure, strapped into a wheelchair, sitting alone in a far corner. My thoughts flowed into hers.

Mother!

She did not look like the vision I had seen through the box. Her black hair hung limply to her shoulders. Her face was gaunt, her eyes vacant. What had happened to her?

A teenage patient, dressed in a sweatshirt with the words Magic Mountain on it, shrieked, "Hey! Look at him! He's a frog. A giant frog!"

I had allowed the projection of Victor to slip. I struggled to draw enough of my mind away from Mother to continue to present the image of a Hispanic student.

Brimley tried to calm the overweight teenager. "There's no frog in the room."

"Yes there is. Look! Can't you see him?" She pointed at me.

Everyone was looking at me. I concentrated on Victor's image, but was having difficulty maintaining an empathetic connection with some of the patients.

An old man, whose mouth puckered around missing teeth, said, "I can see him. Yeah, he looks like a frog, all right. Yep. He's a frog."

Brimley frowned.

I stood before Mother, seeking the contact I had experienced at the lake. I used all the empathy I could spare to peer into her mind. The pale shape of a figure appeared in a green swirling fog.

The other patients gathered around us.

"He looks like a frog, doesn't he?" the teen asked MG with a hopeful expression.

"Sometimes," MG said, without taking her eyes off me.

"She ain't spoke in sixteen years," the old man said. "Pretty, ain't she? Hope she gets better, been wanting to ask her out."

The anticipation of change, like the silence in the forest, caused my eyes to turn in independent scans looking for danger.

An aura billowed from my pack.

"Cruuuuu!"

The sound swirled around the room.

Brimley, nurses, and patients gasped. The teenage girl jumped back, knocking into MG.

A sphere of light emerged from my backpack and floated toward Mother.

Patients screamed and ran.

Inside the miasma, the ancient hunchbacked likeness of Curratta formed and hovered before Mother, a shocking appearance.

"What the...?" Brimley studied the spectacle.

The specter spun into a tight stream that flew into Mother's heart. Straining against the restraints of her wheelchair, Mother's eyes flashed open. The split irises were colored the same jungle-leaf hue as Edgar's when the *tunjo* had possessed him.

Mother groaned. The disturbing bifurcated eyes fixed on me.

Patients cackled and shrieked.

"Carlson. Get Turley and anyone else who's free in here!" Brimley called. "What is this?" he demanded, as if I had put on the display to incite his patients.

"The light! The light!" One of the patients cried.

"Hey, look at that! Lilia is trying to talk!"

Brimley bent over to better study Mother.

She struggled against the straps restraining her and raised a thin arm from a worn terrycloth robe toward me, pointing. Saliva bubbled on her lips. "*Tunjo.*" The voice was Curratta's speaking through Mother, garbled, coming from within and without the frail woman in the wheelchair.

"She wants the necklace," MG said.

I understood now. This was how Mother would lead me to Manoa.

I took the container from my bag and opened the lid. Chacs billowed out in a cloud and flew through a closed window to add their destructive rain to the deluge drowning the Age of Man.

"What is that?" Brimley demanded.

The ghostly forms of Curratta and the witches hovered around me as I stepped forward to place the necklace around Mother's neck.

"She can't have that," Brimley said, and tried to take the amulet from me.

A telekinetic force flung him away, sending him skidding on his haunches across the floor. He sat on his rump, looking dumb- founded.

Patients laughed and tittered.

"Did you see that?" a woman asked.

"Go on, give it to her," MG encouraged.

I hesitated, feeling I was parting with all hope, my most precious possession. What MG didn't know was that with the *tunjo* out of the box, *Inika* was free to exert her full power on the weather and me. I might very well be dooming the Age of Man. I placed the unnatural necklace around Mother's neck and felt my powers wane. The weakness was a shock that caused my knees to sag and vision blur. It was all I could do to concentrate on maintaining the image I was projecting. But nobody was looking at me. Mother's eyes opened, clear and brown. "Take me with you," she gasped.

Quetzal had been right. We would go to Manoa.

"Orderlies!" Brimley commanded, back on his feet. "Get them out of here!"

Two men and a woman converged on us.

Reluctant to let anyone touch me, I backed away from the small, emaciated figure encompassed by a chartreuse hallow, the necklace hanging from her neck.

"You're not going to leave her, are you?" MG asked, her hands on her hips.

What did she expect me to do, overpower the orderlies, sweep Mother up and fly away?

The guards herded us out of the lounge and through the front door.

"What are we going to do?" MG asked.

I looked around the rainy landscape expecting a burst of fire to appear, a sign from *Quetzal* about what I must do.

"Well, do something!" MG said.

"What? We can't just take her."

"The police have been called," the guard from the front desk said. "You are now trespassing."

MG gave her an angry look, then strode toward her car. "Come on we'll think of something," she said.

I looked up at the dark and leaden clouds–disgorging torrents of rain. Where was the Plumed Serpent?

"Your mom is just going to have to check herself out. It might take a day or so, but we'll get her out of there."

In a "day or so" how many cities would flood? The key to the survival of the Age of Man was locked in a hospital, and there was no time to spare.

As we drove past the scowling guard with a walkie-talkie pressed to the side of his face, MG saluted. "I'd say you *stimulated* Brimley's patients. Wouldn't you?" she chuckled.

I felt too confused to respond with other than a weak smile.

The guard stepped out to confirm we were leaving and that the barrier had shut behind us. With the instinct of a forest creature, I sensed a predator. My eyes searched for the danger. My skin tingled and I tensed in the seat. My attention was seized by a sleek red sports car driving toward the entrance of the Institute.

"Shhhhraaaaa!"

The Assassins of Fire!

CHAPTER TWELVE
COMMITTED

The red car slowed on the other side of the road and turned into the gate. I shrank down into the seat with weakness that grew more pronounced the farther I withdrew from the tunjo. My hand burned where Kinchel's flames had touched me on the beach of Lake of the Frogs. I looked down to see a cross burning in the pale skin of my palm. He was near. I rotated an eye over my shoulder to see Nurse Assassin driving a red car. By giving Mother the necklace, I had brought her death.

"Stop!" I said. "Please stop."

"Ready to go back? What do you want me to do?" MG pulled over to the side of the road.

I watched the other car turn into the Balfore Institute.

"I have to go back."

"Gotcha!" MG pulled to where the road curved back toward the entrance to the Institute.

I stepped out of the pickup.

MG called to me, "Don't you want my help?"

"No, thank you. Thank you for everything. There is nothing that anyone else can do. I have to go."

Before I could lose my courage or become befuddled by what I hoped to accomplish, I contracted into a crouch and launched myself over the high spiked fence surrounding the grounds, landing in six inches of water that splashed up, soaking my pants. Bent low, leading with my head, I sloshed across the soggy lawn to the entrance.

Brimley was not going to let me in again as Victor. I had to become someone else. But without the *tunjo,* could I cast a strong enough illusion to disguise myself?

An Asian orderly was opening a car in the parking lot.

The female guard who'd just escorted me out as Victor was sitting behind the desk. I hesitated in a dark area beneath a dripping redwood. Even if I could disguise myself from the staff and patients at the Balfore Institute, there was no way I could hide from *Kinchel* and his Assassins. But what was there to go back to? My only hope was that *Quetzal* would protect me if I obeyed him and sought Mother. Only by going forward did I have the slightest hope of escaping the trap I was in. My mother was waiting for me inside.

The Asian orderly was leaning into the open door of his car. If I was going to go, I had to go now. I seized his appearance, dropping into his thoughts like a night-hunting owl, and holding his image firmly in my mind, moved through the portico into the entrance to the hospital.

"Hey, James, that was quick. Did you find what you were looking for in your car?"

I nodded, straining my senses—telepathic and physical—to maintain the illusion.

The guard turned in the seat as I rushed past her. "James, you're soaking wet. You're leaving puddles everywhere. James?"

The doors to the patients' lounge were locked. I looked behind me to see the real James crossing from his car toward the entrance.

"I'll buzz you in," the guard said, and pressed a button on her desk. The door to the ward swung outward. As soon as the barrier closed behind me, I transformed my appearance to Corporal Bob, the man who had treated my wounds in the park.

I looked to the corner, scanned the couches and wheelchairs. Mother was not there.

"It's the frog!" the teenage patient exclaimed. "The frog is back!"

A female psychiatric nurse tried to calm her. "There's no frog in the room."

"Look, look, can't you see him?" She pointed at me.

The rest of the patients were watching me. I concentrated on Corporal Bob's image.

"Yeah, he's back," said the old man who wanted to date Mother.

Where was the Assassin of Fire? I was losing control over the patients' thoughts. Their out-of-order minds were more difficult to influence than their caretakers' minds.

Brimley stepped toward me. My eyes darted about, looking for an escape, or another image that I could project.

How long could I hold a disguise without the *tunjo?* As long as I concentrated on one mind, I was all right, but with so many people looking at me, the illusion was weakening. The Assassin of Fire was close. Maybe she had only lured me back by threatening Mother so she could kill me? All I could think to do was take the most direct course to the *tunjo.* "Take me to Lilia Moss," I commanded Brimley.

He was surprised by the demand. "Who is this?" he asked a psychiatric aide. "How did he get in here?"

The man looked perplexed and said, "I don't know, sir. He wasn't here a minute ago. I don't know who he is."

The aide moved to seize me. I maneuvered behind Brimley, trying to avoid being touched. Another orderly was positioning himself to seize me.

"I have something to tell her." I hopped away.

The patients were cackling and laughing, incited again to the level of disturbance I had caused earlier. "Wait." Brimley stopped the men from chasing me. "We won't hurt you," he said to me.

"I don't want to be touched," I said.

Brimley seemed to be trying to calm the patients and me. "Nobody is going to touch you if you don't want." He smiled and opened his arms.

"I need to talk to Lilia," I said. "She's in danger here. Someone has come to murder her. You must protect her."

"Cruuuuu."

I heard the witches calling from one of the hallways leading from the lounge. A glare shined from beneath a doorway. I had found the *tunjo* if I could only get there. I maneuvered in the direction of the attraction.

"James, your assistance, please," Brimley called to the Asian orderly whose appearance I had taken in the parking lot.

James cut off my route to Mother's room.

"It's the frog. He's back," the teen tried to explain to Brimley.

The doctor's eyes shifted among the agitated patients. "Sir," he said to me. "Would you mind stepping into my office? I can better help you there." He spoke in a soft, non-aggressive tone, extending his arm toward one of the glass-walled rooms off the lounge. "Nobody will touch you, I promise."

James and the orderlies separated me from the room where I hoped to find Mother and see if she was still in possession of the *tunjo.* They herded me into an office.

Framed pictures of a woman and three chubby children were set on a credenza beneath a painting of a salmon rising to a fly.

"Would you mind if I close the door?" Brimley asked. "We won't touch you," he reassured me.

"Go ahead, Private," I said, imitating Corporal Bob.

I searched their thoughts, trying to find a way to get them to leave me alone so I could change disguises and find Mother before *Kinchel* found us both.

Brimley and James stayed together in front of the door. "I am afraid that we don't know how you came to visit us," Brimley said, as if he had made a mistake I could explain.

My empathy scoured his mind for an explanation of why I was here.

"I was sent here."

Brimley smiled, pleased that he had figured it out before I had spoken. "Has anyone here at the Balfore Institute admitted you? I'm afraid there's been some confusion. Did anyone take your file?"

I looked at him with a blank expression. I didn't know what he was talking about. I was wasting time. I'd never be able to reach the *tunjo* in time to save Mother or myself. "Is there some place I can go? I'm very tired," I said. I looked to where a puddle had formed beneath me. "I'm all wet."

"Yes, I see. We'll take care of that in just a moment. I just need to ask you a few quick questions."

"I can't talk to you now, Private!" I did not have trouble acting disturbed and imitating Corporal Bob.

Brimley leaned toward James at the door and whispered, "Someone must have mistaken him for one of ours. I'll call Crenshaw. Maybe he referred him to me as a consultation. Keep him in iso until I find out what's going on."

"How did he know about Lilia?" James asked.

"He must have witnessed the disturbance."

"Am I dismissed?" I asked.

"Yes, we can do this later," Brimley smiled.

He and James walked me toward the main entrance, away from the hallway where I had sensed Mother.

"Would you mind staying in here?" Brimley held his hand out toward an open door to a padded room. I contemplated my chances of jumping away from Brimley and James, but I was trapped.

"We'll bring you some towels and a change of clothes," Brimley said to me. He turned and whispered to James, "Get him out of his clothes and into some scrubs. Full observation. Suicide watch."

After Brimley had walked away, James smiled at me. "I'm going to lock this door for a minute. If you need anything, we'll be watching and listening to you." He looked up at a camera mounted above the wall. "Once you've changed and dried off, we'll talk. OK?" He locked the door behind him.

For five minutes I paced the floor, throwing out the deception of Corporal Bob, certain that Mother was being murdered at this very moment.

When I heard someone unlocking the door, I moved as close to the entrance as I could, and changed my image to James.

A surprised young woman entered carrying a pile of clothing and towels. "What are you doing locked up in here?" she asked.

I mumbled about a mistake and hurried by her into the hall, hoping that whoever had been watching me through the camera had not noticed the switch.

Passing through the lounge area to get to the wing where Mother was, the other patients were not fooled.

"Going to see your mom?" The elderly man winked at me.

I nodded. He and some of the other patients started to follow me.

"Go back!" I said. "It's dangerous."

They stopped at the end of the hall and watched me with apprehensive eyes.

I went to the door where I had seen the gleam of the *tunjo* and heard the sound of the witches.

Another door opened a crack at the end of the hallway from the lounge. Someone was looking to see what was on the other side. The Assassin of Fire was not far. With no plan other than to reach the *tunjo*, I opened the door and stepped inside.

Mother lay on the bed, the necklace held against her chest. She was dressed in a pair of off-white cloth pajama pants and a pullover. Her eyes were closed, her skin as pale as goose down.

"Cruuuuu."

The talisman called to me.

The witches rustled about her. A corona of magical light emanated from the pulsing eyes of the pendant.

Nurse Assassin opened the door from the hallway. She wore a sleeveless, black t-shirt revealing a tattoo of the snake-wrapped cross on her upper arm.

Our eyes met, we recognized each other. No disguise would hide me. With the back of her foot, she kicked the door shut behind her.

I looked at the *tunjo*, contemplating leaping for it with a desperate hope that its power would give me the strength to defeat the Assassin of Fire.

The Assassin came for me, head hunched forward, red eyes narrowed, ready to fight me to the death.

"Cruuuu."

Mother's body flew past me, flung from the bed. The *tunjo* channeled the full power of the witches into her.

"Shhhhraaaaa!"

"Cruuuu!"

"Shhhhraaaaa!"

The combination of the screams was shrill and terrifying. Mother and the Assassin of Fire clawed and bit each other, like two battling mountain lions.

The intensity of their clash produced a crackling burst of energy in a swirling red and green fog that formed the terrifying shape of *Kinchel*. His dragon heads pressed against the ceiling, flaming wings beating.

From the swirling kaleidoscope of images, Curratta, haggard and old emerged, pointing a gnarled staff of hard wood tipped with a casting of *Tatya-Masi* at the monster. Waves of energy from the mouth of the carving drove the beast back. I crouched against the wall, a helpless spectator at a battle for my life and soul.

The Assassin was atop Mother, her hands reaching for the *tunjo*. Sparks burst and disjointed, ancient voices wailed around the combatants. Mother's eyes were open and jade. As frail and thin as a corpse, she rolled over atop the Assassin. The women's hands were squeezed around each other's neck. Then there was an agonized female scream, a final snap of bone breaking, a gasp, and silence.

The haze cleared and the two women lay motionless on the floor. The Assassin of Fire's head was bent at a terrible unnatural angle over her shoulder. Mother was barely alive beside her.

Was I going to lose her as I had Edgar? The *tunjo* pulsed on Mother's chest like a muted heartbeat.

"What was it? Did you hear that?" From within the ward came wails of fear, screaming, insane laughter, people calling and the sound of footsteps running toward the room.

I swept Mother up across my arms, used the proximity of the *tunjo* to reinvigorate the disguise of the Asian orderly, and hurried out into the hallway.

"What's going on, James?" challenged one of the men who had escorted me out as Victor.

"There's been an accident. Someone's hurt, in Lilia's room."

"Oh my God, look!" A patient pointed through the doorway of Mother's room.

There was a loud explosion from near an exit door to the ward. Nurse Assassin had left a firebomb. A white cloud of chemicals blew across the room with horrendous effect, igniting the ward, setting patients and staff aflame. Screaming, they tried to flee the quickly spreading conflagration.

"Shraaaa." The flames morphed into the nine heads of *Kinchel* the Avenger. The Assassins would spare no life to kill me.

I led the rush to the exit hallway, but Titus Creation blocked my escape. I jumped to the side just as the steel barrel of his gun recoiled with a series of rapid reports, hitting James Li who fell to the ground. Titus Creation then panned the pistol to get a bead on me, as I leapt about the room with Mother's inert body across my arms.

A man ran down the hallway to where the policeman was shooting into the melee. "What are you doing?" he screamed while wresting the pistol away from Titus. The Assassin tried to fight him, but the man struck him on the side of the head with the barrel of a gun, sending Titus crumpling to the ground.

The entire population of the Institute was trying to get out the front door to escape the inferno. I hesitated in the lobby as the crowd pushed around me out the entrance.

Outside, Blond Assassin's pupils shined red as he watched those exiting the building.

The sound of approaching sirens grew louder. Through the din, *Xolo* could be heard furiously barking in the back seat of Titus Creation's patrol car.

Over my shoulder I saw the man with the gun pushing his way after me. There was something immediately familiar about him. I thought he might be my uncle, but if he were, what would he think at the sight of Corporal Bob carrying his sister away?

I changed the image I was casting from that of Corporal Bob to Kare.

I knew I had correctly identified him when he ran up to me a pistol in his hand. His thick shoulders sloped from a wide neck, straining the fabric of his black suit jacket. The steel-plated heels of his snakeskin boots clacked against the polished floor. Chestnut-colored eyes glowered beneath thick eyebrows. "Kare, what are *you* doing here? What is this madness?"

In a perfect imitation of Kare's voice, I replied, "They're trying to kill Lilia. Help us."

"Who are they?" Eduardo squinted.

I nodded toward where Blond Assassin could be seen through the window. "Him."

Eduardo twisted his lips and lowered the gun barrel to his side. "Wait for a moment, then follow me."

Eduardo moved outside to Blond Assassin, and raised the pistol, pressing it against the Assassin's temple. "Give me your gun, now!" he said as I exited in the guise of Kare carrying Mother.

Blond Assassin handed his pistol to Eduardo. Assassin Wolf smashed against the rear window of the police cruiser, trying to get at us. Two more police cars raced up the driveway from the main road, with fire engines following.

With my back-turned right eye, I saw Titus Creation emerge from the Institute's entrance. Bolting across the soggy lawn in long hops, I heard Eduardo call after me, "Kare! Where are you going?"

Holding a pistol in each hand, he ran up the driveway parallel to me.

Blond Assassin moved to the cruiser and released *Xolo*. With burning red eyes, the wolf bounded after me. There was no way I could escape on foot.

Ahead I saw the familiar shape of MG's truck. She threw open her door. "Du! Du!' she shouted across the lawn.

I hurtled toward her as Eduardo ran past the emergency vehicles, his gun still drawn.

Xolo, burning eyes, flagging tongue over his sharp white teeth, was nearly on me when Eduardo fired a shot. Wolf-Assassin's head exploded. Her body flipped backwards. And with an angry growl, the wolf disappeared in a burst of flames.

At the sound of the shot, a police cruiser stopped, tried to turn around but the back wheels went off the paved surface and onto the flooded lawn where they spun, leaving their car partially blocking the driveway.

The red car driven by Hunter Assassin pulled up behind Titus Creation and Blond Assassin in the Calaveras cruiser, lights flashing and sirens blaring in an urgent demand that the responding vehicles allow them to pass. The surfaces adjacent to the driveway were blocked by trees and flooded lawn, leaving no alternative but for the Assassins to wait until the fire trucks moved.

Holding Mother and looking like Kare, I climbed into the seat behind MG.

"I knew it was you," she said. "The way you were moving." She turned the truck around and was starting to drive away when Eduardo wrenched open the back door as the pickup gathered speed.

"It's my uncle," I shouted as Eduardo jumped headfirst into the moving truck. MG tipped around the corner so the door closed, seconds before the passenger-side mirror was knocked off by a gunshot.

The sound of gunfire, the whine and metal ringing impact of bullets striking the frame of the truck, chased us as we hurtled down the road in front of the Balfore Institute.

Eduardo leaned over the front seat. "Lilia! Is she alive?"

I held Mother's frail form across my lap. "I think so," I said. The ferocious strength in Mother I had witnessed was hard to imagine looking at her battered body. The neck of her nightshirt was torn. Her thin shoulder was scratched. The Jewels of Life in the eyes of the *tunjo* dimmed. Even with the power of the necklace to keep her alive, she was dying.

"I thought you were dead too," Eduardo said.

He thought he was speaking to Kare.

"Cruuuu."

"That sound!" Eduardo raised Titus' police revolver, leaned over the seat and stared at the necklace on Mother's chest. "The *tunjo!*" he gasped. An aura pulsed around the necklace. "Es verdad.*" So, it's true*, he whispered.

The specter spun into a tight stream that flowed into her heart. Her eyelids bolted open—the witches' jade on top, Mother's brown on the bottom. She sat up in the seat next to me, her unblinking pupils staring straight ahead.

Eduardo recoiled in horror. "Lilia?"

Her voice was weak and distant as if speaking from deep within her body. "Eduardo, take me home."

"Yes, Lilia. I'll take you home."

She closed her eyes and slumped against me.

His intense gaze focused on me. "What is this? How did you get the *tunjo?*" he demanded.

There was no better time to show him who I truly was.

When I released the image of Kare, Eduardo's brown skin blanched, and his upper lip trembled beneath his moustache. "What are you?" He refused to believe what he knew was true.

"I am Lilia's son. This is the *tunjo* you found in the cave."

"You lie," Eduardo snarled and aimed the gun at me. "What have you done to her?"

My throat closed and the blood rushed in my temples. "They tried to kill her."

"Who?"

"They, the servants of the Lord of Fire." I point to those chasing us. "Will you help us?"

Eduardo gripped his pistol tighter. "Drive down the mountain. There is an airport. I have a plane there."

"Shraaaa!"

The Calaveras police cruiser was drawing closer, now only three hundred yards behind us. Blond Assassin leaned out of the cruiser window and aimed a weapon at us.

We slid around a curve on two wheels. The pickup teetered on the edge of a steep drop. My heart almost choked me. I leaned away from the tilt to keep the truck upright.

"Come on girl," MG muttered and thrust her head over the steering wheel trying to see through the rainwater backing up on the windshield against the insufficient push of the blades. Mud coursed off the steep slopes of the mountainside. MG swerved around fallen rocks and powered through a slide, keeping the truck pointed down the road. The turns and twists flashed by. Frozen moments of terror passed in slow motion, then blurred as we raced down switchbacks, exposed to gunfire followed by moments of relative safety when the mountain hid us.

A stream of muddy water covered a portion of the twisting highway. MG did not slow as she drove into the slick. With a head-twisting jerk, the pickup lost traction and the truck's tail floated toward the edge of the mountainside. MG dropped the gear, accelerated, and steered out of the slide with the gas pedal pushed to the floor. With a twist of the steering wheel, the left side of the pickup lifted off the ground, violently flinging Mother against me. I held her as the truck veered toward the cliff before regaining traction and continuing down the mountain road.

My rearward-turned eye watched Titus hit the slick patch. The police cruiser spun in a complete circle and incredibly flew out on a course straight down the road, only twenty car lengths behind us. *Kinchel's* great powers were at the command of his servants, while all we had to save us was MG's driving skills.

We were now in full view of our pursuers. The next bend was a hundred yards ahead.

"Shraaaa."

Blond Assassin aimed a rocket out the window of the cruiser. With a flash of light and a trail of smoke, the projectile flew toward us.

MG skidded close to the mountainside and cut through the turn just as the grenade exploded with a blast that threw rocks, fire and smoke into the air with a thought-shattering percussion. The impact violently shook the pickup. The windshield popped with a spider web of cracks. MG was lifted off the seat but drove straight through the smoke and fire without hesitation.

I craned my neck, left eye distended to see a boulder falling into the path of the pickup.

"Ahhhhh!" Eduardo groaned as the monster rock rose up in the air at the edge of the road and hovered over the roof of the cab before landing with a jarring crash behind us. The shockwave lifted the end of the vehicle and sent us sliding again toward the cliff before we sped around the next bend.

The mountain road cut along the side of a canyon where I could see back to Titus maneuvering with stops and starts through the rock debris left in the wake of the explosion. *Kinchel* would not be delayed for long.

We'd gained a thousand yards, but when we reached the straighter road leading to a bridge, the Assassins had closed within ten car lengths. The cruiser sped over a hill. Blond Assassin was out the window again, firing a rifle at us.

"Phlunk, phlunk, phlunk." Our rear window exploded, and the bullets traveled through the cab, shattering the windshield, passing us like fiery bees. Rain blew in torrents around us.

Ahead were the blinking red and blue lights of the police cars blocking the road on the far side of a bridge, but MG didn't slow. With the engine whining, the pickup raced toward the blockade, as policemen dove away to avoid the onrushing truck.

"Cruuuu!" An aquamarine, sparkling light rose from the *tunjo* on Lilia's chest and pulsed inside the cab.

The cloud now concentrated around MG. For an instant I thought I saw her pupils split brown and jade.

"The airport is over there!" Eduardo screamed.

MG spun the wheel and launched the truck from the highway. We flew through the air, fifty feet over an embankment, and landed with a jarring crash on a side road.

The detour barely slowed the Assassins of Fire, who jumped the same embankment and followed us onto the old highway. Two police cars, lights flashing and sirens wailing, chased along the parallel road.

A sign ahead read Municipal Airport. The old road was rough and pooled with rain. We hit puddles and streams that slowed one side of the pickup, causing us to be tossed about at different angles. A giant splash thrown up behind the vehicle blocked my view of Titus. MG turned the wheel, sending us across a nearly submerged bridge over a swollen drainage ditch toward a sand pile. Orange trucks with metal plows were parked behind a fence. MG did not slow for a lowered wooden barrier attached to a metal post, past a sign warning of Severe Tire Damage. The truck's impact broke the board and sent it flying over the roof.

Flooded fields edged a wide strip of pavement.

Titus followed, near enough that I could clearly see Brian's calm expression as he aimed his rifle at us.

'Shhhhraaaaa!"

As MG steered toward several airplanes on the tarmac, Eduardo pointed his gun through the empty frame of the windshield at a parked silver truck on which was written Jonathan Jet Fuel. The vibrations of rapid explosions rang in my ears. An acrid, sulfurous cloud blew back from Eduardo's gun. Holes opened in the rounded side of the truck; brown liquid spurted. We sped past just as flames spread toward us, followed by a blast that blew into the passenger compartment with a hot concussion, causing the car to swerve.

"Shhhhraaaaa!"

Kinchel's growl combined fury and frustration as his image was engulfed in flames. Titus could not avoid driving into the inferno. The K-9 car emerged afire and continued to follow us until the vehicle could go no farther. Clutching their guns, Titus and Brian staggered from the fiery wreck, their skin blackened, clothes smoldering.

I was amazed that we had beaten *Kinchel* even to this point, but where could we go now? Police cars were approaching the airfield from different directions. Could we surrender to the police? The Lord of Fire could not possess them all.

We fishtailed to a stop. Eduardo jumped from the door and ran to a white twin-engine plane, pulled down a door behind the left wing, and bolted up a ladder into the curved fuselage.

The feeling of being herded caused me to hesitate at the bottom of the stairs. What choice did I have?

The left propeller started to turn, the engine belching a cloud of burnt fuel.

"Goodbye. Thank you. I love you," I said to MG and hopped onto the steps of the plane.

Without pausing, she followed me.

"No," I cried and turned on the steps. "Don't come," I said. "Surrender to them. You've done nothing wrong."

MG looked back, trying to decide. The plane began to roll. The sound of approaching police cars grew louder.

"Get in," MG pushed me up the steps.

"Close the damn door," Eduardo shouted.

"How?" MG said.

"Pull that cable and push down the handle on the door."

MG did as she was told and was now locked in the plane with us.

Eduardo's hands moved rapidly over the controls. The right propeller turned as the engine started, causing an increased vibration in the plane. We pivoted to the left on a sharp axis. The plane rolled faster, bounced between two parked airplanes, and headed toward a small building.

I followed MG's example, and with Mother across my lap, fell into one of the padded seats, facing the front of the plane.

Eduardo advanced two levers in the console beside him. Outside the round window, we swept by a police officer holding a shotgun.

Eduardo bent across the half-circle yoke in front of him. *"¡Puta!"* he coaxed, and pulled on the wheel. The engines strained to build up enough speed to fly, but to no avail. A yellow metal airplane hanger was directly in front of the plane. Was Eduardo going to turn? Were we going to crash?

I closed my eyes and imagined an eagle catching an updraft on the side of a cliff. I felt a bump as the wheels skimmed the roof of the hanger. We were flying.

"¡Aiiee!" Eduardo exhaled.

Mother's arm flopped limply toward the window as we banked. I looked out to see Titus and Brian running, firing their guns at us. The flames of the fuel truck that Eduardo had ignited reached up into the sky and within them, I saw *Kinchel*, his purple wings spread, his fangs exposed, striking skyward in a furious attempt to reach from the metaphysical world to knock us down.

CHAPTER THIRTEEN
A DANGEROUS MAN

My hands were shaking and my throat was dry. We climbed higher into the dark clouds with such power that Mother's body felt heavier as it pressed against me. Then, the nose pointed downward, and I thought we were going to crash. The steep descent threw me forward over Mother. We fell almost as steeply as we had climbed before the plane leveled off, skimming over trees barely beneath the wings.

"I hope he knows where the mountains are," MG said, gripping the seat and looking out the window.

The angle of wing seemed to match the slope of the hillside. We pointed straight up a rocky precipice, pushing me into my seat. Water streamed across the window as we looped, twisted, and dove back down through a break in the clouds.

"He's a maniac!" MG said. Her hands clutched the armrests of the seat, her eyes closed.

My hearing was sensitive enough to hear Eduardo speaking into the small tube in front of his mouth. His accent was different, more American.

"Calaveras tower, this is one-four-niner Yankee Bravo. Somebody nearly clipped us. I think he might have gone in. Fireball off right wingtip."

A fainter voice from Eduardo's earpiece asked, "Your position now one-four-niner?"

"I'm ten nautical at your one-eight-zero, Calaveras. Pretty shaken up here. Permission to land."

"Negative. Airport out of commission."

"Can you vector me into another airport?"

"Roger. I'll get you into Sacramento. Be aware of heavy military and police traffic in area."

"Can you keep me clear of traffic?" Eduardo pleaded.

"Do what I can one-four-niner."

"Oh man," MG moaned. "They're going to have the air force after our asses for being terrorists. We'll be lucky if we don't get shot down."

The man to whom Eduardo was talking guided him for about 15 minutes. When Eduardo signed off, we flew level until we dropped below the level of the treetops, looking as if we were going to fall onto the ground. I looked at MG expecting to see her sharing my panic that we were about to crash.

"Are we landing?" MG asked.

Then the plane began to climb again and pitched sideways as we reentered the clouds.

The panic had left MG's expression. "That was pretty slick. I think he's trying to fool them into thinking we landed."

Fool whom, I wondered? I used to see planes sometimes in the sky over the lake and regretted ever wishing that I could fly in one.

Eduardo's back relaxed and his shoulders dropped. I began to believe my uncle was in control and we were not going to crash. The moments passed. My focus moved from the front of the plane to the window. We leveled. Clouds pressed close. The engines quieted to a less-strained hum.

Were we now on our way to Omagua? How long would it take to fly there? Rain was falling harder. By giving Mother the *tunjo*, I had released the full power of *Inika*. The Age of Man did not have much time before it drowned.

Shock lay on me like numbing fatigue. Across the narrow aisle in one of a matching set of seats, MG had the expression of an animal that has just survived an attack. Maybe that was how I looked. Why was she here? Why had she come when she could have surrendered? She looked at me, expecting me to explain what had happened.

"I'm glad you're all right," I said, my voice sounding hollow and distant, buried within the vibration and noise of the engines.

"You call this all right?"

Even though she was smiling, I felt stupid and wanted to apologize, but was afraid what I would say would be even less intelligent.

We started to climb again. The nose of the plane remained pointed up until we passed into the first sunlight that I'd seen in three days. Old Sol! Maybe the Earth was not drowning. But below, the land remained cloaked in black and gray clouds that stretched to the horizon. The world I knew was gone.

My eyes turned from the window to the cabin to watch Eduardo flip a switch on the console, pull his headset off, and come back to us. Could a plane fly by itself? He knelt beside me, looking at his sister.

The eyes of the *tunjo* shined.

"Lilia," he whispered, and touched her on the shoulder.

She showed no reaction. The glimmer faded around the pendant.

Eduardo studied her. He reached for the necklace.

"Don't!" I said and reached for him. That was a mistake. He slapped my hand away and drew back his fist to strike me.

I cowered from the expected blow. "It's what's keeping her alive. Her spirit is in Manoa. If you break the link, she will die."

Eduardo looked back at his sister. He had been there when the box was discovered and knew the mythology of the *tunjo*. Perhaps nobody else but he would have understood, believed what I was saying. "La'ku sorcery." He scowled. "Why did you take her?"

I switched to Spanish, speaking in an accent I had learned from Kare that would be familiar to him. "She was attacked. I had to take her."

His complexion reddened. His voice was cold, threatening. "Who attacked her?"

"A nurse. But it was...a spirit. The Assassins of Fire..." I saw I had gone too far, but I tried. "There are forces that oppose the witches, *Kinchel* the Avenger, who are trying to stop us from reaching Manoa."

"And you know where Manoa is?" He asked with an expression of stressed tolerance, giving me one more chance to change my story.

"I think it is somewhere near where you found the box, in the cave."

He started. "How do you know?"

"From Kare."

"Yes, Kare. Tell me of him."

I told him the basic information about my life at the lake. Gradually, the more information I could add that he knew, the more he appeared to believe me.

"Theodore did this?" Eduardo drummed his fingers on the bulge of the muscle within the upper sleeve of his black jacket. "I can not believe this. Tell me who gave her the *tunjo*? Was it you?"

I lowered my gaze and then raised my eyes. "I'm sorry. The Plumed Serpent told me to do it."

Now I had lost him again. It was hard enough to explain about *Kinchel* the Avenger and his Assassins of Fire, but to add another mythological being with his own motivations and methods of controlling me was too much for Eduardo.

His eyes narrowed and his mouth pulled into a tight line of fury. "Take the *tunjo* off her. That's what started the curse. That's what will end it."

"Please believe me. It's what is keeping her alive. If there was any other way..."

He puffed out his cheeks against the tight hold of his closed lips and studied me. I sensed that even if he did not understand the power of the *tunjo*, he feared it. I used all my empathy to let him know I only wanted to do what was best for Mother.

He exhaled in a stream from his puckered lips. "Must you hold her?"

He had never seen me without Mother in my arms.

"No. I guess not."

I put Mother into the seat facing me, but she slumped listlessly forward. Eduardo positioned her against the window. Somebody had to hold her or she would just fall over the next time the plane banked.

MG asked in English. " You got anything to dry her with? Keep her warm? She's drenched."

Eduardo shook his head.

MG took off her heavy leather jacket.

"No." Eduardo touched the sleeve of MG's black cotton blouse. He took off his coat, snapped rain off it toward the rear of the plane and covered his sister. "I'll turn up the cabin heat," he said and returned to the controls.

"I'll watch out for her," MG said and sat on the armrest of Mother's seat.

"Thank you, ah...your name, please."

"MG."

I studied her expression. She looked angry with him, yet I sensed he interested her. I was struck by a pang of jealousy. Suddenly, I hated my uncle. Then, I felt childish and weak, without direction. I only wanted to escape this madness however I could.

  * * *

My lack of movement for three hours in the small cabin and the droning of the engines lulled me from my panic to a state of nervous anticipation. I sat across from Mother and studied her pale face, hungering for the comfort I had felt when she had come to me when I found the box. Where was the beautiful spirit that had appeared to me? Rather than make her better, all the *tunjo* seemed to have done was take possession of her frail body in a manner with which I dared not interfere. Would she ever be better? For their own distinct, conflicting reasons both the witches and the Serpent were using Mother to bring me to Manoa. They were merciless, and I in my ignorance was abetting her harm.

MG was watching me. I looked over at her and said, "You may be right about my mother. I don't know who to trust."

"From what I can tell, there are three sides to this: the Lord of Fire, the Lordess of Water, and the Plumed Serpent. We've got to figure out some way to play one against the other," MG said.

To think we could outmaneuver *Kinchel, Inika,* and *Quetzal* seemed more than audacious; it was futile. I had no confidence that they were not listening to us, reading our thoughts. They were at least two steps ahead. "You think we can?" I asked despite my doubts.

"We gotta know more about who we're fighting if we're going to have a chance. What about your father, this Theodore Moss?"

"At the wedding, Kare gave Theodore Moss *Quetzal's* cross. The cross is how *Quetzal* controls people. My father became like Kare. He had to do what the Plumed Serpent told him to. His life changed. That's why he never came to see me or seemed to care about me. I'm sure he would have been a good father if it wasn't for the cross."

MG looked at me with a sympathetic glance. "Yeah, sure. I'm sure he'd have been a better dad. And?"

"That's all I know."

"You need more information. Didn't you tell me you could read minds? Have you tried reading your mom's mind?"

MG was right. The greatest source of information I had ever had access to about the origins of my dilemma was lying right beside me. "I'll try," I said.

Mother's thin face showed no expression in the eerie light of the *tunjo.* Long, dark eyelashes lay over high cheekbones. Limp lips parted above a pointed chin. The choir hummed inside the necklace. I leaned over and whispered, "Mother? Are you there?" Could she free herself from the witches enough to communicate with me again?

Her eyelids fluttered. The necklace radiated, highlighting her pale neck and face. The supernatural light was an indicator of the energy flowing around, in, and through her. The chanting was parted by a woman's wavering voice.

"*Tatya-Masi.*"

"No, Mother. It's Du. Your son, Du."

The only response was the throb of the *tunjo's* light.

I stared into her face, and opened my mind, using the full power of my empathy to try and reach Mother. There waiting for me, as I feared she would be, was Curratta and the *Xucha* witches.

"Cruuuuu."

The *Xucha* chorus chanted. The misshapen and ancient hags' deformed features were twisted in rapture, ecstatic to be in the presence of their god, mindless of how confused I was.

I pulled back, almost losing my mental connection with Mother. My pulse raced. My skin felt clammy. My stomach churned.

"Where is my mother?" I asked, forcing myself to confront the specters.

"*Koox tun,*" Curratta crooned, and held her hand out to me with the assurance that I had nowhere else to go.

As if dangling by the tips of my fingers from a cliff, I maintained my tenuous hold on the physical plane: listening to my breaths, counting my heartbeats, feeling the cool soft flesh inside my arm. Let me pass. I want to speak to my mother.

The shaman's frog-like face contorted into a monster's grimace. Her lips pulled together. Her large eyes narrowed.

"Mother," I called. Where was she? A chilling dread kept my mind from following Curratta into the light. I clung to the plane seat as if letting go would cast me into the world of the *Xucha* without hope of return.

Yet, I mentally pushed past the ancient hags who floated around me whispering spells into a colorless room.

Mother lay unconscious on a narrow bed. White sheets stirred in a gentle breeze. A sweet scent combining vanilla and other orchids wafted around her.

She was as beautiful as she had appeared to me by the Lake of the Frogs when I had found the container.

"Mother, can you hear me? Mother?"

Curratta's voice high and quavering echoed in a great hollow space. "Become one with Lilia. Learn of your past and the trickery of the Plumed Serpent." Curratta extended her arm as she withdrew into the foggy light, leaving me alone with Mother to share her thoughts and memories.

I felt Mother's presence waiting behind the light and allowed my consciousness to be completely absorbed by the vision.

Then I was joined with her in a complete mental communion, feeling what she had felt on her wedding day, learning about the man who was the Earthly Father of *Tatya-Masi*.

CHAPTER FOURTEEN
NORANE

Mother had long been under Norane's spell. She was enchanted by his stories of the Xucha and Tatya-Masi, a La'ku god to be born from mortal parents. At night the moonlit form of the snow-capped peak of the volcano Mount Susuprina towered over the lake. She heard voices, whispers, cries, chants, and drums that seemed to rise from the jungle that stretched from beneath the giant waterfall that tumbled from the edge of the lake to where civilization had claimed the land up to her family's land. She told Norane of these strange callings, and he explained that the ancients were speaking to her.

She could have told her father, but had not, afraid he would not allow her to go with Eduardo and him on their explorations into the jungle preserve seeking La'ku artifacts. Neither had she spoken about her feelings for Norane, certainly not her fantasy that she and the Indian groom would be the mortal parents of a god.

She'd grown up to become an accomplished archeologist whose childish dreams had almost been forgotten on her wedding day. Her nuptials to Theodore Moss had been a grand affair held at Omagua, her family's estate. The great lands of the Morales family were not what they'd been when their ancestor, Cristóbal de Morales, was deeded a land grant of seventy thousand square miles by King Felipe II. But even in modern times, the family manor was an impressive structure, sitting on a hill overlooking Lago Itza Uo, which meant Place of the Frogs in the La'ku dialect. With alabaster walls, green-framed windows and red clay tile roofs, the two wings spread like open arms from the old mansion, which had housed so many generations of the Morales' lineage. The wedding had been in a garden modeled after the Moorish-influenced castles of old Granada in Spain, with lush tropical plants spread among fountains and pools.

Guests in formal clothing passed by Mother and her new husband in the receiving line. Her thoughts were in the modern world and the beginning of a new life as the wife of an American petroleum engineer, when suddenly, ancient hands had reached across the centuries for her.

Norane appeared in a costume she had only seen in drawings depicting how the ancient La'ku had dressed. He was tall for an Indian, over six feet, with a long jaw and piercing dark eyes. He wore striped cotton pants gathered below his knees, high-heeled leather sandals, and a jaguar-skin vest over his muscular chest. Blue and gold macaw feathers hung from the side of his head and from a leather strap wrapped around his right biceps. Knives with bone handles were thrust into his belt.

In his hands was the silver and gold box he and Eduardo had found in the Cave of the Xucha when they were twelve years old. The shining emerald eyes of the half-man half-frog on the lid hypnotized Lilia, and her hands hovered over the container. According to the myth of Tatya-Masi, the Awkanakuy-Hauakuy, the Warrior-Brother, would give Curratta's box to his true love, the Earthly Mother of the god. She had always suspected that Norane was the Warrior-Brother, but that he would select her, a descendant of the castellanos who had conquered his people, was unimaginable.

Norane broke into the receiving line, bowed and held out the box to Lilia. He whispered, "I have looked into my heart and can find only you."

The moment her hands touched the box, a thrill spread into the deepest parts of her; her spirit separated from her body. One minute she was a happy bride waiting to shake hands with a doctor and his wife, the next she was wafting into a dream from which she could not awake. To the outside world, she appeared to be in a daze. But everything for her was in a sharp focus and she could see the spiritual dimensions of the guests and of all life around her. Her spirit had risen above the scene and with heightened empathy she heard Norane's words in her mind, even as he walked away from her body toward the jungle.

"Come with me, be the Earthly Mother of Tatya-Masi."

She had been bewitched.

"You feel the power because you have the power. You are Xucha, have been Xucha since your baby eyes saw Susuprina. Will you come with me to Manoa?"

There had never been anyone, could never be anyone, but him. "Yes."

Oblivious to the shocked looks and calls of her family, her body hurried after Norane across the estate and along the fields toward the falls.

Her father and brother had caught her and led her body back, but her spirit had gone on with Norane.

After her father had taken her by the hand, Eduardo sped on his motorcycle after Norane. He bounced and skipped, nearly falling over as he raced to the top of the waterfall. Skidding to a stop he hurried to where Norane stood on a ledge, his back to him.

"La'ku bastard!" Eduardo raised his pistol and aimed at Norane's head.

"No!" Lilia's spirit tried to cry out to her brother, but her body was too far away and could not speak.

Eduardo pulled the trigger and the gun jumped in his hand.

Norane's body dropped into the swirling brown water beneath the falls. Norane and Lilia's spirit hands joined and they soared off the cliff. Behind the white water, their souls flew into the Cave of the Xucha.

"Are we dead?"

"There is no death for me where we are going."

"And me?"

"This is the time. I know it, and you are the one, I am certain the Xucha will test you. And if you do not please them..." he hung his head. "You will die." He pleaded with his large brown eyes for her to trust him.

"What must I do to please them?"

"You must be the virgin of the lake."

Even in her dream state, she blushed. "Then, I will please them," she whispered.

"It may not always be so—we must hurry—the Plumed Serpent is trying to seize your body."

The farther her spirit flew into the cave, the more distant she felt from what was happening on the surface. She was able to go back with the small level of consciousness that still remained in her body, and saw what Norane feared.

Her father took her body back to the mansion. Her hands still clutched the jeweled silver and gold container.

Don Carlos led his daughter up the back steps to her room. She did not respond to his questions, jokes, even demands she speak to him, but only stared ahead with a vacant gaze.

The distance between her body and spirit made it difficult for Lilia to stand. She sat in her muddy wedding dress beside the window framing Mount Susuprina.

Though she could not speak, she was aware of her mother, Beatrice, and aunt Tatua standing on either side of her.

Beatrice tried to pull the box from her daughter's unbreakable hold. "Give me that filthy peasant trash," she railed, and sat back, throwing all the substantial weight of her ample rear into the effort.

Aunt Tatua, the same height and fifty pounds heavier than Lilia's mother, also pulled.

"She's bewitched," Beatrice wailed as she and aunt Tatua gave up trying to remove the container from Lilia's iron grip.

"Oh, this is Indian witchcraft, I know it! Know it!" aunt Tatua cried, holding onto Lilia by the upper arm.

"I don't think that she can marry him now," her father said.

With gleams of madness in her eyes, Tatua, who had come home twenty years before after a tragic romance and had never left, mocked her brother. "Marry! Did you say marry?" Her volume rose, defeating their efforts to shield their problem from possible eavesdroppers. "Do you not remember standing in the cathedral this morning before 500 people, not to mention God and the bishop, and hear her take Theodore Moss for her husband? Did you not hear her take her vows with your own ears? What has that infernal box, that Indian magic, done to her?"

Don Carlos' helpless bewilderment was conveyed in a blank expression to Tatua. He knew the myth of Curratta's box as well as anyone in the modern world. He had kept the container in his study after Norane and Eduardo had found it in the Cave of the Xucha. He was not surprised that Norane was the Warrior-Brother, but could not understand why Norane had selected Lilia, a daughter of the race that had conquered the La'ku, to be the Earthly Mother of Tatya-Masi.

Lilia's younger sister by two years, Matilde, opened the door without knocking, and brought Theodore Moss into the room.

"Is everything all right?" Moss asked in his excellent Spanish.

"Of course, of course," Beatrice blustered and moved to block Moss from seeing her demented daughter.

Lilia was happy to see him at first. She wished she could explain to him what was happening, but the nearer he came to her, the more fearful she became. The sweet, understanding man with whom she had fallen in love had changed. With her new ability to see his spirit, she now saw a feathered snake rising from flames inside of Moss.

She heard a rattling hiss coming from a necklace around his neck. There was a red gleam in his eyes, a slight twist to his mouth.

She was trapped. With her spirit outside of her body, she could not resist or scream for help.

"Shhhhraaaaa!"

The sound was as loud as the crack of thunder over the jungle, a storm of swirling lights and cries of pain came from a void behind Moss.

Her father alone among her family seemed to sense the terrible threat. "I'm afraid my daughter is in no condition to travel," he said, despite the glare from her mother.

"Why, she's fine," Moss said in a contradictory tone he would never have dared use to Don Carlos before. "The car is waiting."

Beatrice and Tatua followed behind the bride and groom to make sure there was no retreat. If the rice-throwing guests noticed anything amiss, nobody spoke. A happy Moss waved and ushered Lilia into the back of the black limousine. The door shut and the long car driven by Kare pulled away, trailing the devilish sound.

"Shraaaa."

The back windows of the limousine were tinted so the occupants were hidden from the outside. A one-way mirror separated them from Kare.

Moss was a tool of Quetzal the Plumed Serpent—a rapist.

Through Mother's thoughts, I could not stand to watch as Moss pushed up her wedding dress. Defenseless and uncommunicative, Mother could not deter him.

Curratta's box fell from her hold to the floor of the limousine.

* * *

Mother--poor, poor mother, fought over by two spirits. I wanted to forgive Father. I didn't want to think of him as a rapist. On his wedding day, the Plumed Serpent had possessed the innocent man, ready to honor and cherish his new wife. All my life I had tried to understand how he could ignore me. I had lain awake at night wondering if he would ever come, what I would say to him if he did. I bowed my head and nearly cried. Father had been as much a victim of this cosmic struggle as Mother and me. The man

I had seen in Mother's thoughts was a kind man before Kare had given him the cross. He would never have treated his wife like this. He would have loved his son, even a son like me.

But then, who was my father? Was he Quetzal? Norane? Moss? Maybe they all were my fathers and my lineage was as bizarre and convoluted as my physical appearance. Perhaps this mixed parentage explained my feelings of being torn apart. Now I understood what Curratta had meant when she said I was of Fire. Perhaps my true father, Quetzal, trapped in the body of the conquistador Gabriel Ayala, had been calling me all along to come to the cave where Kare and had found the cross and free him. The myth cascaded through my thoughts. Who was I? What was I supposed to do? I had to know more. If there was any chance for Mother and me to escape the powers trying to use us, I had to understand every aspect of the history and myth of Tatya-Masi. I forced myself to return to Mother's thoughts and journey with her into the Cave of the Xucha to Manoa.

CHAPTER FIFTEEN
THE TEST

I felt the comforting presence, a subliminal communication as Mother led me past the horror of her violation, to follow her soul, as she and Norane swept through the Cave of the Xucha, down the pool where he'd found the box containing the tunjo. They passed through the watery barrier created by Inika's magic, and into the fabled city of King Dorado and the Fountain of Youth.

What would the *Xucha* have thought when Norane brought to Manoa a descendent of the Spanish conquerors, the people they had waited six hundred years to destroy? If the witches knew that Mother was pregnant with Moss' child, a child of Fire, Mother would have never survived the *Xucha's* test.

Set beneath the cauldron of the volcano, the stone ceiling came to a point above adobe houses and temples built into the underground face of the cliff. Once a few thousand La'ku had hidden from the Spaniards here, but now the streets of the underground city were quiet and dark. Walls of buildings covered with gold leaf and inlaid with jewels were evidence of the treasure the conquistadors had futilely sought. Norane's and Lilia's spirits climbed steps covered with gold, and walked down a long hallway upon which paintings heralded the coming of *Tatya-Masi*.

Twin golden doors of Curratta's chamber, eighteen feet high, swung open as they approached. From within came a long chilling wail. I felt Lilia's surprise that she understood the ancient La'ku language.

"Cheeee.......

Cruuuu.....

Cuuuurraaaatttaaaa

Farmer!

Anoint your daughter,

Vanquish the day's sordid sins,

Fury, Light, Power, Green wind,

Spirit, steal the Fire away.

Let your force fly to us today!"

"Cruuuuu."

The calling grew louder. Lilia told herself she was safe as long as Norane was there.

He led her onto a gold mosaic of the sun covered with dark clouds, highlighted by precious stones. Before them was the Bratay, a carving of the frog-god wrought from solid jade laced with gold, an empty stone hand awaiting the lost Cocatamia the Staff of Life.

There was a flash of fire. Four jaguars led a procession through green smoke.

Norane tugged at Lilia's sleeve and together they knelt at the edge of the dry Fountain of Life.

Curratta, the Supreme Shaman, approached them. Four attendants followed her. One carried a thick snake wrapped around her shoulders, another an eagle, the third a golden image of Tatya-Masi, and the last held an immense live frog, the Ra.

The huge beast rolled its eyes toward Lilia. Its tongue flicked out with a slurp and snapped beside her ear.

Lilia shuddered and squeezed Norane's hand.

The chanting grew more intense. Curratta drew closer. She looked older than time itself. A fiery pit erupted in the pool where the Waters of Life should flow. The ancient priestess seemed to hover among the flames. Her withered amphibian face lay in a deformed position over her thin shoulder. Huge, hooded eyes stared at Lilia without blinking or moving.

"Curratta," Norane whispered.

"Slayer of the Oppressor, Prince of Omagua, have you brought a virgin from the lake, the true love of your pure heart, who, as the Farmer said, would bear the seed of Tatya-Masi?" Curratta demanded.

"I have, Holy Mother."

Curratta's expression became dubious. With unmistakable anger and bitterness, she said, "She drips with the seeds of Fire. Quetzal is trying to use her to free himself from Inika's spell. He has seized her body."

"But not her spirit!" Norane pleaded. "Curratta, I have looked hard and long into my heart, and found only her. Did not the prophecy say all the rivers of man would flow into Tatya-Masi?" Norane's voice quavered with the only fear Lilia had ever known him to show. She understood he was afraid for her, not himself.

She was being argued over, without regard for what she wanted. Where was her voice? Who would speak for her?

"Long have we watched and wondered at whom you would choose to love. Give her to this test and you give her to pain without end, should she be impure," Curratta warned.

Norane seemed hesitant, raised his head and lowered his gaze, unable to commit.

The supreme shaman studied Lilia. "Yes, child, we have visited you. You have heard our voices. Now hear this."

As the witches chanted, comprehension swept through Lilia's mind. Curratta was making sure she knew what she faced. If she was already pregnant by Moss and the Xucha ceremony proceeded, the torture for her and the new child would be merciless and too much to bear.

Lilia opened her mouth to speak. Even in her dream no sounds emerged.

Curratta bent so close to Lilia she could smell a strange spice on her breath. A light spun in the large pupils of her eyes. Each word seemed to slice a nerve, causing shocks to jolt through Lilia, leaving her opened and exposed to more torture.

"Why do the fires of Kinchel burn dry the Fountain of Life from whence the Waters of Life should flow?"

Lilia's agony was like being unable to move your hand from a flame. But she knew that the pinching of nerves was minimal compared to what she would experience if she submitted to the Xucha.

Norane chanted. "So shall Tatya-Masi return Cocatamia the Staff of Life and bring forth the Waters of Life to extinguish the fires of the Lord of Fire."

The priestesses repeated the refrain.

Curratta pointed a crooked finger at Lilia. "Daughter, do you deliver your spirit to cleanse your womb of Fire?"

What were her choices—submit to Curratta's magic and the promise of bearing a god, or...? What would become of her if she failed—or succeeded?

Curratta bent and touched the tip of Lilia's nose. A chill ran through Lilia as if she had been sacrificed a thousand years ago in the ice of the summit of Susuprina. Never had Lilia heard as frightening a voice

"Will you bear a spawn of Fire or the god of Water? Decide!"

"Speak for me!" Lilia silently begged Norane. She knew he could not.

Lilia closed her eyes to the fearsome sights and feelings. Even as the Plumed Serpent through Moss possessed her body, she knew in her heart she was still pure. Yes, she knew. The answer was there, had always been there, in her love for Norane, the strange whispers coming through the night, the dream that she would be the one to bear the god.

She raised her eyes to the witch, and spoke without hesitation in the ancient tongue, "I am the Earthly Mother of Tatya-Masi."

Curratta decreed: "You shall be put to the test! If you be of Fire then you shall perish by Fire!" Her breath was now in Lilia's ear, freezing like the snow: "Since the end of the last World of Water, we have awaited you. Deliver your soul and body to the will of Curratta!"

Norane squeezed Lilia's hand and she felt his love as never before. "Willingly, Mother," she spoke with an air of confidence that hid her complete terror.

Curratta began to cackle, a slow rolling laugh that built into a shriek. With the agility of a deer, she leapt twenty feet; water rose to lick her heels. The chartreuse veils she wore ruffled around her like a cloud. Her voice echoed throughout the immense chamber as she floated down.

"To the gates of heaven,

The virgin came from

The halls of man.

From the Fire to

The Water

The daughter of Fire chased into

The Water.

Give us your

Innocence,

To Curratta's magic

Come!"

The sounds of wooden flutes played with the beat of drums.

"Norane!" Lilia threw herself at him. His arms were around her for a last kiss.

Then, his hands disappeared and she was held in the grip of webbed fingers. The handsome face she loved was transformed to a gaping mouth from which a long red tongue extended. Rough and pointed, hard in the center and soft on the edges the frog's giant tongue flicked over her body, each touch leaving a searing pain, a sharp knife piercing her.

I was spying on a memory of the moment of my conception—a contest of spirits fought within the body of a mortal woman. My poor mother, how she had suffered! I had the answer to why I could not make up my mind, why I had no innate loyalty to either side. Nobody knew if I was of Water or Fire—or both.

From the floor of the limousine, a greenish-blue fog billowed from Curratta's box. Simultaneously, *Quetzal* the Plumed Serpent emerged from the cross around Father's neck, and spread his multi-colored wings over Mother.

"Cruuuuuuu."

"Shraaaaaa."

The *Xucha* and Plumed Serpent battled for possession of her womb.

Flames burned away her clothes. She fell naked through a fiery atmosphere. The pain of every shattered cell and separated sinew racked her body as the Serpent sought to claim her for himself.

At the same moment, the *Xucha's* test began to determine if Lilia was fit to bear the god of Water. The *Ra*, the bearer of the seed of *Tatya-Masi*, sought to possess her.

Drums beat a slow deafening dirge. Flutes sounded piercing blasts. The out-of-sync chorus mixed with her own distorted cries.

"The test!"

A wave of warm, milky solution crashed into her, flinging her against a wall of red and yielding muscle.

The discordant chorus chanted in a sickening echo:

"Indian,

Spanish,

Man,

Woman,

Fire,

Darkness

Light

Water."

The excruciation resolved into a magnificent ecstasy rising within her body. All seemed right, her doubts and tears were forgotten. At the height of the emotion, Norane was again in her arms, rolling naked across the clouds. Like a high-flying hawk whose heart is pierced by an arrow, a cold fear killed her rapture and sent her plummeting into despair.

She kept falling until her body landed in a volcanic valley where rivers of fiery magma flowed. A ball of flame swooped down from an opal sky and landed on the summit of a dark precipice, causing the volcanoes to erupt in slow motion. She was on her knees upon this distant spire. The brightness grew, illuminating a plain of steaming streams and pits of exploding fire. The contours of people beckoned to her from pinnacles reaching into swirling orange clouds.

A light brighter than the volcanic flames pulsated against the back of the eruption. A brilliant orb emerged from behind the peak and floated toward her. Closer, the light inside the embryonic shape began to pulse. All around her, the harsh chorus chanted.

"Green, green,

so green,

are we,

can we be

so fluid,

can we flow?

Into the green?

Power green."

The ball of light descended on her and shrank until it outlined her spirit in a sparkling aura. The membrane surrounding her filled with amniotic fluid and lifted her, expanding as it rose until it eclipsed the sky. She could not breath. Salty water filled her mouth and lungs.

Death was coming, when her spirit would never be able to return to her body.

The discordant cry arose,
> "*Tatya-Masi.*
>
> *Tatya-Masi!*"

Lilia curled into a fetal position. Bodies of children within bodies of children—babies within babies—fetuses within fetuses—radiated within her. The beings began to rotate and pulse, disappearing and returning, spiraling faster, until they coalesced into a single form of what looked like a giant tadpole, its legs welded together, fingers and toes joined by webbing.

The chorus chanted with adoration,
> "*Tatya-Masi.*"

The pitch changed from a hollow warble to a shrill scream:
> "The uncaused cause,
>
> The stone that pierces the calm Water.
>
> The first wave of the drowning Water."

The drums pounded faster. The aquamarine sphere carrying her and the frog-child began to roll up the steep incline of the dark peak. A separate aura of light formed around the fetus. It rolled backwards, breaking away from her, carrying away her baby. She reached out. The unborn's hand extended toward her, reaching for her. The light throbbed and grew brighter until its intensity blinded her. She screamed, trying to reach her child. Her aura shrank, pressing, flexing, with the undulations of a giant, pounding heart. In her terror, she thought if only she could hold her child, order would return; her fear, amazement, rapture, and longing would fall back into logic. But she was lost. Time and permanence had disappeared into the inner reaches of the vastness that held her. Gone was all concept of herself: what she had been or what she could do. She floated, unconscious, in oblivion.

The giant form of Curratta looked down at her. A dance of kelly crystalline sparks sung in celestial harmony around the witch, and Mother knew she had passed the test. She was now a *Xucha*, the Earthly Mother of *Tatya-Masi*.

* * *

How could I forsake her after what she had been through to give me life? I now understood why she had not come to me: the reason my prayers to see her had gone unanswered. Mother's spirit had remained in Manoa with the *Xucha* while Moss took her body to the United States and the Balfore Institute.

Our mental union had confirmed my suspicion that her hold on life was as thin as gossamer. The power of the *tunjo* was the only medium through which she could return to Manoa. Without the amulet she would disappear into the spiritual plane and never be able to return. But I still had no idea how we were going to get to Manoa.

I again tried to use my empathy to peer into her thoughts. Where was Manoa? How could she guide us there? But all I encountered was the darkness and random images of a dream.

The nose of the plane tilting down shocked me out of my trance. I was awake, erect in my seat, leaning forward to hold Mother up, looking out the round portal. We continued to drop through clouds. How would Eduardo know where the ground was? The descent grew steeper and still clouds surrounded us. When we broke through, we were low enough to be able to see individual rocks and cacti. Like the rest of the world, the canyons below appeared to be flooding.

"I think we're over Arizona somewhere," MG said, looking out the window by her seat. "Man, it's even raining here. This is the desert, man!"

We flew low over an empty road that crossed one of the flat-top mountains.

Eduardo whispered into a microphone. I strained to understand what he was saying and decided he was speaking in a code. "Toro, Santa Fe, Maria."

A sharp bank pushed me against the cabin wall. The plane found its new heading, leveled, and then pointed down again.

Eduardo turned a small wheel, pushed up two levers, and flipped another switch. A sound of whirling came from beneath the plane. There was a quick lurch. The sensation of slowing increased. I crouched forward and held Mother as we touched down with a jarring impact, bounced, flew for another second, and then landed, rocking from side to side until we came to rest beside a black truck parked on the empty highway.

I could see men with cowboy hats, their heads bowed and collars pulled up against the rain.

The propellers quit turning.

Eduardo passed through the cabin. "Nobody say or do a thing," he said in English and opened the door.

The air smelled moist and clean after what we had been breathing in the cabin.

Eduardo spoke to those outside the plane, causing a quick burst of laughter from what sounded like three men.

The plane moved as Eduardo descended the stairs. I heard another quick conversation in Spanish.

"I had some trouble in California," Eduardo said in Spanish.

"Let's make it fast then."

The plane rocked as Eduardo climbed back in. I rotated one eye in a wide arc to see him carrying a wide leather briefcase. He opened a four-foot high door at the rear of the cabin set in a carpeted wall and began to remove brown paper-wrapped packages, which he handed to the men on the ground.

MG stared straight ahead without looking back at the scene.

One of the men outside the plane asked Eduardo, "You hear about the dam? They say it might go if the rain doesn't stop."

"Take out half of Las Vegas," added another.

"You might be all right in this weather. Most of the airports are shut down."

"Maybe. I've still got to make Mexico. I'd better get going. Stay free," Eduardo called.

Is staying free what they were about? Who was trying to enslave them? Let them deal with the Lord of Fire, and then they would know what lack of freedom was.

Eduardo carried the briefcase to the cockpit and started the engines. We began to move.

MG rose up against the backrest of her seat. "Your uncle's a drug smuggler," she whispered. "If you want my advice, don't ask any questions, man," she whispered as she closed her eyes.

I felt strangely embarrassed for having a family member who was a criminal. After all the hours I'd spent dreaming about my family, now I had the chance to finally learn about them. Would the rest be as different as I had imaged Eduardo being?

I squirmed in my seat and pressed my hands in my lap. There was no bathroom on the plane. We were still on the ground. I prayed Eduardo would stop so I could go to the bathroom. Didn't he and MG have to go too? I closed my eyes, pressing them shut, tearing. We bounced along, retracing the path on which we had landed. I leaned across to support Mother.

Eduardo turned the plane, flipped some switches, pulled a red lever and returned to stand over us. "Perhaps this is the best place for you to depart," he said to MG, not asking, rather telling her to leave. Without waiting for her to answer, he lowered the door.

She stood and faced him. "You going to leave me out in the middle of nowhere in the rain?"

Eduardo frowned. "It is all that I can do for you at this moment. It would not have been wise to leave you with those men. We will be departing the United States and there will be danger."

"Like there hasn't been so far?"

Eduardo smiled, lowering his luminous, round brown eyes.

MG shrugged. "I guess it's *hasta la tardy* time then." She looked at me as if I might want to come with her. I did, but did not move or speak. Would MG be caught if the dam the men had spoken of broke? Of all the deaths I would be responsible for, I could not bear the guilt if something were to happen to her.

"We will have to do without you," Eduardo said.

"Tough luck." They smiled at each other, sharing a joke.

Eduardo peeled off a pile of bills from a roll of money he carried in his inside breast pocket and handed them to her. "This is for your troubles. I ask you not to speak about what you have seen."

MG did not take the money. "You think that's going to do any good if Du can't stop the rain? I hope you know how important it is that you help him and your sister."

Eduardo raised his eyebrows in an expression of surprise. "Don't believe this nonsense. You are too smart, too beautiful."

MG huffed with scorn for him.

"Follow the dirt road. *Adiós, señorita.*"

She turned to look down at me. She seemed to be feeling some of the same emotion I was at our parting. She reached out and touched my cheek, and walked to the door of the plane, turned and said, "Bye, Du. I know you'll succeed. You have to."

The bottom of my eyes pooled with tears. I was confused by the emotions I felt for her. I was just a kid, too young to be her boyfriend. What I felt was nothing like anything I had felt for Kare or Edgar. Loneliness made it hard to breath. Every part of me wanted to be with her. Maybe if I had told her how I felt, she would have understood, even if I did not. I stepped around Eduardo and stood in the doorway, watching her walk alone down the empty highway. Let her go, I told myself. Let her escape.

Eduardo pushed past me, climbed down the steps, and pulled down his zipper. I sighed and concentrated on my immediate needs. This might be my only chance. I descended past him, hopped to the other side of the road where I tore open my pants, and with my back to the plane let the relief flood from me.

The propellers of the plane blew moisture past me. The air stank from burning fuel. I lifted my head and let rain run down my face. The wet drops first stung then relieved the itch as they rolled over dry skin. I wished I had time to find a pool for a good soak.

I thought I heard someone walking on the road. I twisted my head to look, but MG was out of sight.

Eduardo pushed me in the back. "Get in." He shoved me up the stairs of the plane.

I climbed another step with Eduardo following me on the step below. I stopped and craned my head as my senses swept the rainy landscape, searching for MG.

"¡Entre pues!" *Get in*. Eduardo pushed me so hard I nearly fell forward.

"There's someone out there, someone coming. Maybe it's MG. She might be coming back!"

With a final powerful push, my uncle sent me falling into the cabin. He turned and looked out before he pulled the cord to raise the steps.

Through the sound of the propellers, I was certain I heard MG outside.

"Please wait," I said, and pushed against the door with my hand.

Eduardo looked at me with an expression that made me understand the risk I took by resisting him. He was a dangerous man.

"It's her," I insisted.

Showing the first act of kindness I'd yet witnessed in him, Eduardo opened the door.

"Hey, let me back in," she shouted over the sound of the propellers. "I want to go with you."

"Very well," he said. "I will enjoy your company."

She's not coming back for you, I wanted to say to the egotistical man, but when she climbed back aboard, I was so happy to see her I hopped up and down with my back bent to keep from hitting the roof, my smile spreading from ear to ear. I must have looked so preposterous that even Eduardo smiled. I didn't care. Compared to my dreadful emotions of the past day, I felt rapturous.

"I have to see this through," she said to Eduardo.

"My sister can use your assistance," he made clear why he'd relented and pushed down the lock on the cabin door.

I watched MG glance at him and nod. An unknown pain split my heart. I didn't want MG to like Eduardo.

CHAPTER SIXTEEN
IN A WORLD OF WATER

The air in the cabin was drying my skin. One of my amphibian characteristics is that I require immersions at least every twelve hours. Otherwise, my mottled flesh dries, itches, and starts to peel in long strips. The more my discomfort increased, the greater my longing to escape the physical bounds into the all-encompassing transformation of my body and spirit through the tunjo.

Why should I suffer? Why should I feel so helpless if I was a god? What was so great about being a freak, an outcast, when I could rule? Visions of my grandeur played in my thoughts. I am Tatya-Masi Bringer of the Sixth World of Water, a warrior-god of Water, victorious conqueror of the World of Fire.

"Hold me. Wear me."

The necklace's entrancing light danced in the dark cabin. The tunjo was my conduit to the celestial plane, empowering me with the essence of the gods. Not to wear it was to be earthbound when I could fly, to be blind when I could see. Mother had known she was creating a god. She had made her deal with the Xucha. She should obey them and give me the totem. Besides, who knew if I took the necklace from her I wouldn't discover how to share the power of the tunjo with her. I would save her. I would be raised to a station where a thought would be manifested. I would only have to imagine the rains ending and they would stop. I would move within the dimensions of time and space. Be revered. MG would love me because I was strong, stronger than Eduardo, stronger than anyone she'd ever met. MG would look at me as she had Eduardo, only with more love. And she would be gentle and caring as she had been in the automobile driving to Oregon.

I could take the tunjo from around Mother's neck. The power of the necklace was wasted on her. She was not strong enough to use it to defend us against Kinchel. I had to wear the tunjo. I had to make the tunjo my weapon.

"Pick me up. Wear me."

I closed my ears to the Xucha's murmuring and insidious wailing, telling myself I had to be strong. The greater strength was to resist, to find the strength within to stop the rains and free Mother's spirit from the witches.

The nose of the plane dipped. I pressed forward to keep Mother from falling. We were descending through clouds. Out the window, not too far below the dark shape of the wing, passed an occasional light.

"We're somewhere in Mexico. Maybe Durango," MG said.

Beneath the floor a thump was followed by the sound of a machine turning.

Mother remained against the cabin wall, looking frail and deathly pale. The tunjo hung from the chain, dark for the moment.

The plane landed with a hard impact. As we slowed, rain streamed across the windows. The heated air in the cabin had dried not only our clothes but my skin as well. I needed to be outside, to find a lake...that should not be hard to do these days.

Eduardo confirmed on the radio what sounded like directions. We came to a stop beside the dark shape of a larger propeller-driven plane in front of a rounded hanger. Grassy areas beyond the lights of the runway were swamped. If only I could dip my feet and hands into one of the puddles, splash my face and torso, throw water down my back.

Eduardo passed through the cabin, carrying a pistol in his hand, another stuck in the rear of the waistband of his pants. He looked once at Mother, and opened the door. Brilliant light shined through the door, brightening the cabin.

The air smelled different, of a strange land.

Eduardo spoke to someone on the ground.

A cardboard container was handed up to the plane.

A delicious scent made my head float.

Eduardo set the container in the aisle and looked at his sister's corpselike body. "Can she eat or drink?" he asked in a helpless tone that contrasted with his strong demeanor.

"Not on her own," MG said.

"What can be done?" Eduardo asked.

It did not take great empathy to read his stalemate of emotions. While his lips were locked in a tight frown, his eyes betrayed a deep concern and love for his sister. He thought of himself as cunning, but was stymied, as was I, by how to save Mother. Should she be taken to a hospital? No. He knew as well as I, that Omagua was Mother's destination. I wondered how much the witches had influenced him. He had been in the cave, Norane's constant companion. Had the Xucha reached out to him as they had his sister?

He caught me looking at him before I could turn away. Compassion left his eyes, replaced with a cold dislike for me. The Plumed Serpent or Kinchel could just as well be influencing him. He had battled the Assassins of Fire, but his soul was not settled. He was dangerous and unpredictable.

"Do you have a cloth? Something I can use to give her some water," MG asked.

Eduardo withdrew a white handkerchief from the breast pocket of his coat. The handkerchief looked soft, ivory-colored, trimmed with lace. His initials EJM were embroidered on a corner.

MG admired it before picking up a bottle from the container and moistening the handkerchief. She sat on the armrest, and patted Mother's dry lips with the wet cloth.

Why hadn't I thought of that? I was so concerned about my own discomfort that I hadn't thought that Mother would also be parched.

"We will be home by morning. Can she last that long?" Eduardo asked.

"I don't know." MG looked up at him. She had a better sense of the mysterious power keeping Mother alive than Eduardo did.

"May I stand outside?" I interrupted.

"Why?" Whatever kindness had been in Eduardo's expression disappeared.

"I need to be in the rain for awhile."

He shook his head. "Stay in here. We do not need any questions."

Anger rose in me. I stood taller, feeling strong enough to confront him physically if I had to. "I'm not a monster." My voice broke. "I am your nephew, your sister's son. I have to go outside."

He took out the gun, the barrel pointed down the side of his leg. He spoke slowly, in a low growl. "You will do what I say. Nephew, monster, or man, you will do what I say, or I'll throw your dead, ugly ass right off this plane."

I tried to meet his gaze, to gain even a chance of his respect. "I have to..."

His grip tightened on the handle of the pistol.

"Easy." MG patted my shoulder. Her touch dispelled whatever folly had made me challenge my uncle.

"Come on. Have something to eat," she said to me. "Aren't you hungry?"

The fragrant scent of food overpowered my senses. I had not eaten since early in the morning and was starved. I nearly slumped against her touch. "Yes, I'm hungry."

MG unwrapped one of the leaf-wrapped squares in the container and handed the pie to me.

I quickly ate the food, aware that my uncle was watching with a frown that showed his revulsion. A hatred for him caused my shoulders to rise, but not my eyes. I did not look at him.

MG handed me an open water bottle. After I had taken a long drink, I poured water onto my hand and patted my stinging face.

I slightly rotated one of my eyes to see Eduardo studying me. He did not think of me as his nephew, and would kill me if I challenged him.

A voice from beneath the door of the plane called that the fueling was done. Eduardo pulled the roll of bills from his shirt pocket and handed several down.

Two blankets, a pair of umbrellas, plastic ponchos, and a white bucket was handed up to him.

He closed the plane door, took his coat off Mother, and spread one of the blankets around her. "We won't be stopping again," he said and set the ponchos and umbrellas in back of the seats, leaving the bucket by the door.

I looked out the window and saw a man in a yellow raincoat circling with his hand, and then saluting. The engines started.

The plane rolled away from the fuel truck. The cabin was dark again. Lights beneath the wings shined on slanting rain. I dipped my nail into the little water left in my bottle and touched my throat. Let the world drown. In the land of water I would be king.

* * *

The hours stretched deep into the night. On we flew through the darkness. MG snored, sometimes mumbling words that made no sense. Her black leather jacket lay atop her. She had refused the extra blanket, which remained folded on the seat in front of her. I wished I could strip. My clothes were adding to my discomfort.

Eduardo came out of the cockpit and went to the back of the plane where he urinated in the white bucket apparently without shame or concern for MG or his sister.

"Sit beside me," Eduardo said softly as he passed back into the cockpit.

Surprised, I followed him.

Computer screens, gauges, wheels, levers, and dials were arranged around his seat, illuminating him in an eerie reminder of the light of the tunjo.

Standing behind him, not knowing how to start the conversation, I waited to see what he wanted with me.

"Sit down," he said, not looking at me.

I hesitated to move into the empty seat. What if I disturbed one of the instruments?

He looked at me over his shoulder.

I maneuvered my triple-wide heavy waterproof boots over the center console, careful not to touch the two pedals on the floor or the round half-wheel and levers around the empty seat.

Once I had settled, I avoided his lingering gaze. It did not require much empathy to detect his scorn.

"What are you?" he asked.

I glanced at him and then away. My throat tightened with sorrow. "Your nephew," was all I could repeat. "Lilia's son."

He gazed through the windscreen into the night sky. "There is no denying you exist. Have you come to avenge the La'ku?"

The bitterness in his voice caused me to shrink farther into myself. Was he asking if I was Tatya-Masi?

Some tension appeared to relax from his shoulders, and with a quick laugh, he said, "Well, my father will be most amazed to see you, that is certain."

"He's my grandfather." I restated my claim to a family. "I want to meet him."

Eduardo smirked and shook his head. "I should be happy to bring you to him. When he sees Lilia and you, his greatest dream will come true. The least I can do as a dutiful son is to bring you both to him. My mother, I am afraid, will die from the shock." He laughed in the manner of one who could be cruel to anyone. "But then again she was always a snob, and so happy when her daughter married a blond gringo."

I was distressed by the description of my family and what it implied about their feelings for each other. Was it the sight of me that would kill my grandmother? Eduardo felt scorn for both his parents, yet I could sense his absolute devotion and love for them. He was a complex man.

The eastern horizon was beginning to pale. I knew from Kare's stories, my grandfather, Don Carlos Morales, had always believed in the myth of Tatya-Masi. It was to him that Norane and Eduardo had brought the box they had found in the cave, and it had been from Don Carlos that Kare had stolen the container. If there was anybody who could help me, it had to be Grandfather. I wanted to rush to meet him.

"Du," MG called from the cabin. "You'd better take a look at this."

"Uncle," I said, "I know you were there when the box was found. You know its power. If I don't learn how to use it, we will all be destroyed."

We looked into each other's eyes, and I saw for the first time, fear. He was afraid of me.

The hard contraction of his eyes and mouth returned. "Go see what she wants," he said.

Hunching over, I made my way back into the cabin.

MG was leaning over Mother. The tunjo was exposed, transmitting, throwing off balls of light, stirring with magic. The spirits within the necklace shared my impatience to be in Omagua.

"Cruuuu."

With a suddenness that surprised me and left me unprepared to resist, I was overwhelmed by an urge to hold the tunjo, to possess its power, to be united with its spiritual core. Murmuring beneath my hearing, the swarm of incessant harpies called me to join them.

"Cruuuuu."

The mournful chant was a mental itch. Inside and out, I was tormented— out of water, out of place. I inched forward. Green plasma flared when I passed my hand through the aura.

"Cruuuuu."

The chant called me, causing shivers to pulse up my spine, flashing in my brain.

I closed my eyes and felt the tunjo waiting, my unavoidable destiny.

"Hold me. Wear me."

I could not resist the call.

"Hold me. Wear me."

If I wore the tunjo, I would be strong. All would do as I commanded. I would stop the rain, save the lands of the Earth from drowning. I had to wear the necklace.

I lifted Mother's blanket and held the heavy shape in my hand. The jade light pulsed around the representation of the frog-god. I pulled it into the growing light outside the window.

The sensation was like thousands of tiny feet running up and down my arm.

The tunjo rose over Mother's head in my grip, as with its own will. The power of the necklace was stronger than what I had experienced in California. As I placed the necklace over my head, my mind and body swelled with increased senses, awareness, and strength. Dimensions were multiplied. I saw back in time, and forward. Memories became reality as did expectations. My empathy could influence the thoughts of millions without my being in their presence.

Curratta welcomed me. Through me, the Xucha would live again. Within the miasma behind her, thousands of ghouls bowed in supplication before a giant stone representation of me, the Bratay. Ghostly shapes danced in the emerald corona projected from the tunjo.

MG gasped. Was she seeing what I was? Could she hear the hollow chants?

"Tatya-Masi. Tatya-Masi."

I saw a mob within the iridescent fog, led by a king, the mythic Dorado whose kingdom of gold so many European invaders had vainly sought, and his court–dressed in ancient costumes highlighted by bright feathers, carrying spears, bows and arrows.

King Dorado exalted, "Tatya-Masi, with the power to raise the Water. Tatya-Masi, with the wisdom to banish wrong. Tatya-Masi, able to flow, to drown, to sweep away. Tatya-Masi controls us with a thought. Worship Tatya-Masi. Adore Tatya-Masi."

The boy who was Du was disappearing like memories of infancy, replaced by a god.

"Du!" MG screamed from far away.

I started to move to the jungle-colored light and those who worshiped me. The unimaginable power of the ages flowed into me. I was Tatya-Masi.

"Du! Your mom!" MG cried. "She's not breathing! She needs the necklace!"

I looked down from the great height of my delusion. Mother was lying across the seat, lifeless. She had to be sacrificed so that I could ascend.

MG reached for the tunjo, but she might as well have been trying to lift it from the snout of a wild boar. As soon as she touched the aura, she was tossed up against the roof.

The plane rolled, unable to contain the blasting energy.

"¡Hijueputa!" Eduardo wailed.

The plane spun, falling in an accelerating spiral.

"Shhhhraaaaa!"

Lightning flew through the cabin. The nine heads of Kinchel, tongues flicking flames, appeared in rolling red waves across the ceiling.

I faced him, confident the power of the tunjo would give me all the strength I needed to best him.

With the first touch of his fiery tongue, pain swept over me. I shrank from him, and held the tunjo up to him like a shield.

"Shraaaaa."

His cry twined around my body like the coils of a thousand snakes, squeezing the air from my lungs. Too late, I realized that I lacked the knowledge or strength to challenge him. Flames from Kinchel's dragon head burnt my flesh from elbow to hand. Each nerve screamed with its own pain from the torturing flames.

MG, Mother and I were thrown to the back of the plane, now spiraling to the ground. Eduardo cried out in the cockpit. Rolls of lightning arced across the ceiling.

I had no strength to resist the beast drawing the tunjo into flames sprouting from his mouth.

I was doomed. There was no escape.

By chance, the tunjo fell into Mother's upturned palm.

Kinchel hesitated over me, enjoying the moment of the kill.

I fell to my knees, nearly fainting.

From my stupor, I saw Mother rise. The necklace radiated in her hand.

Within the corona of the tunjo, the ghosts of Manoa rushed to her side. King Dorado, ruler of Manoa, home of the Xucha, led a ghostly army in a charge at the inflamed form of Kinchel. A club raised over his head, the king urged his followers on. Faces painted, carrying spears and sharp-tipped picks, the phantasmagoric army rushed from the glow of the necklace into the burning light of the Lord of Fire. Over them flew a coven of witches, led by Curratta, her skeleton face and parched hide aglow with the light of the battle.

The Supreme Shaman aimed a polished stick at the chest of the terrible dragon.

A bolt of energy shot into Kinchel.

"Shhhhraaaaa!"

Kinchel's hiss and rattle shook the plane so hard I feared the wings would fall off.

I clawed myself back to Mother.

With a fearsome growl, the burning light of Kinchel withdrew. The battle scene faded, leaving only bursts of blue-green light and wisps of smoke.

I looked up from where I cowered on the floor, and saw only the roof of the plane. The Lord of Fire had withdrawn for now, but when would he return? I never wanted to feel that pain again.

The plane leveled.

The realization that we'd survived the wrath of the Lord of Fire was my last thought before I fell over mother, too exhausted to move or think. I forced myself not to lose consciousness until I had placed the chain securely around her neck. Only Mother knew how to use the power of the tunjo to protect us.

The last remnants of beryl light were sucked into her chest.

I was vaguely aware of MG helping me to a seat and Eduardo speaking urgently into the radio, "Morales Uno, Venga, Venga, ¡Emergencia! ¡Emergencia!"

My head lolled to the side, and through the small window I saw we were flying a hundred feet over a brown river with dense, verdant jungle on either side.

CHAPTER SEVENTEEN
THE FIFTH FALL

The plane radically tipped, raising the wing on the side where I sat, then suddenly dipped in the other direction, descending with a whirring sound toward a verdurous wall of trees bordering a river. Eduardo's voice was clipped with tension, "Morales one, I am coming in. It is me, Eduardo Morales. Mayday! I can barely fly the plane."

"Negative Morales. Runway underwater."

The plane shot through a break in the jungle. Rain-pocked pools of water surrounded small islands. A herd of cattle bunched around a stand of trees trapped by the rising flood spreading across the lowlands. Crops drowned in submerged fields.

The plane leveled and we flew over a delta. Muddy fingers of water flowed around clumps of partially submerged trees. A flock of white birds banked over the flooded landscape. The sight of the water made me long to be beneath the cool, pressing completeness, out of the howling air that only stung me with teasing wisps of moisture rushing past the open cockpit.

I had never been out of the water this long. My skin, beyond itching, burned and flaked off my body. Growing up alone at the Lake of the Frogs, I had spent many hours fantasizing about the day I would meet my family. How could I make a good impression with my flesh falling from my body, my clothes filthy, and being chased by the Assassins of Fire? Perhaps if I hid how I looked, it might soften the blow on my family of seeing me for the first time. I could project the image from one of the novels I had read. Maybe I'd be a happy, handsome boy home from prep school for vacation.

And what about Father? He would know that I had taken Mother from the Balfore Institute. Was he waiting for me at Omagua, too?

Below us, flames burned atop tall towers. Edgar had told me that my father was in the oil business. Clearly, below me was the work of my father, the work of Fire. Water had risen beyond the metal gates and covered the area between tanks and other structures. Evidence of the ongoing battle between Fire and Water was everywhere.

Past the oil field, the land was in a natural state. Treetops were woven together into a tight carpet broken only by a mile-wide river. This was the La'ku reserve the Morales family had protected since the earliest days of the Spanish conquest.

The jungle spoke to me. Natives from another time, dressed in loin clothes, naked chests, carrying spears, bows and arrows, hair caked with mud, faces painted with ochre, looked up to the sky from the invisible jungle floor, brought back to life by a collective dream of a returning god, a promise made to their ancestors. Tatya-Masi had come to restore their world to them.

I was awed by the pure power of the myth, able to survive when all forces of history had conspired to exterminate its belief and promise. But behind the faith was the terrible truth of the clash of gods. This jungle habitat was only another piece of turf that would be submerged in the new Age of Water. What the La'ku believed would be the final death knell of their civilization. If I loved the land, the people, I would join with the forces of Fire and resist the conquest of Water.

"I am not Tatya-Masi," I repeated to myself. "I may look like the god. I may have gifts that open me to your longings, but I am not your god."

Who was I talking to? No doubt the inexplicable was happening to and around me, but I must not contribute my own delusions to the madness.

"I am a boy named Du," I repeated to block the haunting "cruuuu" that was building in pitch in anticipation of my arrival.

My effort to regain my mental balance was defeated by the horizon where the jungle ended. In opaque light a mammoth cone rose into the clouds–Susuprina–the home of Manoa, the lost city of El Dorado. My knowledge of the cave and the passage within the cloudy peak was as strong as a recent memory.

"Cruuuuu."

Drums, flutes, and rapturous cries accompanied the chant.

I rotated an eye to Eduardo. Could he hear? Was he aware of the building frenzy?

His face was pale beneath the growth of his beard. I sensed in him only fatigue and eagerness to be home. I was alone. Nobody could help me.

The falls at Omagua had expanded to cover an area that far eclipsed Kare's descriptions. White churning water sent up clouds of mist into the gray sky. Separate falls were fed by multiple rivers flowing from the lake around islands of jungle and over jagged spires of rock.

My eyes immediately went to the fifth fall. The Cave of the Xucha was behind the fall that formed only during the heaviest rains. The last time the fifth fall had formed was when Norane and Eduardo had found the box. Here was the passage through which Kare, Eduardo and Norane had entered the cave of the witches. I sensed the presence of the giant vine-covered stone statue of Tatya-Masi at the foot of the falls–another anachronism awaiting its place in the present.

The welcoming chants rose in pitch, and the drums pounded like a deep, quickening heartbeat.

The chanting dimmed as soon as we passed over the fifth fall, and I had the sense of two worlds, one laid atop the other, the ancient pressing up against the modern, like tectonic plates ready to rupture.

A lake without beaches spread across fields consumed by the flood. A quarter of a mile from shore, we banked over an island that gave Omagua its name as the Place of the Frogs. With splayed arms and legs, its back humped, pointed snout pressed to the ground, the island faced a village built on the shores of a cliff that ran beside the lake until it dropped sharply into the jungle.

We banked over a mansion of yellowed stone. Two wings extended from a domed center section of the large house. I knew where Mother's room was, and Eduardo's. I knew the hacienda as if I had spent my life there—Omagua, my family's home.

Five minutes later, Eduardo landed the plane with a jarring splash on a paved landing strip as wide as a two-lane road. The sudden deceleration threw me toward Mother then back against my seat. Water sprayed the windows. The plane rolled past a bunker of sandbags protecting three-on-three missiles pointed skyward. I wondered if we'd landed at a military base.

We taxied on a tarmac and stopped before a round metal hangar. I looked out the window to see two men dressed in camouflage uniforms sloshing through a foot of water toward the plane. Behind them, the streets of an adjacent village had been turned to muddy streams.

Eduardo stepped out of the cockpit, and kicked the now empty white bucket we'd used as a toilet during the long flight. He knelt beside Mother and spoke softly, his gentleness again surprising me. "I'm taking you home. Only a few minutes and we'll be there."

When Moss opened the plane door, humid jungle air, full of the moisture I craved rushed into the plane. I wanted to push Eduardo aside and leap out into the rain, but I stayed in my seat and looked out the window where a man wearing a floppy rain hat trudged toward us through the deep water.

Eduardo descended the stairs to speak to the man. "Are the cars ready?" It was more of a demand than a question.

"Sí señor Morales," the man said respectfully, bowing his head.

My parched flesh was peeling in strips from my arms and face. All the water surrounding us—the heavy moisture in the air, the pools beneath our feet, the sound of the metallic drumming of the rain— incited an unbearable longing to be submerged.

"Will you watch my mother?" I asked MG as I moved toward the door, pushing past Eduardo with no attempt to cast an illusion.

No disguise would fool the Lord of Fire. Xiulu would have all of his forces arrayed on this battlefield. I dropped my overalls, stepped outside in my underwear, and leaned back with my arms spread to expose as much of my body as I could to the sheets of warm rain.

A collective gasp rose from the foot of the gangway as the soldiers gaped at me with undisguised awe.

"Holy mother! Look at that!" One exclaimed as another staggered back at the sight of me.

"It's a frog. He looks like a great big frog."

"No. It's the god, a living tunjo. It's Tatya-Masi!"

Eduardo glared at me. "Get your mother!" he ordered.

I reluctantly pulled up my overalls, lifted and carried Mother outside where Eduardo held an umbrella over her. MG followed us carrying my daypack with the box inside.

We sloshed through deep, brown puddles toward four black SUV's. "Put her in here," Eduardo ordered. I set Mother on the backseat of the lead car, and hesitated before stepping in, soaking up another few moments of rain.

"You ride with me," Eduardo said to MG and nodded his head at the next car.

She moved around to the front passenger door of the car with Mother. "I'll ride with Du."

"As you wish."

With her hair streaming rainwater, MG stopped before getting into the car. "Help Du. He's a god, he's really a god. He can stop the rain."

Eduardo nodded grimly and climbed into the front passenger seat of the second car.

Men from the military base and villagers waded toward us through the water at the edge of the tarmac. In their midst for a moment, I thought I saw Kare. I blinked and the tall La'ku I thought I'd seen was no longer there. Had it been Norane, the Warrior-Brother come to greet his god? His son? I searched the villagers but whomever I saw was gone.

The chartreuse aura of the tunjo billowed from Mother's chest, and unimpeded by the glass or metal, radiated around the car.

"Tatya-Masi!" The shrill wail carried above the hubbub of the villagers. Some of the crowd pressed closer in order to see me, while others hung back, turning their faces away, as if overawed by the sight.

I lingered in the rain as the motorcade formed. Guards and soldiers stepped into the rear two cars.

Eduardo leaned out the window of his car with the pistol in his hands. "Get in!" His lips twisted in fury at me.

I stepped into the dry space. My skin burned, barely relieved by my scant time in the rain.

"Cruuuu."

The sound was stronger, the murmuring voices louder, coming from the land and the air. I was wasting time. I needed to go to the Cave of the Xucha. Only there could I gain the power to stop the rain. I looked at Mother, closed my eyes and used my empathy to commune with her again.

"Cruuuu."

To find her, I had to again mentally pass through Manoa, where the Xucha begin to chant. They formed a semicircle around the statue of Tatya-Masi, and as aquamarine water spouted from fountains. I returned to where Mother lay, bathed in a glowing light.

Curratta held her skeletal hands over Mother's spirit body. The Supreme Shaman spoke to me, "She is weak, Tatya-Masi. She has fought a great battle to bring you to Manoa. Return the Jewels so that the Waters of Life will flow again, or her soul will move too far from her body to ever be rejoined."

The witch had made sure that I knew that to disobey her was to kill

Mother.

The spirit eyes opened and Mother looked at me, her face pale, save the dark circles beneath her eyes and her sage-colored lips, which barely moved as she whispered, "You must find the god in you, Tatya-Masi. I can no longer defend you alone from what is coming. Xiulu Lord of Fire sends Mitnal the Smoking Mirror, a fearsome spirit of destruction. You must join the battle."

Even in the vision, the pain in my burnt arm sharpened at the mention of Xiulu. To obey Mother was to accept that I am the destroyer of the Age of Man.

"Mother, I love this world. I can't be the agent of its destruction."

"Then we are lost."

The effort to communicate with me had expended what little energy she had left, and her spirit eyes closed.

Curratta stepped from the light where she's been listening to our conversation. The witch's large, hooded eyes and trembling mouth displayed her apprehension. "Tatya-Masi, the powers in the tunjo are beyond our comprehension. They are yours to hold. Command the Warrior-Brother, the twelve witches and their special powers. Summon the Hosts of Water. Become what you are."

She moved forward, her translucent hands upraised, pleading. "Take up the tunjo. Find the god in you, Tatya-Masi," she said, and then the vision of Curratta, Mother, and Manoa faded.

I looked out at the verdant, rain-soaked countryside where the battle for the next age of Earth would be fought. The Supreme Shaman must know that if I took the tunjo from Mother, her body and spirit could never be rejoined. And I would be giving up what hope remained of controlling my life in this realm—of becoming whatever I wanted to be, not a god of destruction.

How many people had I killed by opening the container and releasing the chacs? And this was only the beginning. The idea that I could save mankind seemed less likely than I would be an instrument of its decline. As we passed through a section of jungle, my feelings of dread and foreboding deepened. I understood why Xiulu sought my death. From what I saw, Inika Lordess of Water was winning. I had caused the cataclysm and didn't know how to stop it. Questions swarmed in my mind, an endless dialectic without hope of resolution. The myth said I'd have the power to end the World of Fire when I found the other two Jewels of Life in Cocatamia Staff of Life. Would I also have the power to choose whether the next Age of Earth would be one of Water or Fire? If Xiulu should kill me or gain domination over the two Jewels in the tunjo, would the rain stop? If so, was it not best for me to surrender and sacrifice myself to save mankind?

What hosts could I summon? Would the Plumed Serpent speak to me again? Lead me to cave of the Xucha. Would he defend me against the other Fire spirits? I soon would be facing the Fire spirit mother had warned me about—Mitnal the Smoking Mirror who had possessed Kare's cousin Hernando Rosas. In order to survive, let alone conquer the mystical forces that surrounded me, I would be forced to do as Mother and Curratta had told me and find a way to fully access my supposed powers.

A surer way of stopping the rain was surrender to Xiulu Lord of Fire. Our chances of survival seemed so slim on multiple fronts that all I could hope for was the chance of another few hours, to at least meet my family and bring my mother home.

Our caravan of cars was speeding down the middle of a highway. We passed stranded vehicles in soaked fields. A family was trapped on the roof of a small three-room cinderblock house. A horse was tethered to the branch of a lone tree in flooded field. A flock of white egrets banked over the verdant landscape. We crossed a bridge where refugees from the flood had sought shelter. The cars in our caravan did not slow and people dove into the water to keep from being hit. I longed to join them, to be beneath the cool, pressing completeness, out of the drying air. But there was no escape for me, in body or spirit.

We passed through a metal gate and drove a quarter of a mile to a mansion with yellow walls and tiled roof. As deep as my dread of this journey ending in Manoa, my concern was compounded by the thought that I would soon be meeting the other members of my family for the first time. One of my favorite fantasies was that my family thought I was dead. When I returned they would be first amazed, then overjoyed. But just as I had contemplated my family welcoming me, I had worried they would reject me, not believe that I was Lilia's son.

We stopped and I carefully lifted and passed Mother to Eduardo's waiting arms before stepping out into a puddle on the driveway. With one slip I could fall and moisten my skin. I needed to be underwater as much as I needed to breathe.

A boy ran into the foyer when we entered. He was at once beautiful and familiar, perhaps twelve years old.

We looked at each other. "Hello," I said in Spanish.

"¡Coño!" he exclaimed.

"Hi, Carli," Eduardo said wearily.

"Uncle Eduardo, what is it?" the boy asked, looking at me, then Mother. "Who is that? Where did you get the freak?"

"Go back to school," Eduardo said.

"It's closed because of the floods. Haven't you heard? It's raining everywhere. Aunt Tatua says that we must pray for deliverance."

"Don't worry about it, Carli. The rain is going to stop. Where is your mother?"

"She's in Miami. She's worried about the house flooding."

Eduardo spoke to MG. "Please make yourself as comfortable as possible. I must attend to my sister and my family. The servants will bring you whatever you need."

"Stay down here," Eduardo ordered Carli. "Come," he said to me.

"I'll come for you as soon as I can," I said to MG.

"Do what you have to do. I'll be all right," she said.

Thick hand-cut beams of wood supported the ceiling of the hallway. More portraits and tapestries hung on the white plastered walls of the second floor. Eduardo seemed careless about muddying a woven carpet laid down the center of the tiled passage, as Carli crept behind us, cautiously disobeying his uncle.

A woman who I recognized from Mother's memories as aunt Tatua, dressed in a robe, her hair wrapped in a scarf, started to come out of a room, saw me, and slammed the door, screaming, "¡Monstruo! ¡Sofea!"

This introduction to my family had not started well. Who would I encounter next? Father? Smoking Mirror?

Carli giggled excitedly behind us.

Eduardo did not react. He pushed open a heavy wooden door into a musty bedroom—the room from which Father had taken Mother on their wedding day. A doll collection rested on the bookshelves. A framed picture of the Morales family perhaps twenty-five years ago sat on a desk.

Eduardo lowered Mother onto a four-posted, canopied bed. For an instant I felt relief. She was home. I had found my family; now what?

Through a set of tall draped windows, I saw Susuprina towering over the lake. The water was so close, I could be there in minutes if I just left now.

Outside the door, I heard heavy, rapid footsteps approaching. I turned to meet my grandfather.

CHAPTER EIGHTEEN

FATHERS AND MONSTERS

I knew in an instant that my grandfather was not prepared for the sight of my heavy amphibian head stooped over wide shoulders, webbed hands hidden behind my back, hooded eyes staring down guiltily. He staggered and clutched his breast. I worried I might have seriously harmed him.

Carli followed Grandfather into the room with an excited, expectant expression of delight. The hysterical cries of aunt Tatua echoed through the house.

Don Morales stared at me and covered his mouth. Lines marked the corners of his eyes in deep creases. He was as I had imagined him, about the same size as Eduardo, stout, with a strong chest and protruding belly. He wore a sports jacket and a dark shirt with the top two buttons open. A scent of spices and flowers emanated from him.

Grandfather quickly regained his composure. With a quick look at me, he leaned over Mother.

Don Carlos studied the pale, emaciated form of his daughter. "So it's true. You found her. Is she alive?"

"She lives through the power of the tunjo. Have you told Mama?"

"No. I wanted to be sure."

"Aunt Tatua saw it. I couldn't stop her," Eduardo said, nodding toward me. I shrank farther into myself at being referred to as it.

Grandfather picked up Mother's hand. "Lilia, can you hear me? You're home, sweet child. You're home."

The tunjo beamed brighter on her chest.

"Cruuuu."

"Do you hear that?" Grandfather asked.

Eduardo's upper lip twisted. "Yes, I hear them, the witches, the Xucha. There are other spirits too. It calls them the Assassins of Fire. They nearly killed us twice."

Don Carlos locked his hands behind his back and rocked on his heels. "Cruuuu."

An aquamarine halo lifted from the tunjo and formed a ghostly vision of Curratta. She wavered and disappeared into the tunjo.

"Whoa! Did you see that?" Carli exclaimed.

"Curratta's tunjo. Then it's true, all true," Grandfather whispered.

"It's only true if we let it come true." Eduardo's chest expanded and he balled his fist.

"Uncle Eduardo brought home a monster," Carli said.

Grandfather raised his gaze to where I hid in the shadow by the dresser. I was excited to see him, yet lamented the impression I was making.

"Does he understand? Can he speak?" Grandfather asked.

I should have displayed good manners and introduced myself, but did not, staring at him mute, unmoving like a beast. Unconsciously, I scratched my face. Skin came off beneath my round black nail.

"Yuck," Carli said.

Grandfather studied me. "Tsaangu beaichehku." He said with his fist laid across his heart, giving me the traditional La'ku greeting.

I sighed and raised my eyes, speaking softly with my shoulders hunched, beseechingly in my best accented Spanish, pleading for him to believe me. "I'm her son...your grandson. I only found her two days ago."

He pursed his lips. "We never knew. We thought she was dead until she called us five days ago." His expression of sorrow and repentance disappeared when he turned to Eduardo. "How did this happen?"

Eduardo shrugged. "Ask Theodore."

"Yes, Theodore. He has much to explain," Grandfather face reddened and his right fist clenched.

Eduardo frowned and nodded. I understood that they shared the same violent nature.

Grandfather looked at me kindly, again asking for my forgiveness. "If I'd known I would have come for you."

He stepped toward me and held out his arms.

Hesitantly, I went to his embrace.

"Welcome, my son," he said and hugged me.

I lay my head on his shoulder and a deep sob escaped from my chest.

Aunt Tatua could be heard calling for help. The sound of people running came from the hallway.

Grandfather sprang away from me and quickly closed the door. Another woman outside sounded nearly as hysterical as the first one. "What is it? Where are the guards?" she demanded.

"Go outside and calm everyone," Grandfather ordered Eduardo.

"What should I tell them?" Eduardo asked sarcastically. "That Norane's final vengeance has arrived?"

"Keep them out of here until I've had time to think," Grandfather sternly said. "And take the boy with you."

Carli started to object, but Eduardo grabbed him by the nape of his shirt and pushed him out the door.

"Momma, calm down. It's just me. You can go back to your stations, men," Eduardo said.

"What is this, Eduardo?" My grandmother Beatrice asked.

"Papa's taking care of it."

"Taking care of what? Tatua is afraid to leave her room. She says that you have brought home a devil carrying a corpse."

"I'll tell you in a minute. Let's see to Tatua, shall we?"

"Where is your father? What were you doing in Lilia's room?"

Carli shouted in excitement, "She's home. She's in there with a real monster. He's taller than Papa. He's got ugly skin that hangs off him. He's got hands like..."

"That's enough!" Eduardo interrupted the boy.

"What is the child talking about? Is your father in there? Where is he? I'm going in."

Grandfather looked at the hallway. Obviously anxious to hide me from his wife, he stepped across Mother's room and opened a door.

"Would you mind waiting in here a moment."

I shuffled past him, wondering if I should just find a way out of the mansion to the lake. "No, I don't mind."

Grandfather closed the door after me just as Grandmother entered Mother's room.

"My God, it is Lilia! Oh my Lilia! Can it be true?" Grandmother wailed.

"Eduardo brought her home," Grandfather tenderly said.

"But what is this light? What is on her? What Indian devilry is this?"

I had to be in the water. Here or in the lake? A large tub set on metal claws, six feet long and four feet deep, was closer. I would have bathed in the toilet.

I turned a knob and blessed relief streamed from a curved spigot. Tearing off my clothes, I sat in the tub, cupping and pouring the water on the most desiccated parts of my body. Back at the cabin, Kare used a wood-fired stove to warm the water, careful that I never be in sight of any fire. I was delighted at the way I could mix cold and hot water to a perfect balance of volume and temperature. My comfort increased as the tub filled to the brim. I shut off the flow and slipped beneath the surface, bending my legs and rolling to the side until I was completely submerged. Caked, dead skin floated away as my pores opened. My family's voices faded. Thoughts slowed.

* * *

My fatigue pulled the underwater dream-state quickly around me. I barely knew where I was or how long I had been under, when I sensed someone looking down at me.

Reluctantly, waking from my meditation, I opened an eye and looked up through the clear surface to see Carli staring at me with a half-smile.

I closed my eye and almost fell back into the dream, but could not ignore the boy. A sigh expanded my chest. Consciousness brought modesty. I pulled my hands over my genitals.

Smiling as my head rose up above the rim of the tub, I said, "Hello."

Carli pushed his lips into the shape of a kiss and stared at me. His perfect proportions again impressed me. Every part of his body from his eyes to his finely pointed hands was as physically perfect as I was flawed.

I waited for him to speak.

"You're the ugliest thing I've ever seen. What are you?"

I wondered if he had any empathy at all. He might not know how much his words hurt me. "I'm your cousin Du."

He bent back and laughed so hard I felt an insecure pleasure that I had at least amused him.

"Oh yeah?" he laughed. "Who's your father?"

I pushed farther out of the water. Even though he was mocking me, I politely answered, "Theodore Moss."

He stopped laughing. His eyes expanded and his pretty red lips parted. "You're ugly and crazy. Wait until I tell him I have a brother!" He bent over. His laughter echoed through the bathroom. "Oh this is great. Wait until I tell Mother, she has...has..." He was laughing too hard to get out what he was trying to say. "...another son and he's drowning in the tub." His mad high-pitched trill echoed. "You'd better come, brother. They're all waiting for you. Weeehaaa!" he laughed and bent over. "I can't wait for my daddy to come home. What a joke."

He closed the door to Mother's room behind him and shouted, "Hey everybody, wait until you hear this."

A woman, perhaps Grandmother, told him to be quiet. He laughed again and was scolded, sent away with a threat that his father would punish him.

"No he won't. He'll be too happy to see his other son. He he he heee." His laughter trailed him as he ran down the hall.

Was he my brother or my cousin? How could he be both? He had called Eduardo uncle and referred to Theodore Moss as his father. Father must have remarried and had another son.

There were too many questions to be answered for me to remain in the water. If my family was waiting for me, I should not delay. I only hoped that I could make a better impression than I had on those I had met so far.

The towel was the largest and softest I had ever touched. I wished I had some clean clothes, but I'd left the pack with MG downstairs.

My muddy overalls and boots were heavy and rough looking. I quickly patted the monk's ring of short hair around the dome of my head. The steamed-up mirror reflected the image of the monster that had terrified my family. Blotched and striped flesh the color of an unripe tomato hung from my face.

"Shhhhraaaaa!"

The death rattle of Kinchel shook the air. Fear clutched my throat. I felt defenseless. I flung open the door to Mother's room to confirm what I dreaded.

The necklace had been removed from her neck!

My heart clenched. Mother was dead. Who would defend us now?

She lay pitifully small, pale and unconscious on the wide bed. A doctor and priest stood on either side of her, Grandmother and aunt Tatua at the foot, Grandfather beside Eduardo by the door.

"Shhhhraaaaa!"

Grandmother cowered against aunt Tatua who repeatedly crossed herself. "¡Santa *María*! ¡Sálvame Dios!"

Grandfather moved to his wife's side.

The doctor dropped Mother's wrist and stepped back, his eyes on me.

The priest held an ornate bottle of holy water.

My eyes danced in separate arcs looking for the necklace, finally focusing on Eduardo. He should know the danger of removing it. "Where is it? The necklace!" I demanded, shocking myself at my own impertinence.

Eduardo reached for his pocket. He pulled out a pistol. His eyes locked on me in a deadly glare.

"Cruuuuuu."

Where was the necklace?

A greenish-blue glow emanated from the pocket of Eduardo's coat.

"Shhhhraaaaa!"

The sound of Kinchel cracked like lightning. I heard a distant chattering sound of many blades slicing through the air: the thump-thump-thump of helicopters approaching.

Eduardo raised his gun, taking aim at my head.

"No," Grandfather cried and moved to protect me.

"Give me the necklace," I pleaded. "I know you want it. That's the way it works. I want it too. But your sister is the only one who can control its power. She's the only who can protect us. She will die without it."

"Give him the tunjo, Eduardo," Grandfather ordered.

Reluctantly, Eduardo pulled the radiating object from his jacket pocket.

"Shhhhraaaaa!"

The black barrel of the pistol followed me as I took the necklace from him.

I had to fight the attraction of the tunjo. The only way I could save Mother was to return the necklace to her.

The priest crossed himself and fell away from me, his words quivering, "Honore sanctificatum et optimum domino ad omne opus bonum." His eyes bobbed so fast they gave the idea he was being shaken.

"Save us from the devil!" aunt Tatua wailed.

"Hold me. Wear me." The necklace was hungry to be around my neck—for me to fulfill the destiny for which it had been created. I twisted toward the volcano Susuprina framed in the window, and held the tunjo above my head.

"Tatya-Masi." The witches chanted.

The Jewels of Life glinted and their ferromagnetic attraction increased.

Jade light streamed from the top of Susuprina into the effigy. The witches had waited six hundred years for me to unleash this power on the world.

The tunjo flared. Those in the room gasped and cried out in fear and amazement.

The witches, ancient women with frog-like faces, shrieked spells at me. Gaseous forms streamed from the totem and swirled around the ceiling, casting off bursting globes of light. Grandmother pointed in amazement at the sight while aunt Tatua frantically made the sign of the cross on her chest.

Protoplasm coalesced into the form of Curratta.

The witch extended a skinless finger toward me, emitting a bolt of emerald energy that struck me in the heart.

I was Tatya-Masi, avenger of the La'ku.

The urge to unite with the Xucha, to become a single force to battle the Lord of Fire—a chance once and for all to be what I was created to be—was nearly irresistible. No! I would not forsake MG and the Age of Man.

My arms shook as I pushed the necklace away from my head toward Mother. The witches raged with frustration and shrank away from me. They weakened enough so I could stagger to the bed and lay the necklace on Mother. She shuddered and twitched as the alien presence returned to her body. Her eyes flashed open and stared at me with split pupils. The spirit of Curratta was back in Mother.

"Andebichi-woho'nee Bide'pe!" she spoke in a hollow voice that rose from deep within her.

I shared her alarm. Kinchel was near.

The priest rushed from the room crying, "I am not qualified."

Grandmother reached out to stop him, and then turned to the doctor. "What is it? What happened? Tell me my daughter is alive."

Mother's eyes closed, shielding the power inside her. Nobody spoke. The doctor's mouth was agape, his eyes large beneath his glasses, staring at Mother.

"Oh my poor baby, what has happened to you?" Grandmother wept, but did not touch her. "Take that abomination from her," she ordered, but nobody moved to touch the necklace shining brightly on Mother's pale skin.

"I would not," Grandfather finally spoke looking quickly at me for confirmation. He turned to the doctor and said, "Thank you for coming. I would appreciate very much your discretion."

"I understand, señor." The doctor bowed, looked once more at Mother, then at me, shook his head, and hurried from the room.

"What are we to do?" Grandmother cried.

Grandfather lifted the tunjo from where I had left it on Mother and gently placed the necklace around her thin neck.

"¡Válgame Dios!" aunt Tatua's voice quavered.

A painting of the Crucifixion hung on the wall above Mother's bed. My gaze rose to the holy women and monk praying at the foot of the Cross. Why was it always death that brought belief?

"What did we just see?" Aunt Tatua looked at me, but was speaking to Grandfather.

"The power of the tunjo, I believe," Grandfather said and put his hands behind his back, watching the now dormant amulet, waiting for the next apparition.

"Please, Carlos, I beg you…take him away. This is more than I can bear," Grandmother said.

Grandfather curled his lip beneath his upper teeth, angry at the way she'd spoken of me, and then relented. "Yes, you must be hungry," he said to me. "I'll have some food brought to my study."

Short of stopping the rain, he could not have made a better offer.

CHAPTER NINETEEN

12

Hunger made me hop rather than the awkward forced walking motion I can do as I accompanied Grandfather into his library. I recognized the room I'd seen in Kare's memories. MG stood before a glass case containing metal, wood, and bone tunjos. Displayed on black velvet covered tiers, each was illuminated by a spotlight. They were inanimate imitations of the tunjo with the Jewels of Life upstairs. In various ways, they all looked like me. But of course, it is I who looked like them.

Grandfather was gracious to MG, and welcomed her in heavily accented English. 'You will please excuse and understand our extreme family situation. I'm afraid I must speak to my grandson and my English is poor."

I was thrilled to be referred to as his grandson.

"No go ahead. I understand."

"Thank you." Grandfather stood close to me and emphasized his words speaking rapidly in Spanish. "Please tell me as much as possible."

I understood what he needed to know was not where I had been for the past sixteen years. I told him about the rain, the Serpent, finding the container, "...and Mother came to me as a spirit. She was beautiful, dressed just like her wedding day."

"And she said that you are Tatya-Masi?"

I closed my eyes. "Yes." I opened my eyes and, with all my sincerity said, "Not that I want to be. You know about Manoa?"

"Of course."

"That's where she is, I mean where her spirit is."

His mouth contracted. "Manoa! It does exist!" He looked toward Susuprina. Only the lower slopes of the volcano were visible through the mist. "I have long thought that we would have to journey to Manoa to find those who placed this spell on Lilia. Eduardo will show us the way to the pool where they found the box. That is where we must start."

I doubted it. My brief empathetic connection with Eduardo had been enough to know that he feared the Cave of the Xucha. I could not imagine what would make him go back. What did Grandfather mean by we? Did he intend to go with us to Manoa?

"Have you tried to use the tunjo? Have you fully opened yourself to its power?" Grandfather asked.

He didn't know what he was asking me. He couldn't possibly fathom the longing I felt to submit to the tunjo. I shook my head. "It would require me to take it from Mother and you saw...." I did not finish, seeing that Grandfather understood.

"Of course." He frowned. "There must be some other way."

"The necklace has powers that go beyond Mother and me. When I opened the box, it started raining...all over the world."

"Don't blame yourself, my son. You might only be the harbinger of the inevitable. We would not be the first world to perish by flood. Perhaps like all life, civilizations have their cycles. The arrogance of our age is that no one before has ever obtained what we have, or known what we know. Within the jungle and beneath this land are the ruins of one civilization built atop the other. Do you think the Aztecs thought they were inferior to the Spaniards? Do you think the Incas thought they could be overthrown by one hundred and eighty conquistadors in one afternoon?"

The way MG nodded I saw her Spanish was proficient enough to understand what was being said. I didn't know if Grandfather expected me to answer his questions, and listened closely hoping he was working his way through the problem and would find a solution other than going to Manoa where the Xucha were waiting to make me Tatya-Masi.

"Come, let me show you something."

Through a door at the rear of his study we entered his laboratory. Grandfather led us to a stone wheel the diameter of a rear tractor tire.

Grandfather turned on a spotlight that illuminated his great artifact. Spiral eyes and a thick broad mouth smiled up at me in an amused but cruel manner from the monolith. I recoiled at the monumental intrusion from the past. Carvings of humans were depicted running from monsters that bore fearsome features: wavy eyes, snake tongues, shark teeth, bear claws. Carved panels of jaguars, eagles, crocodiles, insects, stalks of corn, and winter constellations framed the bestial representations.

"This is the Wheel of Life. The people who made this believed gods fought for the world and when one prevailed, life on Earth was destroyed and started again. It shows the worlds that came before—one destroyed by Fire, the next by earthquake. This world, the one in which we live, is to be destroyed by water. The Mayan calendar, the most accurate in antiquity, says this world will end when the Sun rests in the eye of Sagittarius."

How could the Mayan have known? What was their relationship with the La'ku, I wondered?

As if sensing my question, Grandfather said. "Cultures do not arise from nothing. One succeeds the other, and who knows what is new, what has been taught, and what has been discovered? Your mother and uncle were with me on the expedition that brought this back. They are good archeologists."

Mother, uncle—the words cut through my fear. He had accepted me as his grandchild. My throat constricted with gratitude. I wanted to be part of this family, not its destroyer.

Grandfather led us to a glass-covered case in his library and removed an old leather bound book, "This is from the Codex Morales transcribed by our ancestor, Bartolome Morales, the first Protectorate of the Indians."

He flipped through it and donned a pair of reading glasses before reading,

"The Sixth World, the final World,

Sign of 12 (Water)

It is the World of Water,

Because it flows.

According to what has been left to us,

Said by the old,

In the time of Tatya-Masi

Rain will fall without end,

And we shall perish."

The prophecy stung me like a curse. We shall perish: my family, the world, everyone—was there no way to stop it?

The door opened and servants wheeled in two white-cloth covered tables arrayed with dishes of food. I swayed on my feet, and it was all I could do not to leap for the bread, pastries, fruit, and silver-covered dishes.

Eduardo hurried into the library. "Theodore is here with a squadron of soldiers."

Father. Now I understood why I'd heard helicopters.

CHAPTER TWENTY
SMOKING MIRROR

One look at the pistol in Eduardo's hand and I doubted my father would be alive for long. Though he had abandoned me, I felt compelled to defend Moss. "Grandfather," I said. "My father is possessed by a spirit."

"Enough of this madness!" Eduardo shouted, looking ready to shoot me. "A monster calling my sister mother, village idiots and their superstitions. I won't hear any more."

"Be calm, Eduardo. You must control yourself. These are difficult things to understand," Grandfather said.

"*This* is what you want." Eduardo extended his hand toward the illuminated display of *tunjos*. "Your dream is to see the dead rise, to see the myths, the nattering nonsense of primitives come true. I will not be a part of this madness."

"Careful, Eduardo, that you are not fighting the wrong war. We have the chance to save our civilization, our race, our family!"

"I will fight for our family, whoever our enemies," Eduardo said, and with one last malevolent look at me, strode from the room.

He may have bravely thought he was fighting mortal men, but I knew that we would all soon be facing *Xiulu*.

"Cruuuu." The witches were an invisible presence in the room.

Grandfather knew who our real enemy was. "Will you stop the rain?" he asked me.

"I will try."

"Gurrrurrrlll!" It was the sound of true evil.

I was seized by fear. I'd never heard such a sound before. It was the fearsome spirit of destruction Mother had warned about—*Mitnal* the Smoking Mirror. Father was now under the protection of *Mitnal*. Eduardo would have no chance against them. To survive and protect my family, I needed to forsake the boy in me and become *Tatya-Masi*. I had to go to Manoa.

The beat of the helicopter propellers over the house shook the library. We all looked toward the windows. And then there was a collective, almost audible, flinch when someone rapped at the door. "*Patrón!*" called an urgent voice. "Soldiers are at the front gate. Helicopters are landing on the driveway!"

Gunfire erupted.

Grandfather's face contorted with anguish. We all knew that it was Eduardo who was shooting and being shot at. Grandfather leaned toward the door before pivoting to face me. "Are these soldiers guided by *Xiulu?*"

"They are," I said. "I am certain of it."

Grandfather struck a fist into his palm, as Eduardo had done. "Then we shall never beat them unless we deploy our own spiritual alliances. But how can we reach Manoa?"

I answered with what he'd already proposed. "We must go to the cave where they found the box with the *tunjo.*"

Grandfather stood more erect, an excited gleam in his eye. "If the *Xucha* want us to go, then they will guide us. Better than bowing our heads to *Xiulu*. Horses will be our best hope of reaching the falls. Can you ride?"

"I've never been on a horse."

"He can ride with me," MG said.

Again I was torn between wanting to protect the woman I'd met in California and the knowledge that MG was now *Xucha*. She had already been drawn into the realm where the risks were beyond pain and death, a world of ghosts and spirits that controlled and manipulated the living. At that moment, I envied Eduardo's strong sense of free will because I could no longer resist the forces pulling me to the destruction of all I hoped to be.

While Grandfather went to get Mother, MG and I ate as fast as we could. With my mouth full of fruit, I followed Grandfather who carried Mother across his arms into the dining room.

Grandmother and aunt Tatua walked beside them tearfully pleading with Grandfather. "Carlos, please, I beg you. Stay here with us. Let Lilia die at home."

"Beatrice, please, there's no other way. This is what Lilia wants."

"How can you believe in this blasphemy? How can you do this to me?" Grandmother covered her eyes and wept.

Gunshots reverberated outside the house as Eduardo and his men battled Rosas and his troops.

The *tunjo* grew brighter on Mother's chest and haloed around Grandfather.

"Care for yourselves please. Keep away from the windows until the fighting is over. Goodbye, dear," he said.

Aunt Tatua glared at him. "How can you leave us in harm's way?"

"I must. There is no alternative."

Grandmother sobbed. "Oh this is the end, the end of everything, I know it."

With a banana peel crunched in my hand, I paused to look into her eyes, trying to pour all my sincerity and love into my words. "We go to stop the end of everything."

As we exited the house through the servants' entrance behind the kitchen, aunt Tatua spat at me. "Animal. Satan!"

With that final curse ringing in my ears, I left my family home and followed my grandfather into the rain.

CHAPTER TWENTY-ONE
COCATAMIA STAFF OF LIFE

We crossed a laundry yard and into a covered walkway that led to the stables where Kare and Norane had worked as youths. A servant rushed from a row of stalls facing a central walkway sprinkled with straw to meet Don Carlos

"Saddle four horses. ¡Rápido!" Grandfather ordered as the sound of gunfire came from multiple directions.

Four grooms ran to obey him.

Domination was a lesson I was learning; it was not that dissimilar from the laws of nature where the big eat the little, where whole civilizations are eradicated by vicious gods and spirits for whom human life is expendable. Grandfather feared no man, but he was now facing a ruthless god. Our lives were of no consequence to Xiulu in his battle for domination of the next Age of Earth.

"This is where I keep my exploration gear." Grandfather entered a room as large as one of the stalls. Packs, coils of rope, picks and shovels hung from the walls. MG donned a yellow slicker. Grandfather a long raincoat and cowboy hat. He covered Mother in a hooded poncho and carried her to where an Indian groom held the reins of a large black stallion in the paddock. I remained outside in the rain.

Grandfather swung onto a heavy silver-inlaid saddle. His horse reared, watching me with wide frightened eyes. Grandfather controlled the stallion and positioned Mother in front of him on the saddle, holding onto the reins with one hand. "Harrrraaa." He urged his horse into a trot.

MG sat on a stripe-hooved Appaloosa, led from a stall marked with the nameplate Tigger. Her horse whinnied, anxious to be after the other horse.

"Get on behind me," she said.

My strong wish was to stay off the horse, a sentiment that I'm certain Tigger shared. The horse looked at me with flared nostrils and twitching ears. Nevertheless, I hopped and landed squarely on her back behind MG. The mare reared and would have thrown me, but the legs that can propel me twenty yards at a leap powerfully squeezed, so hard that Tigger groaned and sagged.

MG loosened the reins and Tigger sprang after Grandfather's horse, pursued by barking dogs.

I clung to MG as we raced toward a squad of soldiers, squeezing my thighs so tightly Tigger complained with an angry snort and jarred me off center. I had to use the rear of the saddle to pull myself back into position and hold onto MG.

"Out of my way," Grandfather yelled. "I am Don Carlos Morales!"

The brown-faced soldiers, looking no older than I, scrambled clear as we all raced by.

"A man should be able to ride on his own land, shouldn't he?" Grandfather shouted, galloping away from three helicopters landing on the road.

"Gurrrurrrlll!" The growl of Mitnal the Smoking Mirror warned that Rosas was on one of the helicopters. I rotated an eye to look over my shoulder where I saw two soldiers, rifles ready to fire, jump from the largest of the helicopters.

Hernando Rosas was how I imagined him to be from Kare's descriptions and recollections. He was tall and thin, with an angular face and eyes that seemed to express that nothing could harm him– that you could trust and follow him.

A man in a military uniform followed Rosas from the helicopter. I recognized him as one of Kinchel's nine heads, Soldier Assassin. The Fire spirits were joining together to kill me.

Rosas pointed at us and they climbed back into the helicopter. With my eye turned rearward I searched but could not see my father.

Grandfather's horse jumped a fence. Tigger followed, throwing her one-and-a-half tons into the air. I held MG around her narrow waist and would have fallen off if not for the death grip of my thighs. The horses galloped across the soggy pasture. Tigger pressed her head outward, lungs filling and exhaling through flaring nostrils. The motion flowed from her outstretched hoof, rose into her spine, lifted and stretched, falling and rolling in waves. Mud splashed across Tigger's wide chest. I learned how to balance in the saddle by using a gentle pressure with my knees. The pleasure of being so close to MG thrilled me. Her rain hat fell back over her head, and I relished the musty scent of her wet hair and the touch of her body.

We reached the road where Eduardo had chased Norane on the day of Mother's wedding, and galloped past herds of longhorn cattle huddled in flooded pastures; then we leaped a four-board white fence as high as Tigger's shoulders. This time I was prepared and more coordinated with the movement of the horse.

Men and women harvesting bananas gaped at us as we passed. A man shook a machete over his head and ran after us. I achieved a complete telepathic union with him. His name was Agusto Raymi. The exultation of seeing his god was overwhelming to this humble fieldworker and father of a young family. The myth of the returning god leapt from his dreams into reality. I knew his life was forever changed.

"Tatya-Masi! Tatya-Masi!" he shouted as I rode away, and his shock was followed by the hope of a true believer.

We turned onto a road that ran at a right angle to the Cristóbal School and raced toward the great series of waterfalls emptying from Lake Itza Uo.

Keeping one eye on the road ahead and the other behind, I saw an open-top vehicle carrying two figures slide in the mud around a turn in the road a quarter mile behind us. I strained my senses to confirm that the man driving was Kare. I knew without a clear sight of him the man in the passenger seat was my father, Theodore Moss. It was all I could do not to attempt to turn my head to see them. But being on the horse was too treacherous and difficult for me to give my father and Kare the attention I wanted.

Our two horses galloped along a dirt path that ran parallel to the cliff. Exposed roots and stones protruded from the escarpment. Tigger slipped down a steep mud bank carved by the flood, but the surefooted mare quickly regained her balance. MG guided Tigger along the bank of a cascading brown river too wide for me to leap and too wild to swim across. Fifty yards ahead, the roar of falling water and mist marked the crest of the fifth fall.

Grandfather swung off the saddle with Mother in his arms. MG stopped too, and I hopped off Tigger.

The percussion of the falling water had grown to a pounding roar. Even the exaggerated image of Kare's telling when he'd made this descent as a ten-year-old and his brother Norane had found the box could not match the reality of the cascade pouring through the pinched gorge, throwing mountains of muddy water into the air, smelling of dirt and ripe vegetation. The shore was disappearing in avalanches, swallowed up by the brown river of boiling cataracts. One slip and we too will be sent flying over the falls.

"Gurrrurrrlll!"

The sound of Mitnal penetrated the white swirling mist shrouding us. A helicopter flew beneath the low-hanging rain clouds, its blades beating. I saw a soldier in the open bay fire a machine gun.

Bullets chopped up the leaves on nearby trees as Grandfather led us on a run into the frail shelter of the jungle canopy.

I needed the power of the Jewels of Life to fight the forces gathering around us, but to take the necklace from Mother when we were so close... so close to what? Close to Manoa? Close to the final reckoning when I must prove myself to the god Tatya-Masi, or we would all soon be dead? That I was the god, I now had no doubt. My powers might not be as concentrated without the tunjo, but they were still mine. I closed my eyes and opened myself to the spirits I'd sensed when I'd held the Jewels of Life. "Wind and rain, rain and wind," I whispered.

A dark funnel cloud dropped out of the sky.

"Cruuuu."

The faces of witches and spirits of ancient La'ku warriors appeared in the swirling waterspout. It caught the helicopter and spun it toward the lake. A soldier was thrown from the side-bay and fell out of the copter headfirst—my first victim as a vengeful god.

But Xiulu was not so easily thwarted and he had his own spirits to command. A lightning bolt struck the waterspout. The pilot righted the freed helicopter. Meanwhile, I would not use any of my powers against the vehicle, which was now close enough for me to see clearly carried Kare and Moss. My father looked as I remembered him in the distant recollections of my childhood, as I'd seen him in Kare and Edgar's thoughts—a bit older, graying at the temples, intelligent eyes behind round glasses, handsome in a studious way. As the servants of Quetzal perhaps they'd come to take to me to him so he could fulfill the scheme in which he'd protected me, where he would give me the other two Jewels of Life in the Cocatamia in exchange for my freeing him from Inika's curse. But there was no time to confirm their intentions.

The mist closed, hiding us, as the helicopter flew over us its machine gun firing through the clouds. Bullets struck the ground around us as Grandfather led us along a dirt path to the cliff.

We stopped at the edge of the precipice where the river was pouring over the cliff. Grandfather handed Mother to me, and then removed a coil of rope from his backpack and tied it to a tree.

"I can carry her from here," I said.

"Give me back my daughter."

I could not see how he was going to rappel down the cliff beside torrential falls and keep a hold on her, but there was no arguing with him. I passed Mother to him. She was so light that he balanced her body over his shoulder.

"I'll show you the way," Grandfather shouted. "I've been climbing these cliffs since I was a boy. Just follow me. It looks harder than it is."

I swallowed the argument that Grandfather had never climbed down the cliff with the Lord of Fire chasing him.

Holding Mother with one hand and the rope with the other, Grandfather moved expertly across and down the face of the cliff–finding holds, jumping and sliding. He looked like a young man and got so far ahead of me that he disappeared into the mist.

MG, wide-eyed with fear, gritted her teeth, grabbed the rope and followed Grandfather down the side of the waterfall.

As I was removing my boots, I looked back to see Kare and Moss run from the truck. Kare shouted at me, but I could not hear what he was saying, and was too concerned about MG to wait for him. I hopped to an outcropping of rock, down the face of the cliff, using natural agility to stay close to MG as she held the rope, moving down the sheer, wet face into the thick cloud of mist and rain that hid Grandfather.

Unable to see above or below, I inched across the cliff looking for a space to jump, my eyes darting between the treacherous path down and the way back. A fetid stench of rotting plants and muddy water rose from the jungle. The crack of a lightning bolt raised the hair on the back of my neck. Thunder shook the air, followed by the cry of a jungle cat in the howling wind. Twigs and branches whipped against my face.

"Cruuuu!" The witches' chant rose above the roar of the falling water.

"Shraaaa!" The agents of my destruction responded to the witches' challenge from the top of the cliff, their metaphysical callings piercing the natural sounds.

Lightning split pea-colored clouds when the celestial and temporal worlds collided. Thousands of stars spun in the vapor, casting off spirals of bursting light, as the Age of Man struggled to survive.

I slid my bare feet along the cliff face's rounded, slippery surface, looking for another landing spot. Wind generated by the falling water parted the fog, and I saw Grandfather below me. I jumped and landed on a hazardous perch, teetering before digging my nails into cracks in the rock to right myself.

Above me, Moss and Kare, no doubt guided by their master Quetzal the Plumed Serpent, were quickly catching up with us. I hesitated before going farther down the cliff, to use my empathy to try to reach into my father's mind, to know more about him.

Through the mist, I saw the burning jewel eyes of the Serpent's cross on Kare's chest. The Castilian-accented voice of the Plumed Serpent whispered to me below the level of hearing.

"Come to me. You are near. My servants will bring you to me."

Implied in the Plumed Serpent's words was the Fire spirit's careless disregard for human life. Kare and Moss were only slaves carrying out his bidding. Quetzal expected me to abandon MG and Grandfather. His freedom and the Jewels of Life contained in the tunjo were what mattered, not a few puny human lives.

I used my empathetic connection to ask him, "Will you help us to reach you?"

"I've done all I can. When you've united the four Jewels, it will be Xiulu who fears you."

There were no new assurances in his offer. He could not help us reach the cave where he'd hidden the other two Jewels. And if we did escape the killers closing in around us, the bargain would remain the same. I'd bring him the tunjo and he would reveal where he'd hidden Cocatamia Staff of Life.

"I, too, must trust you," he responded to my unspoken doubt.

We were in a classic Mexican standoff—a gun pointed at each other's head. Neither of us could win unless we both won, and only one of could win. If he gave me the Jewels and I freed him he would try to kill me. It was a fool's gamble, but what choice did I have?

Above, I heard the chatter of an automatic weapon being fired. I didn't think the Assassin could see us through the mist. The blind shooting sent bullets ricocheting off rocks, causing Moss and Kare to press against the rock face of the cliff.

"Gurrrurrrlll!"

With no noise, just a blinding flash, a lightning bolt struck. I was close enough to feel the shock and was paralyzed for a moment. I watched Grandfather slump and release the rope. He and Mother tumbled backwards through the rock spires and spume into the boiling whitewater below.

I felt a numbed detachment. Trying to will myself to move, my limbs didn't respond until MG's touch released me. I hopped down the face of the cliff, holding the dangling rope for support. Fifty feet above the surface, I knew I had to jump if I was to have any chance of saving Don Carlos and my mother.

"Croar!" I bellowed and leapt to clear the outcropping of rocks; dropping feet-first I landed in the water. Immediately, a spinning cataract caught and pushed me beneath the turbulent surface. I was sucked into an underwater cyclone, a drowning machine that violently spun me into the center of a vortex where all slowed.

Mother and Grandfather floated face down beside me. I pulled Mother to my chest, held Grandfather by the back of his raincoat, and attempted to breach the wall of spinning water, but was thrown back.

We were trapped. We were going to drown. Hanging in a realm of equilibrium, I marveled how I could perish by Water not Fire. The struggle for the Age of Man was over. I would no longer be the agent of Fire or Water. My battle was finished. Acceptance brought a sense of peace. I held my mother and grandfather and gave up to the water as we drifted into death.

"Cruuuu."

Mother's spirit spoke to me one last time. "Command the waters, Tatya-Masi. Become the Water."

With her words, my focus was drawn back into this world. The tunjo was now floating in the swirling cocoa-colored water within its own bubble of sparkling chartreuse light. The Jewels of Life shined in the eyes of the likeness of Tatya-Masi.

"Cruuuuu."

I reached out and the tunjo floated into my hand. With the touch of the amulet, I renounced my humanity and became the god. My fear disappeared. Strength expanded my muscles. I was Tatya-Masi.

I closed my eyes and held out my hand. Streams of verdant light shot from my fingers, parting the fierce waters, and I was able to pull Mother's and Grandfather's limp bodies from the maelstrom with no more effort than sliding my foot through a slow stream. With strength I'd never known, I lifted Grandfather onto a narrow beach.

As I climbed onto the muddy shore between the jungle and waterfall, Mother seemed as small as a child in my arms. Her wet hair clung to her pale face. I searched but couldn't find her spirit-self. Could the tunjo still keep her alive? I quieted my internal argument that I needed the tunjo to defend us, and forced myself to place the necklace over her head again. I saw Mother's chest rise as she took a breath.

Grandfather was pale and unconscious. MG, soaking wet, had made it to the bottom of the falls and was followed by Moss and Kare. They moved around the muddy edge of the pond toward us.

"Are you all right?" MG reached me first. Again, just the touch of her hand on my shoulder filled me with warmth.

"Come, we're near," Kare said. "Follow me. Quickly!"

My eyes went irresistibly to my father.

Moss' lips twitched when he looked at me. I leaned closer straining all my senses to gather every impression, plunging into his mind like a thief ransacking a drawer to look for valuables, seeking to know this man whom I had imagined every day of my life.

His thoughts were on the Lake of the Frogs where his own father had taken him to their fishing cabin. With a flash of insight, I achieved an empathetic connection to the young man who had married Lilia Morales, but was overridden by the torment of his freewill being commandeered by the Plumed Serpent, and then Mitnal for the promise of protection and wealth. I was trying to find his body among the reflections in a hall of mirrors.

"Father." I reached out to touch him, trying to keep my voice from breaking, pouring every honest bit of love and forgiveness I felt for him into my greeting.

He focused on the olive skin mottled by tawny blotches on the back of my hand. "Come, let's be done with this. I must bring you to Quetzal," he said as if that would explain everything he'd done and I suppose it did.

"Cruuuuu," the Xucha chant sounded more mournful, as if they sensed my coming betrayal.

"We must leave Don Carlos," Kare said. "He won't be able to manage in the cave, and we can't carry him."

"I can carry him," I said and went to lift him, but without holding the tunjo I did not have the strength.

MG also wanted me to go to the cave. "There's a better chance that someone will find him and care for him out here then in the cave," she argued.

Despite the strong empathetic connection we'd always had, her motives were suddenly difficult for me to perceive. Is this what she believed or were the Xucha, who needed me to retrieve Cocatamia Staff of Life from Quetzal, speaking through her?

"Don Carlos would want you to go on," Kare argued.

"Shraaaa."

Grandfather would not have abandoned me. "No. I won't leave him," I said and tried again to lift him, but he was too heavy.

"Help me," I plead with Moss and Kare.

MG knelt beside Grandfather and placed three fingers on the side of his neck. "There's no pulse. He's dead," she said.

She was right. His spirit had left him. The Assassins were nearly at the bottom of the cliff.

With a sob, I left Grandfather's body on the wet ground.

"Come," Kare said with a hand on my back.

I was surprised how tenderly Moss picked up Mother, and carried her to where the outer edge of the falls formed a veil of water. I'd seen this route in Kare's memories of the day he'd found the cross. The witches, the Serpent, Moss and Kare—all had brought me to this point. My dream of being a regular boy must end. There was no other choice for me. With one last look back at Don Carlos' lifeless body, I took the step I'd dreaded since finding the magical silver and gold box, into the Cave of the Xucha.

CHAPTER TWENTY-TWO
THE FATAL WAY

My eyes quickly adapted to the dim light. The waterfall thumped in the echo chamber of a cavern the size of the cabin back home at the Lake of the Frogs. We squeezed through a crack in the rear wall where Kare's flashlight illuminated a skeleton and the shards of broken clay pots. Kare led us through the glistening stone corridor until he held the light on a narrow rock bridge over an underwater canyon. Moss carried Mother across and I followed MG. The feeling of déjà vu grew stronger as I retraced Kare's childhood journey into the depths of the cave. What I knew and what I should know grew harder to distinguish. Was it the sense of having been here before because of my shared memories with Kare or a deeper self-knowledge that one day I would come here? Was I coming for the first time or returning?

The sounds of our footsteps, our breathing, and the plop of water into rock basins created a rhythm that made the cave seem animate. Rock walls pressed around us. Stalactites dripped from the roof. After fifteen minutes of navigating the twists and turns of the cave, I heard the flow of an underground river and knew we were close to where Kare had found the cross.

When we entered the conquistador's crypt, I felt as if I could have found the way by myself. Gray light from the cloud-covered terrestrial world pierced the darkness through a slit in the high stone wall, casting a illumination on the skeletal remains of Gabriel Ayala. For an anticlimactic moment, nothing stirred except the sound of our breathing.

I looked at Kare and waited. He lifted the snake-wrapped cross hanging from his neck and held it to the beam of light shining through the crevice.

Although I was expecting it, I gasped and stepped back when the Plumed Serpent arose from the cross in a fireball, towering over us, his ruby eyes burning brightly. By the light of his flame-tipped wings I saw eleven more skeletons in ancient armor lying against the walls where they'd died five hundred years ago in their failed escape from Manoa.

His reptilian head turned on a long scaled neck and faced me. My heart raced and all my thoughts were exposed. Despite my previous encounters with Quetzal, the depth of our empathetic connection shocked me. In an instant I knew that I'd been a fool to trust him. All I'd accomplished was to bring him the two Jewels of Life in the tunjo. With all four Jewels at his command, his spirit would rule the Sixth and Final World of Earth.

I searched for an escape route while trying to imagine how I could keep Quetzal from seizing the tunjo.

The Serpent's voice echoed in my mind. "Remove the tunjo from the witch," he ordered Kare.

"No," I protested and moved to protect the Jewels of Life, our only weapons against the forces of Fire closing in on us.

"I must," Kare whispered and reached for the tunjo. The same telekinetic force that had repelled Dr. Brimley when he'd tried to touch the necklace at the Balfore Institute sent Kare tumbling across the dirt floor.

"Take it," Quetzal ordered Moss.

"I cannot," Moss said and flinched as he paid the price of speaking the truth.

Quetzal roared in rage. A stream of fire flowed from his fanged mouth, driving Moss with Mother in his arms to the precipice of an underground cliff, until Moss' heels were over the edge.

I leapt between him and the apparition. Heat singed my skin. Quetzal might not be able to manifest a body in the material world, but he could still generate fire. I held up my hand. "Stop. We cannot defeat each other."

Quetzal's flames diminished. He knew that Moss was not strong enough to remove the tunjo from Mother. His powers in the temporal realm were limited by the weakness of his servants. The Serpent's eyes studied me with a hostile glare. His voice in my mind had a mocking tone. "Mitnal the Smoking Mirror and Kinchel the Avenger are near. You will not be able to stop them from taking the Jewels from the witch."

"Give me Cocatamia Staff of Life and I'll free you."

"Never. Here I will remain—Water's prisoner in a World of Fire before I will allow a god of Water to possess the four Jewels."

Too late he realized my trick. While Quetzal had been in my mind, I'd been in his. I hopped to where the skeletons of two conquistadors guarded Cocatamia.

In a rage Quetzal formed a flaming barrier to protect his hiding place.

But I saw with Quetzal's eyes and spoke with his hissing tongue, "La vida es sueño." I said the spell to open the portal to where he'd hidden Cocatamia Staff of Life.

The rocks opened and flames surrounded a baton the size of my forearm. The silver scepter was crowned with a golden likeness of Tatya-Masi. In its eyes, the Jewels of Life shined with the colors of the ocean. The Staff of Life cast off blue-green and red orbs of light that rose in effervescent bubbles, creating a frothy chorus of wavering voices.

Quetzal's serpent tongue flicked flames. Amber light glinted on his ivory snout. His voice was not so certain now. "Cocatamia Staff of Life is protected by the flames of Xiulu Lord of Fire. No creation of Water can withstand the flames of Xiulu. A servant of Inika will never possess the Jewels."

"You forget that you are my father. I am of Fire." Even as I spoke with bravado, my arm ached at the memory of Kinchel's burns I'd suffered that morning in the plane. Despite my words, I agreed with him. I was of Water and only by Water could I overcome Fire. I hesitated and looked back at

MG. I must succeed for her, but what was success? Xiulu would stop the rain with Cocatamia and the tunjo. The Lord of Fire would surely kill us all. But should I not be willing to sacrifice all my loved ones and myself to stop the flood and save the rest of mankind?

In the end, I was confronted with a pure will to survive, to save my family and friends. I knew what I was and what I must do. I was Tatya-Masi Bringer of the Sixth World of Water. The Lord of Fire would not beat me.

"Wind and rain, rain and wind," I whispered. A small dark funnel of clouds spun through the air. I mentally guided the waterspout into the fiery vault. Water steamed as the flames evaporated the funnel. I concentrated harder, hearing Mother's voice, "Become the Water."

With a deep breath, I reached into the flames. My flesh burnt as I penetrated the barrier. With bones and tendons exposed, the pain was nearly unbearable.

"Cruuuu," the witches chanted their encouragement as Cocatamia Staff of Life floated into my grasp. And with the touch of the baton, I ascended to a new higher level of existence. Fear disappeared. Strength expanded my muscles. The flaming barrier exploded.

I held the power of life in my healed hand.

The Plumed Serpent, resplendent with his colorful plumage, spread his wings over me. "Your power is great, Tatya-Masi. Free me. Quickly. Kinchel and Mitnal come. Use the Jewels to give me freedom and we will stop Inika's rain."

I hopped to where Moss held Mother.

Quetzal demanded my attention. "You attend to the witch-mother but not me?" His wings erupted in flames that rose to the ceiling. Moss and Kare backed away in terror.

"Silence," I commanded with the new power of the Jewels coursing through my body.

Now Quetzal shrank to his most beguiling form and the flames disappeared. Opal feathers folded over his silver chest, he bowed his golden beak and said in the courtly voice of Gabriel Ayala, "I bear no harm to you or those who serve you, Tatya-Masi."

Energy arced between the four Jewels of Life. What I'd barely glimpsed when I'd held the tunjo, the intricate dimensions of the spirit world now nearly overwhelmed me with their immediacy. I saw Quetzal the Plumed Serpent as a trapped nova captive in walls of Water. I saw the chains of Fire that bound Moss and Kare to the cross and by the cross to Quetzal.

I pointed Cocatamia at Mother's chest and her elemental selves were reunited. With a blur, her spirit flew from Manoa into her body. Muscles firmed, she leapt to my side, strong and vibrant, ready for battle.

"Gurrrurrrlll!" the bloodcurdling sound of Mitnal the Smoking Mirror shook the air as Rosas led the Assassins of Fire into the grotto, their guns firing.

With only a thought, I raised a wall of water. Their bullets traveled into an infinite volume until they fell harmlessly.

Rosas and the Assassins stopped shooting their weapons and stared at the instrument of their defeat.

"Cast the bridge," Mother said. "Call forth the Hosts of Water. Summon the Warrior-Brother, the twelve witches and their special powers."

The arc between the Jewels, uncontrolled by me, formed a dimensional breach between the celestial and temporal realms. Frog-faced chacs, rain spirits, poured through the passage and flew out of the cave, into the leaden sky.

Quetzal's voice was in my mind. "You doom this World!"

I turned an eye to the high opening in the rock wall. The intensity of the rain was overwhelming man's last defenses. The Age of Man was being swept away. I heard the desperate cries of a threatened species, of a dying civilization. I saw Bert and his family fleeing into the mountains as Calaveras was destroyed by raging floodwaters.

"Free me," Quetzal pleaded. "Only I can show you how to stop the rain."

Rosas and the Assassins morphed into a wall of flames as the Water spirits attacked them. The chacs sizzled and spit, throwing themselves against the fiery barrier.

Mother sensed what I was about to do and begged, "Do not trust Fire!"

But I knew that without the help of Quetzal I would never be able to stop the rain. I held up the scepter into the meager sunlight shining through the crack in the cave wall. Kare faced me. The Jewels of Life formed a single intense beam of light that struck the ruby eyes of the gold snake wrapped around the Serpent's cross. I waved my hand and closed the passageway to the celestial realm.

A beam of light refracted into twelve rays that penetrated the skeletons of Ayala and his men and swept away the watery chains that held them.

The dark space of their empty eye sockets beamed with burning red orbs. With the clack of rejoining bones and sinews, jawbones and teeth, flesh grew and covered sternums and skulls, filling empty armor as the conquistadors, dead for five centuries, came back to life.

Then, with my attention diverted by this horrendous sight, Rosas leapt from behind the steaming front line between the forces of Water and Fire, and with a single-minded determination, reached for Mother and seized the tunjo. The hair and silver chain burnt through and the totem fell into his hands. Mother resisted, but Rosas threw her off him with a back swipe of his hand.

Before I could stop her, MG leapt to defend the tunjo. Rosas raised a pistol. He fired and the sound echoed in the cave. As the moment froze in my sight, a bloody wound opened on MG's chest.

"No!" I screamed. My back arched and I threw my head forward with a mighty blast from my enlarged chest. "Croar!"

"Believe," Mother beseeched me. "Become Tatya-Masi. You have the answer. You've always had the answer. Use your gift!"

Finally, in the white heat of my passion, I understood. The answer was not to overcome, but to become, to shut down and open myself–completely, wholly–use the empathy that had given me the ability to hide to reveal myself.

With a final rush, the current flowing through the Staff of Life gave me the knowledge to command the forces of Water. I spun away from my enemies, heedless of their weapons, and with two hands aimed Cocatamia toward the interior of the cave, toward Manoa.

"Chac sis na!" I cried in the language that I finally understood. "Arise, soldiers of Water."

"Cruuuuu!"

The sound was like a flight of eagles diving by my head. On a cold, damp wind, the ghostly shapes of the witches, their skirts trailing sparkling swirls of blue and verdant waves, swept into the grotto.

The banshee shrieks of the warring spirits created a hellish racket as they mixed with the clanking of the reborn conquistadors struggling to complete their reconstitution and join the battle.

"Shraaaa!"

Kinchel arose with flaming wings spread across the roof, razor teeth exposed in nine snarling mouths to cover Rosas as he ran from the cave with the tunjo.

A figure hurtled past me and threw himself at Rosas. I recognized Norane, the Warrior-Brother, looking unchanged from the vision I'd seen in Kare and Mother's memories of her wedding day.

"Shraaaa!"

"Cruuuuu!"

The two cousins wrestled, their muscles taut with effort. The sounds of their cries and solid thud of flesh hitting flesh echoed in the cave.

The witches, ephemeral shapes of light and haze, spread around me, spitting spells from their wrinkled mouths.

"Bin tin nah ka binex! Bin tin nah ka binex!"

Gabriel Ayala, the farthest along in recomposition, swung a broad two-edged sword at Norane and though he missed, the conquistador was growing stronger and more coordinated with every thrust.

Rosas pushed Norane's hand away from the tunjo, and, locked together they teetered on the edge of the underground cliff. The skeleton of Gabriel Ayala threw himself at Rosas and Norane.

The impact carried the three over the precipice.

"Raaaaaaaaaaaaaaaaaaaaaaaa!" Rosas' scream trailed him as he fells carrying the tunjo into the darkness of the depths of the cave.

I doubted that Quetzal and Mitnal the Smoking Mirror had sacrificed their temporal bodies to gain the tunjo, but without its power we were losing the battle with the Assassins and reconstituted conquistadors and our best hope of survival was escape.

Norane caught the edge of the cliff with one hand and swung back into the cavern to face the conquistadors closing in on Mother and me. The balance of the battle had shifted. Without the tunjo, my strength was diminished. The water shield was steaming and disappearing. I fell back, tried to stand but crumpled to my knee as Kinchel and the conquistadors moved in for the kill.

The nine heads of Kinchel poured fire at me. "Santiago!" the conquistadors shouted their ancient battle cry.

"To Manoa!" Mother cried.

Yes, Manoa.

I held Cocatamia Staff of Life over my head. The Jewels of Life in the protruding domed eyes were poles through which celestial water spread, creating a bubble that surrounded Mother and me in a thin luminescent film. The individual shapes of the Xucha witches and Norane merged into the sphere.

I lifted MG and with the burning flames of Xiulu chasing us, we left the temporal world.

CHAPTER TWENTY-THREE
MANOA

Floating in the center of the bubble, MG lay pale and breathless in my arms. The pulsing Jewels of Life on Cocatamia were what kept her soul from leaving her body. I might have stayed, given up the Jewels to stop Inika's rain, but now I was going to the only place I might restore life to MG.

With a pleasing sensation up my spine, tingling on the back of my neck, and across my shoulders and into my chest, I had a feeling of being in a dream where anything imagined became reality. But MG's blood on my arm kept me focused on why I was here.

Suspended, drawn into the light as others have described the passage between life and death, we floated through the Cave of the Xucha. Carried down the pool where Norane had found the box and into the depths of the lake, we dropped beneath Lake Itza Uo, past rock pinnacles and submerged cliffs. Gaseous balls spun off lime plasma as we passed. Minute plankton-like particles reflected eerily in the beam of the Staff of Life. On the floor of a deep underwater valley we passed through a translucent film. The bubble carried us into the center of Susuprina, and like a Nassesalar corpse bearer I carried MG into Manoa.

Cocatamia's head shined brighter, as the Jewels recycled their power through me. My overalls transformed into a cape of shimmering quetzal feathers. A python skin codpiece fit perfectly around my exaggerated features. An emerald-studded gold wreath adorned my head.

Mother was vibrant, rejuvenated. Her poncho dissolved, replaced by a jade habit of light, airy fabric. Norane's chin was thrust forward, his muscles taunt as he appeared to be caught in mid-step returning with his god-son to Manoa.

The interior of the Temple of the Fountain of Life lay under centuries of dust. In the dim light I saw the empty ruins of structures and streets.

The orb deposited us in the center of the central square atop the gold and jeweled mosaic of the sun being eclipsed by clouds where seventeen years before, Norane had taken Mother. Before us was the statue of Tatya-Masi, its empty hand awaiting the return of Cocatamia Staff of Life, from which the Waters of Life would once again flow—the Waters that I prayed would heal MG. The Ra, a massive jade carving of a frog stood opposite, its head pressed to the ground, an extended blue tongue curled at the edge of a barren pit of dark dirt.

A dozen sarcophagi, standing coffins embossed with depictions of La'ku totems and hieroglyphics, formed a ring around the pit.

With our arrival, life returned to the temple. A rainbow of swirling colors erupted into waving curtains of light as each sarcophagus lid opened and the Xucha emerged from their half-century hibernations.

A thunderous cymbal sounded and pulled my attention to the frog statue where Curratta, in a jade gown like Mother's, dried flesh stretched over veins and bone, moved in a rolling walk down the tongue ramp. The Supreme Shaman pointed her gnarled spell stick at the Bratay. The restoration of the Fountain of Life could not come too soon for the ancients, the dead, or for MG.

The peeping melody of cane flutes resounded. A chorus of drums began a slow regular beat.

Mother and Norane locked hands behind my back and walked forward, gently escorting me toward the waiting stone image of Tatya-Masi. I rotated my eyes in separate arcs to see over each shoulder. Mother appeared resolute, her gaze straight ahead, her pale complexion flushed with excitement.

Norane, shoulders square, radiated rapture–all he'd dreamed was about to come true. To him I was perfect. He could not conceive of my human weaknesses and trepidations. He had no idea I was here only to save MG. If not for the murderous Rosas, the Jewels would be in Quetzal's hands by now.

"Cruuuu." The Xucha incantations grew more intense and higher pitched. Globes of lit water pulsed with aquamarine light along the path leading to the Bratay.

I gently deposited MG's body at the foot of the dry basin of the statue. If this worked, the Waters of Life would flow again and Manoa would be reborn. The Lordess of Water would flood the globe with Water spirits. Rain would fall without end until the fires of man were extinguished. What was not already destroyed would be submerged and in two years, when the sun rested in the eye of Sagittarius and the temporal and celestial planes were the closest, the spirits of Water would flow into the temporal plane and Inika Lordess of Water would reign supreme. Yet, I was willing to risk the fate of the Age of Man to save MG.

I shrugged my wide shoulders, hung my great head, and with the fatalism of one performing what he must, hopped forward and placed Cocatamia Staff of Life into the waiting stone hand. I took a breath, surprised to find myself the same. A slow rumble built from beneath the floor of the temple.

Fountains burst from crevices. The spirits of long dead La'ku in the Staff of Life swirled upwards, twirling and intertwining, their high voices a cacophony of jubilation. The stream of souls grew brighter and tighter until they touched the center of the reflective dome a hundred feet above us. The beam was refracted through jewels positioned around the city and for the first time in five hundred years, Manoa was lit with intense beryl brilliance.

A trickle and then a spout of water traveled up the base of Cocatamia Staff of Life. The flow grew until it gushed around the scepter. From any angle the Waters of Life looked like a rainbow of sunlit sparkles. As brooks babbled, the souls contained in the Water bubbled and erupted in a chorus of voices crying with longing to be reborn.

I dipped a silver chalice hanging on the fountain into the Water and poured shimmering rainbow water on MG's wound. The Waters effervesced in bubbles that lifted the blood and restored her flesh. When I touched the cup to MG's lips, her beautiful eyes opened with an added gleam in their turquoise irises.

She sat up, looked at me, and then around. "Whoa," she said. "I don't think we're in Kansas anymore."

I smiled with manic relief. Whether we were alive or dead, Kansas or Manoa, I could see and hear her for at least awhile.

"Nice outfit. You look like something out of a Mardi Gras parade."

She looked around at the magically lit monuments and city. "Let me guess. We made it. We're in Manoa. They got any pizza and beer here? I'm starving." She looked at the filthy clothes she'd been wearing since I barged into her life four days before. "I could also use a change of clothes and a bath."

"Might not be necessary," I said.

In the same manner Mother and I were clothed, with a thought MG was now dressed in the jade gown of the witches. Her blond hair was braided and wrapped around her head.

"You have to be careful what you wish for here," I warned.

"I always said I'd ask for world peace if I got three wishes."

"Well, if we don't do something it is going to be very peaceful."

"Still raining?"

"More than ever."

"Oh boy. I feel strange, but OK."

"You're Xucha now. Ever since you held the Jewels, and now that you've drunk the Waters of Life, your powers have been growing. I didn't know what else to do. I'm going to get us out of here though."

MG twirled so her skirt flared around her. "Take your time. I feel fine.

No, better than fine. Last thing I remember was being shot and now I'm ready to run a marathon."

"I bet you'd win."

Curratta moved past us and dipped a finger into the Water of Life. The change in the witch was barely noticeable. Her figure remained ancient and twisted like the branch of a bonsai tree, but her aura flared brightly, and when she moved, she appeared to float.

When Norane drank from the fountain, his muscles expanded and bulged against the leather strap around his arm.

Mother took the cup and drank. Age and sickness reversed. Her beauty matched MG's but radiated with an added glow. In her thoughts I saw the source of her contentment was her love for Norane, but more than that, the promise of Tatya-Masi. When Norane had given her the box and taken her to the hidden city, they'd given up their lives in the world so that I could be born. Now her faith had been rewarded: she was reunited with Norane and I was here.

The dead of Manoa, desiccated mummies, staggered toward the fountain.

"Holy jeez," MG said and backed away from the procession of ghouls moving toward the Waters of Life.

Skeleton fingers touched the Water and brought the life-giving fluid to their skulls. Bodies formed around the ghastly shapes, pressing against ancient gowns. Muscles and hair grew. Eyes formed and brightened in hollow sockets.

Mother and Norane followed MG and me until we were standing beside the barren bed of earth before the statue.

"Tatya-Masi," Mother said.

Her adoration embarrassed me. "It's Du, Mother."

"Tatya-Masi." She refused to acknowledge my worldly name.

Curratta hovered behind her with Norane attentive at her side.

"Hello, Lilia." MG stepped forward.

Mother did not take MG's extended hand, forcing MG to give Mother a quick pat on the back.

I reminded Mother that MG had been shot fighting for her.

"Do you wish to serve Tatya-Masi?" Mother demanded.

"I serve no man," MG said, anger creeping into her voice.

"This is not a man."

Curratta and Norane were listening to their conversation with expressions that clearly indicated that in Manoa everyone's words were understood, no matter what language was spoken.

Norane knelt on one knee before me. In the halo of the refracted light, he was the living presence of the forces that had brought me to and would keep me in Manoa. "Tatya-Masi, will you accept me as the Warrior-Brother?" he asked with reverence in his voice.

I glanced at MG. Here was the moment of truth. If I was a god, then a god must be obeyed. I mimicked the tone Grandfather had used when he'd ordered the soldiers out of his way at the stables. "We're leaving. Take us back."

Norane raised his head to glance at me, confounded by my behavior.

Mother looked at him and explained, "He knows very little. The Plumed Serpent kept him isolated and weak."

"Take us back." I increased the authority in my voice.

"Back?" Norane stood and looked at Curratta. For all his physical strength, he appeared helpless, failing at the role for which he'd been selected by Inika—to be the Earthly guide of Tatya-Masi.

Curratta silently studied me.

"You can do whatever you want," MG said. "Nobody will stop you. They exist only to serve you."

I looked to Mother. If anyone knew how we could leave, she did.

"You saw how I lived," Mother said. "If you can call that living. Is that what you want to return to?"

"But your soul was separated from your body. Is there a way we can leave with our souls?"

Mother turned to Curratta, the final and only authority here. I looked into the witch's large eyes and tried to connect with her, but it was like trying to empathize with myself. She was I, and I was she. Maybe MG was right and they all just existed only as part of my imagination. What I didn't know about myself, she could not tell me.

How wrong I was became clear when the shaman spoke.

Curratta stepped between Mother and MG and faced me. While rejuvenated, Curratta hardly looks any less hoary. Her callow skin stretched over her bald head with patches of white hair protruding from the sides. She was a terrifying specter, and I feared angering her as she bowed her head slightly from her raised crooked shoulder. I tried to maintain my gaze into the spiraling core of Curratta's huge irises.

The Supreme Shaman spoke hesitantly, yet her voice scared me. "Tatya-Masi goes back into the World of Fire to unite the four Jewels of Life. He will take his servant with him."

The twelve Xucha spread in a semicircle around the Supreme Shaman and lowered their gaze in reverence. Still, their shock at what was transpiring was evident in their hollow expressions. None of their expectations of what would happen when their god returned included him leaving them.

The witches bowed their head and closed their newly reformed eyes.

Curratta said, "We all live by your grace, Tatya-Masi."

"I too will accompany Tatya-Masi to the world," Mother said.

"Your new life will not last long there, daughter." Curratta rasped.

"I have lived there before, I can again," Mother answered with rebellion that surprised me.

Curratta paused, and then gravely nodded. "For you to leave, a soul from the outside world must remain. Here is one who can take your place."

I followed her gaze to where Don Carlos was being led to us by two witches.

"Grandfather!" I exclaimed. He wasn't dead. Or if dead, he was in Manoa where he could live again.

Don Carlos appeared stunned.

"I am so happy to see you again," I said.

He looked around in wonder before saying. "Kare Kuwaru'wa is carrying my body home, yet my soul is here. This is where you have been, isn't it, Lilia? All these years when I felt you so close, when I looked at the lake and thought of you. You were there," he marveled.

Mother smiled, but her joy at their reunion was tempered by the understanding that they must soon part again. Her eyes glistened as she looked at him. "One of us must be the bridge to the living. One of us must stay, Papa."

This is what I had asked for, yet I didn't want to leave Grandfather here any more than I did Mother. I'd just found my family. Was I now to lose my grandfather? I wanted us all to leave together. "Is that the only way?" I glanced at Curratta.

The witch observed me with her deep-set, large eyes. I knew the answer. Grandfather would be held here, so I would return. I might be their god, but they didn't trust my human side, and thought that I'd been contaminated by Quetzal.

"Will you stay here, papa, so I can go back to life with my son?" Mother asked.

Grandfather looked at the blues, red, and red-jeweled light dancing on the white walls of palaces built into the inner wall of the city. "We are in the City of Eternity now. Time doesn't matter here, yet I'll miss you every minute we are apart." He looked at me. "I'll miss you both." His expression grew somber. "I see much now, what we have before us. Listen," he said to me. "Rosas lives. He now possesses the tunjo and the Jewels of Life. He will rule our land without pity. He is a cruel man possessed by a terrible demon."

I nodded. Grandfather was reporting what he saw with his physical eyes just as Mother had when her soul had been separated from her body. If Rosas had survived the fall in the Cave of the Xucha, then Gabriel Ayala and the spirit of Quetzal the Plumed Serpent had too. The La'ku prophecy that in two years, when the Sun was in the eye of the Sagittarius, a new World would begin, could still be true. I knew that Xiulu would not cease his efforts to assure that the Sixth and Final World was a World of Fire.

Grandfather continued, "The land, our land, Omagua, and all the lands around us, will suffer under the tyranny of Rosas." Grandfather set his jaw with the strength of will I'd come to admire so much. "You must stop him, my son. You are the heir to the Morales line. You will have my blessings in all that you do."

The thought of being part of that great family gave me as much strength as the power of the witches and the magic of the Jewels of Life. "Thank you, Grandfather. I will always be proud to be a Morales."

He put his hand on my shoulder. "When the battle comes, your trials will be great. I will do what I can for you. If staying here is what will help you, then gladly I will remain." He looked about at the fountain and rejuvenated witches. "Manoa," he marveled. "In Manoa."

Mother took Norane's hand. I sensed the great love and passion between them and Norane's torment over the loss of the time for us to be together as a family. We could leave, but he could not. Norane wanted to be the one to teach me, to share what was left of my youth, to be my father.

"Will you permit us to leave, Awkanakuy-Hauakuy?" I asked him, using his formal name of the Warrior-Brother.

A quick smile lightened his dour expression, before he gravely said. "I will be there when you need me."

Curratta floated to the fountain and dipped a golden tubular vial attached to a chain like the one that had held the tunjo. The witch barely rose up to the level of Mother's eyes, but with her head back, her enormous eyes looked like the deep waters of a well. "I believe that you are upon the path that the Lordess of Water has set you." Curratta levitated above Mother, and with a skeletal hand placed the necklace around her neck. "Your soul was detached from your body for too long for you to live in the world. The Waters will last until the sun enters Sagittarius. Then you must be in Manoa."

Curratta was making sure I had two reasons—my mother and grandfather—to return for the final battle for the Sixth and Final World in two years when the Sun rested in the eye of the Archer.

Curratta addressed Mother: "As long as the Waters last you will be able to live in the world, but be warned. Mitnal now possesses the tunjo. He will seek to use you to discover the way to the Jewels of Life in Cocatamia. You will always be in danger and there is little the Warrior-Brother or we can do to protect you in the world. Remember, always, you are Xucha. You carry the lessons and weapons of our sisterhood. Use them well to serve and defend Tatya-Masi." She whispered, "Teach him our ways."

Curratta shifted her intense focus to MG. "And you. We've never had one like you, but this I know. Inika Lordess of Water is strong in you. Serve Tatya-Masi well."

Mother lowered her head before MG. "Forgive my rudeness, sister. We serve the same master."

"I understand, Lilia," MG said.

I shifted my feet, wanting to leave before they changed their minds.

"Goodbye," I said to Grandfather.

"Go with strength, my son." He patted me quickly on the back, before giving his daughter a quick hug.

I looked at Norane, and then back at Curratta. "I do not leave in weakness. I do not shun my fate. My decision to live in the world is to better know the world. And when I know the world, I will know how to leave the world."

Mother raised the vial containing the Waters. A corona radiated around the tube, forming the same bubble that brought us to Manoa.

"Cruuuuuu."

The witches' chant was now a dirge, bidding a sorrowful farewell.

MG and I stepped close to Mother. The last thing I saw as we left the ancient city was that the purple cap of a mushroom had pushed up from the earthen pit facing the Bratay. Manoa too would have new life. How long our lives would last depended on my ability to survive and return with the other two Jewels of Life.

The bubble lifted and took us back through the dome covering Manoa and up to the passage that emerged on Frog Island in Lago Itza Uo.

When we were in the night air, the bubble transporting us dissolved leaving us alone in the dark. I was saddened but not surprised that the rain was still falling.

We climbed cautiously onto the muddy bank among reeds bent by the incessant rain and winds. Lights showed the positions of Rosas' soldiers on the grounds of Omagua. The mansion was brightly lit. Before I could say anything or hide, I sensed a familiar presence.

Twelve pairs of burning eyes surrounded us. Quetzal the Plumed Serpent had found me.

CHAPTER TWENTY-FOUR
DEVIL'S BARGAIN

Iturned to face *Quetzal*. Mother and MG stood on either side of me ready to fight. In the dim light, I saw Moss and Kare behind the Plumed Serpent. Surrounding us were the eleven half-life conquistadors. Their skin was the color and context of parchment. Hooded black cloaks covered their skeletal bodies. Red lights burned in the hollow eyes of their skulls. If the Plumed Serpent had survived the fall in the cave, then surely Rosas had too, and grandfather's prediction would come true.

"You've given away your power," *Quetzal* said. His voice remained that of Gabriel Ayala, but had a raspy quality as if spoken from a dry throat.

"Not all of it," I said, trying to sound and think with confidence.

"Rosas has the *tunjo*. Where are the other two Jewels?"

"Where I can use them when I need them."

Quetzal glanced toward the lights of Omagua and then at me. "You see the condition you have left me in. I am only partially freed. *Inika's* chains still bind me to the Earth."

"You said I've given away all my power. What can I do?"

"What you've squandered may yet come back to you. I will protect you as I've done before if you give me your word that you will release me when and if the Jewels are returned to your hands."

"And if I refuse?"

"We can kill you now or let you go; without my aid you won't get far."

"You've betrayed me before, why should I trust you now?"

"That you are alive speaks for my word. I want your future, not your death. As long as *Mitnal* possesses the *tunjo* and you do not hold the other two Jewels, Smoking Mirror will not search for you, and as long as I protect you *Kinchel* the Avenger will not find you. Only I will know where you are. Do we understand each other? Shall we agree?"

"What of the rains? In what kind of world will I live?"

The Plumed Serpent hunched his narrow shoulders and bowed his cloaked head. "This rain pains me and it does you. The *chacs* are your spirits. Call them back."

I would if I could, I thought, but between *Quetzal* and me a thought was as good as spoken words.

He extended his boney arm from the wide sleeve of his tunic. "Let us join Fire and Water. These spirits cannot resist our united will."

I took *Quetzal's* desiccated hand. The heated flesh was alive with the energy of the union of our minds.

Spirits and gods hovered in and around us: manipulating, battling, hurting and healing–recognizable if I opened my senses to their presence. I was *Tatya-Masi*. I closed my eyes and took a slow breath, focusing the power I possessed.

"Stop the rain," I whispered.

There was stillness in the air. Water and Fire came to perfect equilibrium. Then, the wind shifted, and with a howl the dark clouds formed into a massive funnel over Lake *Itza Uo*. The spinning spout reached into the atmosphere until it was as wide as a continent. The suction pulled the monster-faced *chacs* from the atmosphere by the thousands. Their fanged faces wailed as they were drawn into the void.

The clouds broke and for the first time since I'd found the box, I saw stars.

EPILOGUE

Whatever power I possessed over the spiritual world did not extend to the everyday struggle for food and shelter. The roads were ruined and we survived by eating what we could catch or find. We had no money and couldn't return to Omagua, now the stronghold of Rosas. While I could disguise myself, we couldn't risk anyone recognizing MG or Mother, and I would not leave them.

Mother guided us into the jungle preserve where our family had sheltered the La'ku since their conquest by our Castilian ancestors. Built around a pyramid, the village of K'aáx Chumuk was the last place anyone was paying attention to in the country. Able to take what they needed to survive from the jungle, the native La'ku in many ways resumed a normal life more quickly than the people in the modern world.

After we'd been there a week, Mother got word to Eduardo who had escaped Omagua and had formed a guerilla army in the jungle. He brought us to the coast where a boat took us to the United States.

The weeks of rain left great physical damage in every country, but greater was the trauma on the collective psyche of mankind. Neither science nor religion could completely satisfy mankind's need to know why the rain had come, and if they would return. The legend of Tatya-Masi spread, as did the La'ku prophecy of a coming battle for the Sixth and Final World when the Sun rested in the eye of Sagittarius.

The near-collapse of social order allowed us to enter the United States without being challenged. Jerry Forrest was there to meet us when we were put ashore in Florida. And six weeks after the worldwide rain ended, Mother, MG, and I returned to the Lake of the Frogs in California.

As the months passed, it becomes clear that Grandfather's prophecy had come true. In the post-deluge turmoil, Rosas through the power of Mitnal the Smoking Mirror had been able to create his own country, which he named Nueva Granada, New Granada after the old viceroyalty of the colonial era. In that manner, Xiulu Lord of Fire preserved his control over the battlefield where in sixteen months the Sun rested in the eye of the archer of Sagittarius, the final battle for the Sixth and Final World would be fought.

Among the reports we heard back from Omagua was that the legend of Tatya-Masi grew in proportion to the misery of the people. Images of the god were common in the Indian villages and native bazaars. Every La'ku in the countryside seemed to have either seen the god astride a great white horse, or knew somebody who had.

That Quetzal the Plumed Serpent had joined forces with Mitnal the Smoking Mirror was evidenced by reports of twelve wraiths that enforced his rule, killing all who spoke the name of Tatya-Masi. Despite the terror, many still whispered that when the god returned, Tatya-Masi would drive away the Castilians, and once again the land would belong to the La'ku.

I often thought of Kare and Moss. While I sympathized with their bondage to Quetzal, I knew that I could not risk helping them. Only when I freed Quetzal the Plumed Serpent would they be freed. Until then, I was going to enjoy what freedom I'd found to live as a man, not a god. Soon enough I'd have to become Tatya-Masi.

The Waters of Life in the vial Mother carried from Manoa kept her active and buoyant. At least for a short time, I had a family. Quetzal kept his word and gradually I became confident enough to venture out, mostly in the disguise of Victor Magallanes, the boy who I saw die while he was robbing the gas station.

But perhaps my greatest joy came when MG asked me to be in her band.

One night when we were playing at the rebuilt Roadhouse, MG turned back to me with her guitar slung over her shoulder. "When are you going to let it rip like you did last Halloween?"

Seated behind a keyboard, looking like Victor, I frowned at the memory.

"Come on," she encouraged. "The disguise is holding. Let's take it up another level."

"You want me to be Tatya-Masi?"

"You are Tatya-Masi. Play music like him."

Well, why not? After all the damage I'd brought to the world, maybe I could play a good song or two.

I reached into the minds of the small audience, felt and reflected their musical desires back to them, and took them where they wanted to go.

ABOUT THE AUTHOR

Jeffrey Marcus Oshins is a writer and musician recording under the name Apokaful. He lives in the mountains above Santa Barbara, California.

Read the sequel to *12: A Novel About the End of the Mayan Calendar*

AND WE SHALL PERISH

You can also check out Jeffrey Marcus Oshins on Facebook, Twitter, Pinterest, Wordpress. Visit the website @www.12novel.com

Listen to the band

APOKAFUL

YouTube.

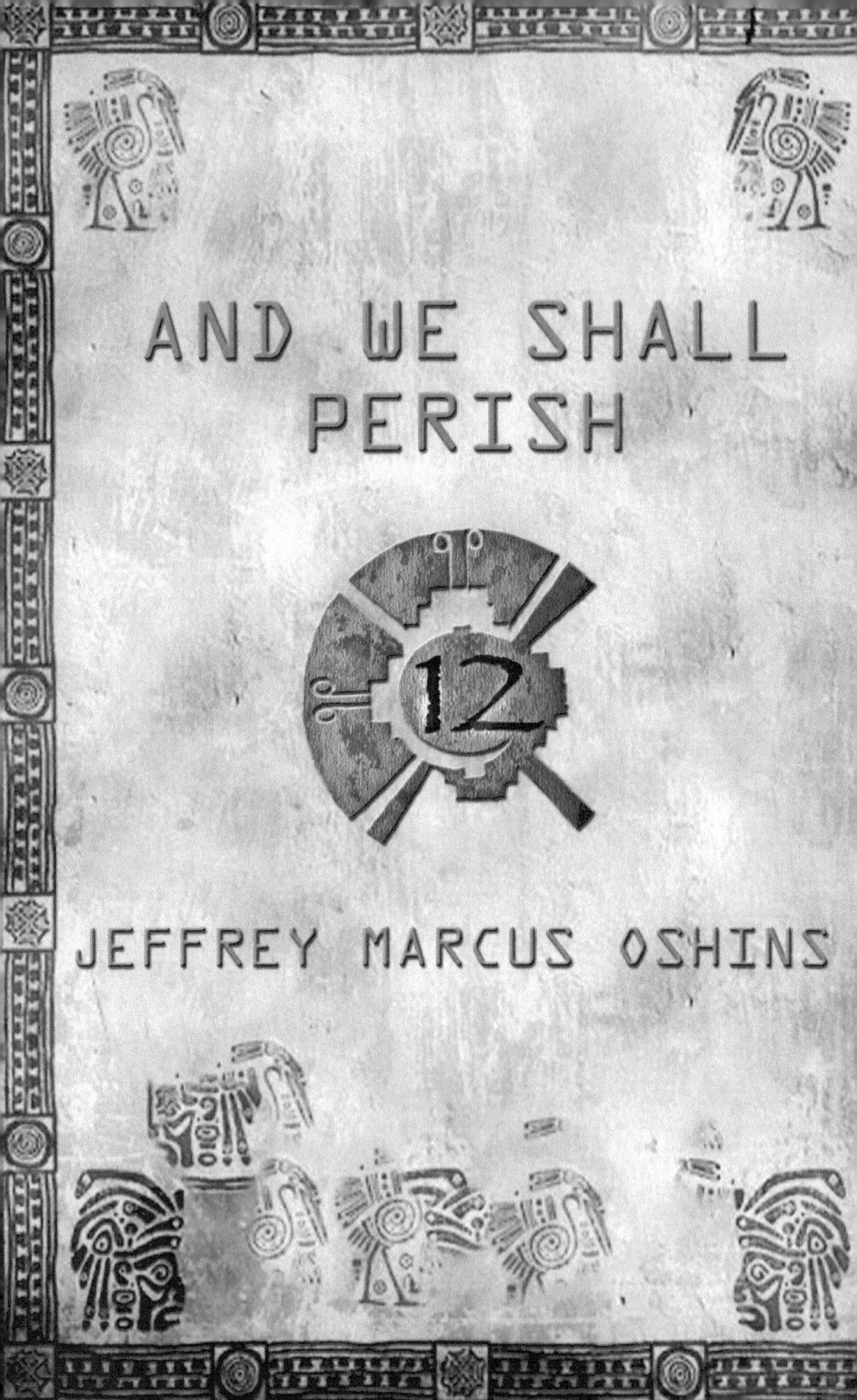

AND WE SHALL PERISH

12

JEFFREY MARCUS OSHINS

READ THE BEGINNING OF
AND WE SHALL PERISH
THE SEQUEL TO
12: A NOVEL ABOUT THE END OF
THE MAYAN CALENDAR

Ceaseless Worldwide Rains and Ruin

Modern civilization is helpless as ancient gods battle for the Sixth and Final World of Earth. Whole cities are being swept away by a worldwide flood. The fate of humanity depends on the courage and indomitable will of two orphans from one of worst slums of South America. Their love for each other must be powerful enough to survive the wrath of a ruthless dictator and the magical powers of celestial beings intent on the destruction of the human race.

And We Shall Perish

Jeffrey Marcus Oshins

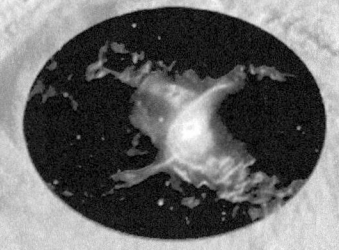

DeepSix Publishers
Santa Barbara, CA

An account of the battle for the Sixth and Final World of Earth.

I

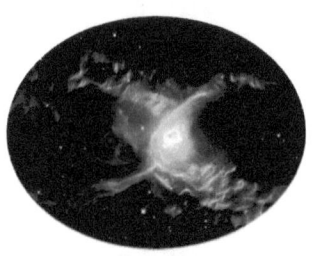

THE ORPHANS OF FIRE

The rains came a week before the god was to appear. How could Anta not know the date of Tatya-Masi's return? Her father's devotion to Tatya-Masi was what had gotten him killed; why twelve-year-old Anta, her twin brother Koya, and her little sister Ati had been left without a father in the slums of Quesada.

The clouds swept in from the eastern jungles and beat various rhythms on the roofs of Us'me, a squatter camp behind the Quesada city dump. If you were fortunate enough to have a metal roof there was a pleasing resonance to the rainfall. To those with only cardboard over their heads there was a dull plop and soon a drip as rain seeped in.

Anta rolled over and tried to find a dry spot beneath the loose cover of cardboard, wood and plastic, but Death was looking for her little sister Ati.

Uma, their mother, pulled the three-year-old onto her lap. "Spit, spit." She slapped an urgent beat on Ati's narrow back.

The tiny girl gasped for air and her eyes widened in panic.

Uma shook her. "Spit."

Koya reached over Uma and hit Ati hard between the shoulders. Her small head shot forward and a foot-long roundworm fell from her mouth onto the newspapers bedding.

His thin lips pressed tight with anger, Koya spoke in the dialect of the street where there was no time for wasted words. "No eat dump food."

The city garbage dump gave them a place and a way to live, but you had to know what green mold could be knocked off a piece of bread or fruit, what meat could be boiled clean of worms and other things that could kill you. Anta blamed herself for not making enough money or finding enough good food for Ati.

Uma held Ati against her shoulder, massaging her back. "Light," Uma said.

Anta lit a candle she'd stolen from a church. The flame flickered over the broken chair and crates; clothes and tools pushed against the upper wall to thwart thieves.

No going back to sleep now, Anta carried the soiled bedding outside and threw the still-glistening white worm into the embers of their cooking fire.

Street lamps lit the city spread out below the mountainside dump. Anta's eyes were drawn to the distance where an electric snake with fire wings flapped atop a tall building. Always the fire snakebird flap-flapped but never rose, stuck like she was. She silently cursed the pitiless gods who'd put them here.

Like every day, Anta thoughts were on how she'd make the money the family needed to beat Death one more day. The first garbage trucks would be arriving at the dump in two hours. There hadn't been enough rain to fill the water buckets, so she had to buy the day's water before starting her hunt for things to sell.

Clothed in a man's shirt tied with a belt and a pair of knock-off athletic shoes that Koya had stolen, she moved down the muddy hill. The empty paint buckets knocked against her skinny knees when she jumped over the open sewer that ran behind their shack.

Their neighbor, a woman who made her money reading cards, called from the open window of her kitchen. "Dear Anta, bring one water."

Anta picked up an empty bucket and wondered why she didn't wake her lazy son, Gypsy, to stand in line.

"*Tatya-Masi* protects you," the card reader called after her.

Anta shuddered and stared into the dark. She wanted nothing to do with the god *Tatya-Masi*. He was the reason the red-eyes had killed her father.

For a year, the family had traveled the countryside while her father had preached to groups of *indios* that the god was coming and this world was going to end. One night while camping on the side of a road, the family had awoken to what sounded like monsters clearing their throats to swallow you.

"Shraaaa." The voices of the red-eyes echoed from the bottom of their graves. "Let no man say the name *Tatya-Masi*." Three red-eyes took their father in their skeletal hands. One last shriek and Death took her father.

Anta ran the bad thoughts from her brain. Fear made you weak. The weak and stupid died first in Us'me. Demons were near everyday. She needed to think about paper and metal, a few centavos to pay for some Top-Ramen.

A half-hour to dawn, a line of women and girls carrying plastic containers stood by a white wall. They endured the rain in the open with the dumb acceptance of cows and horses. A bird's nest of electric wires ran over their heads.

Something–though Anta could never say what or why–made her feel a better life was waiting for her than standing in line to buy a few cans of water. By the time she'd hauled the water up the hill, the sun was out. She fixed the coffee Koya had brought home last night and poured the first serving into a jar for him. No taller than Anta at five feet, he took the coffee without a smile or thanks. Her brother was a gangster.

They stood outside by the cooking fire in front of the shower curtain that covered the entrance to their hut. The bare ground was littered with scraps of wood and discarded wrappers. A company of parrots complained from the spiral branches of ciebas trees in the hillside forest.

"Have one sugar." She poured the white grains from the packet she'd found behind a restaurant yesterday.

"I feel in one good way today," Koya said after a sip. "Tonight I go by Rosas' store."

Was he joking? Why would the richest man in the world have a store? Rosas had a country, this country–New Granada.

"Need I help?" Anta asked. Sometimes he let her go with him to whistle if trouble came.

He ignored the offer and gazed down the mountain at the city.

She wanted to ask more about Rosas' store, but the day was getting old.

* * *

Koya kept an eye on his sister until she disappeared behind the shacks. If things went right tonight, he would do a job that would make him rich enough to take Anta and the family away from Us'me. They'd drink coffee at a café from white cups with as much sugar as they wanted. Maybe they'd go north to Los Angeles where they made the movies and the shirts and caps with the pirates and red bulls on them. He knew a world beyond this hard life. He'd seen it in the DVD's at Emilio's, the fence who bought what Koya stole. Guns that fired flaming rockets, tanks, grenades, cars that always survived when the ones chasing you crashed; men who kept fighting when they had been hit and kicked so hard they should be dead. Tough guys like him.

He liked his sister all right. But he didn't show it. Anything you liked would get taken from you. He couldn't spend all day protecting her. Anta could take care of herself.

* * *

The rotten-egg and burning-flesh smell of the dump grew stronger as Anta reached the bottom of Us'me. Dark-winged vultures and crows sat amongst the piles of paper, old food, plastic bags, and everything else the *ricos* didn't want. *Indios* waited to be the first to meet the arriving trucks. Children with bloated bellies and the red hair of those too far gone to live long ate whatever they could find.

Anta concentrated on collecting metal, newspapers and magazines not too wet from the rain. She found a metal sign, filled two bags with aluminum cans, slung them over her back and walked for a half-hour to where the streets were paved and the electric buses ran.

Nura, the junk lady, lived behind a white wall with broken bottles cemented on the top. Inside her open gate were cleaned backpacks, washed foam rubber for mattresses, tires, auto parts, forks, knives, spoons, tops of jars, glasses. The *mestiza,* fat from beans and lard, did business behind a wooden counter. She had brown teeth and a dirty mop of stringy hair that hung around her shoulders. As usual, she insulted Anta, telling her that she stank and was filthier than her dog Pepe. Anta pretended not to hear, wishing that she could eat as well as Pepe, a strong black brute who slept in the corner with an eye open.

Anta put the aluminum cans on a scale. There would be no haggling over that. She hoped she might get a good price for the sign and set the square piece on the counter.

"What is this?" Nura used her fat lips to show how much she didn't like something. "Why do you bring me this useless trash?" Nura lifted a corner of her lip toward her ear. "You know what it says? Course you don't. Says stupid girl. So I know it's your sign. Ha, ha." The fat *mestiza* looked at her dog to share the joke.

Anta's expression remained blank like she really was a stupid girl. She was smart enough to know that Nura was going to give her some money for the sign.

"I'll give you five *centavos* for it." The lip twisted over brown teeth.

"Ten."

"How many people you think need a sign says stupid girl, stupid girl?"

They settled on eight *centavos,* and fifteen more for the cans. Nura gave her small round brass coins, enough for the day's water and some bread. Anta would have to carry ten bags of cans to Nura to earn enough for beans or rice for the family's dinner.

She made three more trips to the junkyard, getting an extra

thirty *centavos* for a part of a car and a dry book she found behind a school.

Near evening Anta crept into a garage where boxes of vegetables were put into trucks. Some squashed tomatoes lay on the ground behind the trash. Anta rushed to pick them up, but was chased away by a *mestizo* who hollered, "Dear god, why are these filthy people on the Earth?"

A thousand poor were lined up at a church waiting for bread. Anta knew better than to stop. A hundred would be lucky to get a few rolls. Better to find candles in churches than bread. Sometimes there would be rows of burning candles and without anyone looking she could steal ones that still had plenty of wax.

The trashcans outside restaurants where the *gringos* ate were best for bread and other food, but you had to be quick and know when to be there. Otherwise you could be in for a beating from the *gamines*, the orphans who lived on the street. They smoked *basuco*, coca paste, their eyes wide, skin drawn tight on bones, giggling idiots. Last week, Anta had seen five of them dead in the dump with bullets in their heads.

Anta cut off the day's work to go home, knowing Ati would be waiting for the packages of dried noodles she'd bought in the *indio* market on the other side of the dump.

Uma had a bone boiling with corn and a soft carrot. Ati waited by the fire, her eyes never leaving the food. The worm had left her hungrier than ever. When the soup was done, Anta let Ati have more than she took.

Karla came over looking for a meal. She sat on a wooden crate and held Ati in her lap. "Do you know what day it is?" Karla asked her.

Wide-eyed, Ati shook her heads.

"The twelfth month. *Tatya-Masi* is coming." Karla began to hum, and then sing softly.

"Move, move to *Tatya-Masi*

Twelfth month, Water washes the Fires away

Move, move to *Tatya-Masi*

The twelfth quarter moon

Move, move to *Tatya-Masi*

To the Temple-By-The-Sea

Move, move to *Tatya-Masi*."

Uma pulled Ati by the arm away from Karla.

"What be the matter, dear Uma?"

Uma looked about to make sure no one was listening. "No words by these things."

"But this day be one better day for all us La'ku," Karla said.

Uma took Ati inside the hut.

Karla sang louder to bug Uma.

"Move, move to *Tatya-Masi*

Twelfth Month Water washes the Fires away

Move, move to *Tatya-Masi*

Tatya-Masi of the *Water*

Move, move to *Tatya-Masi*

Tatya-Masi, the one truth

Move, move to *Tatya-Masi*."

Anta saw the fire snake growing brighter in the distance. There is only one truth she thought, Death–Death always there, waiting for you to slip, to get sick, to be too weak to run, to fall into the dark hole. The rats lived better than they did. How could they ever *move-move* to *Tatya-Masi* or anywhere else?

Koya came out of the hut. He had extra plastic bags in his rear pocket.

"Where go by?" Anta asked.

He pulled his lucky pirate hat tighter over his head. "Go by I-work," he spoke in the slang of the barrio, and sauntered down the hill.

Anta followed him. "I come?" she asked.

"No job for one little girl," he said, as if they were not the same age.

Anta didn't follow until he'd cut through a row of shacks on the dirt path to the city. He might be a better robber, but she was more careful. Last month she'd stopped him from snatching a purse just as a cop who would have shot him had walked around the corner. She was better at following people too. She hid behind walls and peeped around corners to see where Koya was going. Every time he checked over his shoulder, she was hidden. She tracked him from Us'me to where the land flattened and *ricos* lived in brick houses covered in white plaster. Paths became roads. Electric lines ran across the streets. The smell of cooking pork on hot coals came from a market where sometimes Koya would buy her cooked meat and sweet drinks when he had good luck. Cars and trucks blew dark smoke from their exhausts. Drivers sped a few feet, honked, and cursed when they stopped.

Anta saw a street orphan use an old trick to steal a watch. The *gamín*, younger than she was, stuck a lit *cigarillo* on a taxi driver's left arm. When the driver slapped the burn, the kid lifted the watch off his right wrist and ran. The cursing *mestizo* yelled, "I'll find you and when I do..." He did not have to finish the sentence. The *mestizos* and cops hunted *gamines*, shot them and left them in the dump or the river.

The distraction caused her to lose sight of Koya. She hurried in the direction he'd been traveling, past a blonde *gringa* on a big sign that told *ricos* what to buy. In an alley near a store with windows, where plastic people showed dresses and suits, Anta had to pass up a cardboard box that would have been just the thing to repair the hole in the shack's ceiling.

By the central market was a place with a fountain in its center where *mestizos* and *indios* sold blankets and other native clothes, weavings, and carvings to *gringos*. Deformed young begged here. Sometimes, Anta wished that her feet grew out of her ears so the *gringos* would leave *centavos* on her blanket.

She reached the *Plaza de los Mártires*, the oldest part of the city, and still could not see Koya. He'd said something about robbing Rosas, so she went to the side of the plaza where the General lived.

* * *

Koya's street sense told him he was being followed. He ducked behind a vendor's stall, and saw his sister moving through a group of *mestizas*, young schoolgirls in their uniforms. They were a chattering flock of birds in blue skirts and white shirts, the kind he'd rob just to make them cry. If one of the *mestizas* were his sister, he'd not let her walk alone on these streets. He hated the *ricas* schoolgirls. What did they know about life? Anta was better than any of them. After tonight when he was *rico*, Anta would go to a church school and be a happy, empty-headed, weak, *niña* in a blue skirt.

* * *

Anta stuck her head around a corner in case Koya had seen her following him. But he wasn't in the alley that ended at the rear of a government building.

A hand fell on her shoulder. She gasped and tried to spin away, before seeing it was only her brother.

"Why be here?" Koya pressed his face close to hers.

She leaned away from him. "Rob I Rosas store."

"Quiet. Want all cops in the Quesada to know where we go?"

We, he had said *we*. He was going to let her in on the job.

Koya hesitated and then smiled. "Come by me."

She loved it when he smiled at her, but kept her expression serious so he didn't change his mind. She followed him a hundred steps up the alley to a store with dark windows.

Koya reversed his hat on his head, and went to work on a heavy padlock on the door. He fit two shims he'd cut from a can around the top loop and worked them until the lock popped open. He had more trouble with the door lock. She watched him carefully put a straight piece of metal into the keyhole, take it out, shave off more of the metal with a file.

Her heart beat loudly in her ear and her arms trembled. He was taking too long. The alley was a dead end with nowhere to run. She turned her back to Koya. People were walking past the entrance to the alley. Cars drove by on the boulevard. This was the center of the city. They couldn't just spend all night breaking into a store, particularly if Koya was right and it was Rosas' store. With a click the lock opened.

"Move," Koya said.

They stepped inside the dark store and Koya closed the door behind them. What if there was a dog or an alarm? Why had Koya said this was Rosas' store? Someone who lived in a palace would not work here. Maybe Koya had it wrong or she didn't understand. She peered over his shoulder to see the shapes of machines and rolls of cloth stacked on shelves.

Koya lit a candle and held it high.

In the glow of the flickering wick, she saw a machine with cloth lips. They'd have a great night of stealing if they could carry that away.

"There be one door here," Koya said and ran his hand along a wood-paneled wall.

Anta saw nothing but a wall.

"Locked." Koya cursed.

"Rob one thing and move from here." Her voice quavered. They'd be killed if anyone, especially General Rosas, found them.

Koya put his hands on his hips and thought out loud. "Be on street last night. One man walk by. See I big *jefe* Rosas. Follow Rosas down one alley, keep I very small and quiet. Rosas look round and then move by this place. I come by window and look in. There be one space to see inside."

Steel bars covered a blackened window. She hoped nobody could see them through whatever space Koya had been able to see Rosas through. How did Koya know Rosas was not here now or about to come in the door?

Koya's thin shoulders tightened. "It be Rosas. There be one door behind this wall."

Was Koya *loco?* Rosas lived in a palace guarded by *Fierros* and red-eyed skeletons who'd killed their father.

"I no move in when he be here," Koya said.

Anta saw a big pair of scissors on a table. She could get 30 *centavos* for them.

"Rob these one time." She picked up the scissors.

"That be!" Koya said. "Rosas move by these. Rosas pull down one time by this."

Koya reached past her and closed the top of the cloth mouth machine.

To her amazement the wood-paneled wall opened to reveal another door. Koya handed her the candle and put the two points of the scissors into two holes in the wall and twisted. A door opened before them. "Oh Anta, I be so happy you come by here."

Anta blushed at the rare compliment. Koya took the candle and stepped into a dark hallway. Maybe if she'd been thinking less about compliments and more about staying alive she could have said something to stop him.

She followed him along a cement wall, trying not to make noise but their feet echoed in the hollow space. A gust of wind blew past them and caused the candle flame to flicker. She smelled oil. Ahead the darkness ended. Please stop, she wanted to beg him, but followed close as he crept forward to the edge of a garage. Koya put the candle in his pocket, and boldly stepped forward.

"Whew, whew," he whispered. "I told you this be Rosas place. Sure be one Rosas place."

Bright bulbs shined on a small tank and a fat-tired racing car that looked fast enough to fly.

Koya walked toward the car in a trance, and ran his hand along its red side. "Whew, if I could rob this one," he muttered.

Anta didn't know he could drive.

"How Rosas move car and tank by here?" he asked. "How go by street? Sure there be one more secret door."

She'd seen tanks before in the parades, daddy tanks to this puppy.

Koya walked around the tractor wheels. "One time we move by this," he said. "You drive. I shoot."

"Shoot?" Anta asked.

"Shoot machine guns, rockets and one big gun."

Koya was in a dream. Nothing could make him leave this place without the tank or car.

"Move by here, rob and move," Anta said and kept her eye on another doorway behind the tank.

Koya also saw the other path. "Rosas be by here. One truth now!" Koya said. "Move that way to the palace under the plaza."

He walked to a pair of open steel doors. "See we move by here under the *Plaza de los Mártires*. This be Batman place. This be way to Rosas Bat Cave. Stay by here."

Koya lit the candle and stepped into the dark passageway.

If somebody closed the doors, Koya would be trapped. Anta hurried after him.

"No move by I," Koya said over his shoulder.

She ignored him and stayed close to him and the candlelight.

With his hat brim facing back, Koya walked fast like he knew where he was going. The sound of their steps seemed as loud as shouts to Anta.

The long stone hall slanted down, taking them deeper. Anta imagined the Cathedral of the Apostles and the Presidential Palace over their heads. After a city block, the tunnel flattened. Ahead was another bright room.

Koya pressed against the wall and glided forward. Anta rocked on her feet ready to run. Koya stepped into another room as big as a store.

"Whew, whew," he said.

Anta stayed close to him. What was this place, a house, police station? Tubes ran across the ceiling. There was a bedroom, a glass shower stall, and guns, lots of guns. Soldiers and red-eyed skeletons would be near to so many guns. Anta studied a table with a big lamp over it. Beside the table was a barber's chair with leather straps. Drills and sharp metal tools hung on a wall. This Bat Cave was one scary place.

"Be fire rockets. Be grenades." Koya pointed to things hanging off the wall and in boxes. He lifted a heavy pistol and held it like the gangsters in the movies.

Anta studied four small video monitors on a desk that showed the stone hall they'd come through, the inside of an elevator, and rooms more *rico* than a hotel lobby. She searched for a camera. Somebody could be watching them.

On the far side of the room was another pair of open steel doors. Three underground tunnels, steel doors everywhere, what kind of place was this?

"Rosas' palace be up there." Koya looked for a button on the wall, and then pulled on the shiny doors of an elevator. She was glad he couldn't make it open.

"Look by there." Koya examined a narrow slot at the side of the elevator. "Be one money machine elevator."

"Rob one thing and move by here," Anta again pleaded. The gun alone could get them enough for the family to eat for a month. Nura would pay a lot for the tools.

Koya pulled his ear. "We rob by Rosas Bat Cave more times."

I hope not, Anta thought, but didn't say it.

Koya opened a center drawer in the desk that held the monitors. "Whew! Whew! This sure be the money machine elevator card. Rob I Rosas palace by this." He pulled out a piece of plastic hanging from a necklace. His eyes glistened like he had a fever. Anta hoped the credit card wouldn't open the elevator, that they could grab some loot and escape this cave.

Koya pushed the thin plastic into the slot. The door opened with barely a sound.

"No go by I," Koya said. "Move back one time for you."

She sidled through the small gap as the door closed.

Koya scowled at her and pushed the top button sending the elevator up so fast her stomach rose to her throat.

"Why come?" Koya shivered. "No place for one girl."

She pushed herself into the corner, Koya the other.

They stopped rising. The door opened. Anta was sure this was no place for a girl or a boy.

II

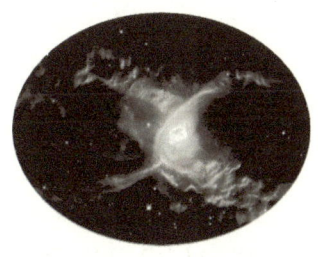

ROSAS' JEWELS

Why had he let Anta come? If Rosas or a Fierro tried to capture him, he'd kill them with his new gun or be killed. But what about Anta? He didn't want her to die. The job would be that much harder, but he wouldn't stop. Heroes never stopped.

His guts twisted as he stepped from the elevator and swept the gun in front of him. He'd been right. The cave was only the beginning. This was Rosas' room. He knew it.

Rico clothes hung from bars. Shelves held enough shoes for a department store.

At the end of the clothes room was a closed door. He pushed it a crack and peeked out to see a *rico* bed as big as a house. That had to be Rosas' bed.

There was a movement. Koya retreated and motioned for Anta to duck behind hanging clothes.

A boy as tall as Koya but twice as wide, wearing only underpants, his *tetas* jiggling, came in the clothes room.

From behind a curtain of dresses Koya recognized Enrique, the son of Rosas. How could he not recognize him? Enrique was the prince. Every boy in New Granada wanted to be Enrique. He was always on television having so much fun, winning at soccer, riding a horse, playing with all his *ricos* friends.

Enrique took a dress off the rack, almost exposing Anta's hiding place.

The prince was a princess. Koya watched him step into the gown and tie a pink sash around his waist. Enrique reached with a flabby arm and spun a dial to open a wall safe. He took out a handful of jewelry and went into the bedroom.

Koya peered from his hiding place, could not see Enrique, took a deep breath, and went to the safe. He stood on his toes to reach inside and pulled out a thick wallet. Rings and necklaces followed. He was glad Anta was there to help him carry so much loot. They loaded their plastic bags as fast as they could.

The last thing to come out was a beautiful box. Jewels in the eyes of *Tatya-Masi* sparkled on a gold lid.

The box glowed. Was he crazy? He felt stronger, could hear and see things better.

"Cruuuuuu."

Koya twitched at the faint sound. His sister was shaking. Was it an alarm? Was a camera moving to see them? He couldn't take his eyes off the carving of *Tatya-Masi* on top of the box. He put the gun down and held the treasure in both hands.

"Put in, now!" Anta said and held open a bag.

Her voice broke the spell and he slipped the box into his plastic shopping bag and picked up the gun.

The door to the closet opened.

Enrique squealed and ran the other way. The high-heeled shoes he was wearing caught in the rug and pudgy boy fell on his face.

Koya went after him. "Quiet one time," he said, waving the gun.

Enrique whimpered and pushed himself along the floor, but didn't say anything.

"No move," Koya warned. What should he do with him? Tie him up? Hit him over the head with the gun, or shoot his way out?

The bedroom door opened and a woman screamed. Koya recognized *Señora* Rosas followed by General Hernando Rosas.

Koya was too scared to use the gun. He ran through the clothes room to the elevator where Anta was waiting.

"Push the button," he shouted.

The door was closing too slowly.

Rosas, worm-lips twisted, eyes burning with rage, lunged and grabbed Koya by his red bull shirt.

"Run." Koya tossed his loot bag to his sister.

* * *

The last thing Anta saw of her brother was Rosas dragging him through the closing gap of the door. She pressed her elbows against her ribs. Her mouth opened in a silent scream. Why had they ever come here?

As the elevator carried her down she sobbed. Her brother was dead. The plastic bag he'd thrown was heavy with loot. Maybe if she gave it back to Rosas they might only get a beating. Her hand reached for the up button, but she didn't press it. Who would help their mother care for her sister if both she and Koya were in jail or killed, a couple of *gamines* left in the dump?

Koya's last word to her was to run. When the elevator door opened she fled toward the tunnel to Rosas' store.

Steel doors on both sides of the Bat Cave shut. She was trapped.

On one of the small monitors, she saw Rosas coming down in the elevator carrying a rifle.

Anta set the bags of loot on the desk and pushed as many buttons as fast as she could. The door at the rear of the Bat Cave opened.

Anta swept up the bags and ran past the elevator door just as Rosas stepped into the room. She raced by him carrying a plastic bag in each hand, through the rear door and into a hallway carved from rock.

This new tunnel was the scariest one yet. Lamps set in the floor and ceiling shined on holes in the wall where skeletons with dried skin, long cobweb hair and yellow-curled fingernails stared down at her. If she was not already as scared as she could be she'd have run.

"Put-put-put!" Firecracker sounds snapped in her ears. Pieces of rock flew near her head. Each breath punched from her lungs. Fire ran up her legs. She didn't care about the dead bodies dried up like old rats or carvings of monsters. Her pumping feet carried her through the underground graveyard.

The rock passage came to a room with a round stone roof. In the middle of the floor was the top of a head. Anta ran downstairs along a wall that wrapped around a statue of *Tatya-Masi*. She heard Rosas' heavy breathing and saw his black boots two steps above her. The stairs ended at a rock wall. There had to be some way out of here. A six-inch crack in the rock was the only place she saw to go. She twisted sideways and forced herself through the narrow break until there was no room for her head.

"Vermin," Rosas shouted.

Anta pushed with all her might until her head felt like it was being crushed, and squeezed through into a dark space where she was blind. Rosas' gun blazed. Flashes of fire lit the crack in the rocks. Bullets made whining noises as they flew by her. She retreated another step and there was nothing to stand on. Her arms whirled with bags of loot in each hand, but she couldn't keep her balance and fell backwards into a deep hole.

She gasped. Her head hit the ground causing a pain that shot up her spine into her eyes. Koya's bag fell from her grasp. All she could see were spinning stars, and then nothing but darkness—darkness blacker than the darkest night.

"Cruuuuu."

Ghostly light rose from the ground in a blue-green cloud filled with small bubbles.

Something was with her, a spirit. Had she fallen into the underworld? Her fear had discovered new limits. Her breath came in gasps. She felt weak and wanted to cry.

"Cruuuu."

The sounds and light were coming from Koya's bag. She reached out and touched the plastic. What was in there? Her racing heart slowed until she could think. She felt stronger. Her fear quieted and she could breathe again.

Grateful to have anything to see with, she took out the box. A picture of *Tatya-Masi* was outlined in burning gold on the lid. The god's eyes shined with inner brightness. Warmth radiated from the metal.

"Cruuuu."

The calling surrounded the box.

"Cruuuuu."

Her shaking hand carefully lifted the lid.

"Cruuuuu."

A cloud with its own light the color of sage wafted from the box. Inside each drop within the haze was a winged frog-faced monster the size of a bee. She'd heard about them from her father. These were *chacs,* water spirits that brought the rains.

The magical shower lit a gold *tunjo* inside the box. A pendant of *Tatya-Masi* was attached to a silver necklace and lay on a bed of woven *indio* cloth. Jewel eyes of *Tatya-Masi* shined with their own brightness.

Rosas would not stop trying to get back his treasure. She would trade the box for Koya.

Then there was a new sound—a mixture of a growl and hiss that took her back to the night the red-eyes had come for her father.

"Shraaaaa."

In the dark, two red-eyes, then four, and then six moved toward her.

The red-eyes had come for the necklace holding the pendent of *Tatya-Masi*. She closed the lid and bent over, trying to shield the box with her body.

"Shraaaa."

The eyes of the *tunjo* darkened as if to help her hide.

"Shraaaa."

The nightmare wail lessened. First one pair of red-eyes blinked closed then the others.

Great magic and danger were inside the container. She should leave it and run as far and as fast as she could. But what would she trade for Koya? She put the magical container inside the bag and set about finding a way out of this dark place.

Using her hands as her eyes, she felt her way along a slime-covered stone wall. Rats ran over her feet. Water dripped into puddles she waded across.

Hours passed. She inched forward until she heard the flushing sound of a river. The echo of whatever was ahead made it hard to judge the distance in the underground night. Where was she? How could she get out of here in the dark? Should she use the *tunjo?* No, she'd gotten this far with her own eyes and ears.

She held out her foot and felt nothing. There was no way

forward and she wasn't going back. She pressed against the wet wall and felt with her hand that she was at a corner, reached around with her foot, and stepped onto a narrow ledge. She swung around the sharp bend and crept onto another path.

She kept moving until her outstretched hand felt cold steel on the wall. It was a ladder. Climbing up, she heard a car splashing a puddle, smelled the fresh scent of rain. So close to escape she could see the car lights through small openings in the steel manhole cover. Pushing up with her shoulder and hand, she tried but could not lift the lid.

The ladder shifted beneath her, pulling free from the wall. She didn't move, willing her body to be completely still, took a breath and then with as much balance as she could find on the teetering perch, stepped down, shifting her weight in tiny increments to keep the ladder from tipping until she stepped on the ground.

There was nothing to do but keep going along the path, shuffling her feet, running one hand along the wall and holding the bags of loot in the other until she found another corner with her hand and stepped around with her face pressed against the wet, cold wall.

A foul smell filled her nose with every breath. At least she thought she knew where was she was going now. The sewer came out in the river where the poor washed their clothes. Would Rosas and the red-eyes be waiting there for her?

She moved toward the sound of rushing water. Drops flew up to her face. What if she had to swim? She'd drown if she fell in.

At last there was a change. At first she thought the light was something in her mind. Then she could see that she was on a narrow ledge in a pipe carrying stinking water. When she came to where the sewer flowed into the river, the night air smelled as sweet as a rose. She stayed in the pipe and scouted for signs of the red-eyes or Rosas. A soft rain was falling. Everything sounded quiet and peaceful. She guessed that it was an hour before dawn. A stabbing pain in her heart quickly replaced the joy of her escape from the underground world. Koya had been with her when this night had begun. How was she going to save him?

* * *

Koya was strapped to a table in the gunroom beneath the palace.

Rosas showed him the cruel claws of a pair of pliers and slowly lowered them toward Koya's tied hands. Koya sucked in his breath and waited for the pain.

"Where is the *tunjo*?" Rosas demanded.

"No I *tunjo*."

"Who was she?"

He wasn't going to tell him. He would not rat Anta, but then another of his fingernails was pulled out.

"I-sister."

"Where do you live?"

"Us'me, on first hill, by dump. Go I, find I-sister." He blubbered like a girl.

Koya didn't know if Rosas believed him but the torture stopped.

Koya hated himself for being weak. He'd betrayed his family. Better to die, to end this pain—in his head, in his hands. No! Do not give up, he told himself. Be a hero. Find strength. He would say no more, no matter what Rosas did to him. His life was now dedicated to one goal—to survive and have his revenge. Anything Rosas did to him would only be added to his debt.

His eyes were nearly swollen shut from the beating he'd received, but he could see Rosas at the desk with the monitors, talking into a phone.

"I want a construction crew," Rosas ordered. "Take the wall down behind the underground temple. Tear it apart from top to bottom, every crack. I want a family named Raymi brought in. Turn the dump barrio upside down for them. Just do it!" Rosas ordered.

* * *

All was hopeless. Koya was gone. The weight of his loot was heavy in Anta's hand. She found a dark doorway and opened Koya's bag.

"Cruuuuu."

The lit cloud plumed from the beautiful box with *Tatya-Masi* on the lid.

"Cruuuu."

The sound was here and nowhere, up and down. She checked the street for a sign of the red-eyes. She wanted to see the necklace again, to feel the strength she'd felt when she'd held the *tunjo*.

She opened the lid.

The verdant steam billowed upwards. Anta gasped and reflexively closed the top. *Chacs* flew out of the cloud into the night sky. Rain fell harder.

Here was deep, old magic. Koya had stolen a great treasure.

She put the box in the bag and took out the fat wallet stuffed with money, not *centavos* but *gringo* dollars—the best kind of money. There must be hundreds of the bills. With this, they could eat steak and potatoes for the rest of their lives. They had more money than a drug dealer now. They were rich. Koya had made them rich.

All her life she'd thought that if only they had money, she'd be happy, but now felt only sadness. Should she save Koya first or protect the family? Koya would tell her to make sure the family was safe. Rosas would be coming after the family. She had to take them where Rosas couldn't find them. Then she would trade everything: the box, the money and jewels for Koya.

She had dollars but no *centavos* to pay for the family to escape. What was she going to do with the box? The magic cloud would tell Rosas where she was.

Hurrying through the dark city, shivering and dripping from the soft rain, Anta came to the junk woman's closed and locked gate. She didn't have time to wait for Nura to open for business. If Anta made too much noise, she might get caught. If she tried to climb over the wall, she'd cut herself on the broken bottles, and if she made it she'd be attacked by Pepe, or shot by Nura.

Anta hit her fist against the metal door.

Pepe barked, wanting to bite her.

"Nura!" Anta called softly.

Pepe barked louder.

"Nura!" Anta shouted.

Other dogs on the block began to bark. A light came on at the end of the street.

"Nura! Wake now." Anta called more loudly.

"Who is it? What do you want?" Nura shouted from inside.

"Have one good thing for you," Anta called.

"Come back later. I'm closed for business."

"No. Have one good thing now."

More lights shined in windows on the street. Every dog in Quesada now seemed to be barking. A door opened down the block.

"Move now Nura," Anta called.

"I have a gun," Nura warned from behind the gate.

"Nura, be Anta stupid girl. Know you stupid girl."

A view hole slipped open.

"Stand where I can see you," Nura said.

Anta stood on her tiptoes.

"You? What do you have?"

Anta held up one of the bills.

"What is it?" Nura asked. "Paper?"

"Money. Dollars," Anta whispered.

"Are you alone?"

"Only I one time."

There was the click of a lock being opened and the metallic complaint of a latch being pulled.

The gate opened slightly and Anta slipped through.

Pepe wasn't the lazy dog that slept in the corner during the day. His back was arched and his teeth bared. Nura held him in one hand and an umbrella in the other. The dog pulled free and shot forward.

Anta shrank from the dog.

Pepe didn't bite her, but barked and kept his snout aimed at her throat.

Nura locked the gate from the inside. "*Hijo de Dios*, you smell worse then ever."

Nura led her into her office, closed the umbrella, and turned on the light. "Stay there near the door where I don't have to smell you."

Even to Anta, used to the scents of filth, she reeked worse than dead bodies in the dump. She didn't care.

"Give me the money," Nura said.

Anta reached across the space until her arm was almost completely outstretched. She hoped the light or spirit sound didn't come from inside the bag with the box and loot.

Nura took the bill from her and examined it. Her narrow-set

eyes bulged over her fat cheeks. "That's a hundred dollars," Nura said. "Where did a dump rat come by dollars?"

"One *gringo* move dollars by I."

"What do you want me to do with it?"

"Make *centavos*."

Nura's lips twisted around her yellow teeth. "You stole it. I know you did. I should give it to the police. I should have you arrested."

Anta tried to keep her expression blank. "More dollars again."

Skin rolls deepened on Nura's forehead. "How many more?"

"Give some *centavos* and move I more dollars by you."

"What is that in the bags? You have more here, don't you?" The junk woman leaned across the counter.

Anta couldn't stop herself from swaying. She was ready to run if Nura came around the counter.

"Give *centavos* for dollars." Anta kept her voice firm.

Nura's lips twisted. "You stole these dollars. You know you stole them. What keeps me from keeping it all? I'm one nice lady when I give you two hundred centavos."

"Four hundred. One book bag."

"A backpack? All right, a nice backpack and three hundred for the dollars and then you're lucky."

"And one large plastic bag," Anta said.

It was like they were arguing over an old tire, but this was more than all the tires in the dump. Anta knew how far Nura would go and settled for three hundred and fifty.

The *mestiza* made Anta wait beside the old boards of her counter as she held an umbrella over her head and hurried among the piles of junk. Bending over to hide her secret places from Anta, she collected money from old cans and bags of coins hidden in different places in the junkyard. She brought Anta a plastic bag heavy with bills and coins and another larger empty plastic bag.

Anta peered inside the moneybag.

"It's all there," Nura said. "Here's your backpack." She picked up a bag that Anta had found in the dump a few weeks ago and sold to Nura for 10 centavos. It was pink and on the outside was a picture of an angel with a magic wand.

Anta could tell by way the junk woman's thin smile that Nura had given her far less than three hundred and fifty, but still it was more money than Anta had ever seen. She gripped the bag of money at the top and took the backpack.

"You have more?" Nura leered at her.

Anta pivoted and headed to the gate with the growling dog stalking her.

Anta waited for the junk woman to unfasten the latch.

"When will you bring me the rest? I'll have money waiting for you and more clothes. You're rich now. You can dress like me," Nura said, smiling like she was Anta's friend.

"Later more dollars," Anta lied.

Nura held the umbrella over her head and opened the gate.

"Bring me more dollars. You won't get a better deal," Nura called.

Anta ran onto the street with the book bag, *centavos,* and loot.

"And go to the baths," Nura said as Anta rounded the corner.

As soon as Anta was sure the junk woman was not following her, she stepped into an alley, looked around to make sure nobody was watching. She stuffed as many *centavos* that would fit into the woven bag she wore around her neck, put the box and the rest in the pack. She tore holes in the top and sides of the large plastic bag to make a rain poncho and pulled it over herself and the backpack.

Beyond the alley, she heard the sound of many engines. She moved to the avenue and saw, in the first light of dawn, cars with big guns driving past. Behind the gun cars came tanks nearly as wide as the street. Helicopters buzzed overhead. Trucks carried soldiers in a long parade of death going to Us'me.

She didn't have to be told what was happening. Rosas had come for her. She had to save the family.

Anta took all the shortcuts. Day came with dismal gray clouds heavy with rain. The chaotic sound of multiple gunshots came from Us'me. Anta ran faster, her chest heaving, her stomach crying from hunger. She was too late. Fires arose from the hills. The flames spread together until they lit the mountainside. Rosas was burning Us'me.

Anta pushed through a crowd fleeing in the opposite direction, and came to lines of back-to-back soldiers. One line faced Us'me,

the other, the city. Nobody could get in and nobody could get out.
Inside the barrier, soldiers shot dogs, people, anything that was
alive.

Rosas and a thousand soldiers could not keep Anta from her
family. She hurried across the dump past a *gamín* who was pulling
trash over himself, digging in like a dirt beetle.

A hand reached out from the frame of a burnt car and seized
her. She wrenched away, but the grip was too strong. Her attacker
pulled her to him.

It was Gypsy, Karla's son, their neighbor. The fires reflected in
the scared eyes. Rain and sweat reflected off his shiny forehead.

"Hide, Anta, they want you."

"I-family?" Anta cried and tried to pull away, but Gypsy held her
tight.

"All family dead, all dead." Tears rolled down his cheeks into the
black stubble of his beard.

"No!" Anta dragged him from the protection of the old car.

A quick "put-put-put," and insect-sounds whipped by Anta.

Gypsy pressed her to his body, sighed and fell forward atop her,
crushing her into the yielding pile of trash.

Anta pushed up with her hands to get out from under him. She
felt him shiver and then he was a still dead weight on her.

Anta squirmed to get out.

"Cruuuuu."

The box gave her the strength to lift him off her.

"Shraaaaa."

The sound of the red-eyes stopped Anta. She let Gypsy's
corpse fall on her and hid beneath him in the bed of old food
and discarded paper. From under his arm she looked out to see a
skeleton in a dark robe sifting through the dump. Fire in empty
eye sockets floated toward her. The dark shape of a skull rotated to
where Anta hid. She did not breathe—silently praying the spirits in
the box would not make a sound.

"Shraaaa."

The red-eyes lifted the body of an *indio* lying atop a pile of
garbage and tossed him aside like a cornhusk. Nothing she'd seen or
heard that night compared to the fear that now gripped her heart.

"Shraaaa."

The red-eyes roved past her.

The sounds of terror were all around her as people were dragged from their hiding places and shot by the soldiers. More bullets rocked the dead Gypsy's body atop Anta. His leaking blood grew cold and then sticky on her.

Anta lay beneath Gypsy for the rest of the day. Her burrow filled with water; she became so hungry that she ate the core and seeds of an old apple from the garbage in which she hid.

At dark, the shots and explosions stopped, replaced by the sounds of misery–crying children, moaning, pleas for help and doctors.

When Anta could stand it no more, she pushed out from the garbage grave and stood in the warm rain. By the light of the burning fires she saw black, crusty bullet holes pockmarked Gypsy's corpse. He'd been killed trying to protect her. One more weight was added to the sorrow crushing her heart.

Us'me was still there. It would take a year of soldiers to kill the slum. The dead were being buried or eaten. Those who had survived were taking what the dead had owned. Those who lived would go on until it was their time to die.

Anta knew better than to go closer to her hut. In addition to the red-eyes and Rosas, all of Us'me would be hunting for her, hoping for a chance to earn a reward. Nobody had a friend in Us'me when ten *centavos* were on the table. Still, she had to know, she had to be sure.

Anta darted from shadow to shadow, avoiding light and the soldiers prowling through the remains of Us'me. She came to the slop of mud and burned cinders where the hut had stood, stooped and picked up a small corncob doll Koya had made for Ati.

Gypsy was right. All the family was dead. Anta's eyes filled with tears. Pain in her throat made it hard to swallow. Everything that she had loved in this ugly world was gone.

The rain fell and hissed on the embers and splattered against her plastic poncho. Anta swore to *Tatya-Masi* and the *Christo* that she'd never go back to this smelly dump, and crept down the mountain for the last time.